HYDRANGEAS ON FIRE

A. C. AHN

Copyright © 2015 by A. C. Ahn

Cover illustration & design © 2015 by Elaine Ahn,
    www.elaineisahnline.com

ISBN: 1502772469

ISBN-13: 978-1502772466

Printed by CreateSpace, An Amazon.com Company

For my brother

So vast, so limitless in capacity is man's imagination to disperse and burn away the rubble-dross of fact and probability, leaving only truth and dream.

—WILLIAM FAULKNER

HYDRANGEAS ON FIRE

1

May, 2015.

I watch through the open door and smoke, as he staggers away on the floor below. He's clutching his left leg, which is leaving behind a trail of blood. "Where are you going?" I cry. "Don't leave me here. Don't leave me here to die alone." He doesn't respond, and continues to slither away until the smoke thickens to the point where I can no longer see the yellow light glisten in the tiny pools of his blood.

"What have you done?" I hear myself say. I run to the door, hoping to try to escape as well, but the fire is now large enough to guard the entryway and trap me in the empty room. My lungs tighten due to the lack of oxygen in the air as smoke races into my mouth and fear begins to cloud my mind. If I can't keep myself from panicking, then I will surely die.

My first thought is to call for help. I feel for my phone,

hoping maybe someone is close enough to get me out (like Josh, but he's in another borough, or better yet, Dan or Pam), but only find my handgun, and I suddenly remember disposing of both the little spiky-haired man's cell and my own before coming here. What use is this gun to me now? "You brought this upon yourself, you crazy—" I try to yell, but instead cough uncontrollably into my fists. When I regain control of my breathing, I mutter under my breath, "Idiot."

I pause as my desperation to survive compels me to focus and ignore the hot, stuffy air about the room. I've long since abandoned my foolish commitment of dying in the fire. I manage to somehow kick the heavy door shut and rush to the small balcony window and slide it open, welcoming fresh air into my lungs. The light chill and scent in the breeze summons memories of happier times: of summers in southern California and winters in my crappy but homely apartment in the West Bronx. In an instant, I'm overwhelmed with emotions, too many to process, and feel sick. I climb out, stumble to the railing, and peer over the side ready to puke, but not before I jump back, startled by the view; it's only a three-story drop from where I stand to the cold, concrete pavement, but it seems like it's three-hundred.

I hurl, watching yellowish lumps grow smaller and smaller, like sinking marbles in a pond, but I don't feel any better. I slump down against the cool metal railing and think back on my life—about all of my proudest moments, most miserable days, and dumb regrets. When did everything go so wrong?

I pull out my pistol and shoot the remaining rounds into the closed door across the room. The bullets lodge themselves into the material (which is some sort of hardwood, maybe mahogany). The sight relieves a bit of my anxiety for some reason, despite the fact that I'm still trapped in the room where the fire was started. I laugh at the irony of the situation—being forced to breathe in smoke so soon after I've resolved to quit smoking. I guess there's no getting around it for someone like me.

I get up and peer over the railing again and look at the empty gun in my hand. I pass the Glock 19 from hand to hand, feeling the magnitude of its vacant power with each toss. "I no longer have any use for you," I sputter, and with all my might, throw it over the balcony.

Now, what can I do next to save myself?

I hold my head in my hands and concentrate, thinking back to my training days as a cadet and all of the fire safety pamphlets I collected as a child. There must be something there. I must have experienced, watched, or read something useful.

I decide to impulsively reenter through the window. When my feet touch the floor I feel a chill rush up from the soles of my shoes to the ends of the hair on my head, so I take a moment to shake the strange sensation. When I open my eyes, I spot a small table in the corner nearest to the door that I'm sure wasn't there before. I crawl across the room to it anyways and grab the vase sitting on top of it, which is full with a colorful assortment of flowers resembling pom-poms. I recognize them, but can't seem to recall their name. I take a quick whiff in the hopes a scent will help me remember, but I can't make out anything but smoke. I decide to leave them in the vase as I pull off my jacket and scarf and start to pour water from the vase onto the clothing. By now, the room has acquired its own climate, as clouds of smoke conceal the ceiling. Once my jacket and scarf are significantly drenched, I replace the vase with the nameless red, burgundy, purple, blue, pink, and white flowers on the table and throw my jacket over the point where the fire was born and is at its largest. At first, it seems to have a favorable effect, quelling a majority of the fire, but soon afterwards, even the jacket becomes fuel for the flame. I then wrap the soaked scarf around my face, covering my nose and mouth, and tie it tightly in the back. I bite on it with my teeth to help hold it in place and proceed to breathe through my nose.

Standing, I survey the rest of the burning room. I didn't notice before when I had first walked in, but there's an accent table positioned at every corner of the room. And on each table, there's a vase with flowers in them. I've already handled the one closest to the door. The other vase on the opposite side in front of me has a sunflower in it. I turn and see that the one directly behind me holds a single rose of unusual color. Finally, the last one in the far corner, nearest to the opening of the small balcony window, contains two lilies, both dark, both practically identical, but one contains a tint of life the other lacks. I hunch over and make my way to the lilies, desperate for a smell other than smoke, when something else catches my eye only a couple of feet to my left. I pick it up to discover that it's a golden reed with a small white gem in its center.

I stumble back out the glass window, onto the balcony, against the railing, clutching the reed, and stare down the bullet-riddled mahogany door, which is being slowly whittled away by the flames. It's becoming difficult to breathe, even out here now that the rest of the house is burning down, and the heat is unbearable. A lulling cacophony of far off sirens and fire truck horns seeps into my ears as my eyes stutter close.

"Now you wait. Someone will come for you," I assure myself. "Someone always does."

2

May, 2005.

"Sorry to hear about your father."

I'm about to shrug it off, but stop myself upon seeing Mr. Pezza's heartfelt expression. "Yeah, I don't really want to talk about it."

"No, no, I understand, kid. The death of a parent can be a really hard thing to handle, especially for someone so young."

"I'm not that young," I tell him.

"Yeah, I guess you're right. You're a lot older than I was when I lost my father. I was only a five-year-old boy when my father died. It was during the war, the war of your people." I scrunch my nose and inadvertently roll my eyes. "My family never recovered. I had to work as a delivery kid before I even entered high school."

"I think you told me this before," I say while taking a sip of my soda. "You delivered pizzas from this very restaurant when it was owned by the previous owner."

"Yeah? Well it's a bit more relevant now. Doesn't hurt to tell it again." Mr. Pezza goes back to the ovens and pulls out a large mushroom pizza. He divides it, then throws a slice onto a paper plate and slides it in front of me. The smell of greasy, hot pizza causes my stomach to stir with excitement and begin to eat itself. "A slice of mushroom pizza. Your favorite, eh? Perhaps it will put your mind off of life for a while."

I sprinkle on a handful of Parmesan cheese and dried pepper and devour the slice without hesitation. Pezza's Pizza is the one place that has never failed me, in terms of food. The handmade pizzas of Pezza make the chains look like they're dishing out melted cheese on cardboard. Sure, it's not exactly the healthiest thing to eat around here, but for just two and a half bucks, you can get the juiciest slice in all of New York. And the atmosphere isn't so bad either. The same black-and-white pictures of famous people from years ago hang on the walls. Naturally, the pictures mostly consist of people of Italian descent, such as Sofia Coppola, Robert De Niro, and Liv Tyler, although I'm not too sure about the last one (whether she counts as being Italian or not). Mr. Pezza is obviously a cinephile when it comes to Italian actors, which is a fairly common attribute for first generation citizens who harbor an abundance of ethnic pride. I, on the other hand, don't really have that much pride for my motherland, mainly because my motherland doesn't view me as one of her own.

"You know, I don't think I've ever asked you about those photos," I say with my mouth half full. "Did you actually meet any of those people? Those movie stars?"

Without even glancing up, Mr. Pezza replies, "Nope, can't say I have. Those pictures right there were taken by my brother. He was a—what do you call it—a paparazzi photographer. He loved the idea of following around actors and actresses and taking pictures of them. You could say his calling was in lights and photos and red carpets, while mine was in cheese and dough and brick ovens."

"I never knew you had a brother."

"Well, it never really came up," Mr. Pezza says. During all those times Mr. Pezza told me stories of his past, he never once mentioned that he had a brother, although I should have assumed.

"So, does he still take pictures of famous people?"

Mr. Pezza stops kneading dough for a split second. "I'm not sure. My brother and I, we don't really talk anymore."

"Oh, I'm sorry to hear that."

"It happens, kid. It's sad though." Mr. Pezza gets back to the dough, pressing even harder than before, which tears the dough in two. "He should be here, running the family business together, living with the family. Everybody's here in New York, our mother, our sister, our cousins, our aunts and uncles. But he's off somewhere in LA, most likely living alone. I can't help but worry about him from time to time. It breaks my heart."

"I'm sure he's all right," I say as I get back to my slice.

"Yeah, I guess so."

After finishing my meal, I pay Mr. Pezza, but he insists on it being on the house. If there's one thing I know about Mr. Pezza upon seeing him interact with his customers over the years, it's that he is more stubborn than he likes to admit. I thank him for his hospitality and leave the pizzeria, but not without taking a final glance at the photos on the wall. The black-and-white is unnecessary in this time and age, but I guess it frames the people displayed as being somewhat timeless, that old age can't affect what's already in the gray. And that idea seems to fit with Pezza's Pizza pretty well. I just hope that years from now, I'll be able to come back to this exact pizzeria and enjoy a freshly baked mushroom pizza in the company of movie stars.

For a moment, I think about calling up Barry, but then I remember that his parents sent him away to live with his grandparents in Seattle. I guess they just got tired of watching their indolent son waste away the prime years of his life, and the fact that he is their youngest child obviously didn't help his case all that much. Some parents just can't wait to be left with an empty nest, and really, I can't blame them. Children are like unexpected houseguests for the most part—overstaying their welcome for eighteen plus years, spending money, and causing trouble. I think it's crazy that some people actually plan out to have kids.

A pair of sparrows flutter by with light twigs tucked in their beaks, riding along a cool spring breeze. After months of unrelenting snow and chilling temperatures, I must say the arrival of spring is a welcomed sight. On this particular day, every year, my father would actually sober up and take me out to the mall, where he would buy himself a new suit or a nice pair of shoes, and I would be able to enjoy window shopping for various items that I planned on buying later when I grew up. I'm not entirely sure as to why my father would even bother with new clothes, especially since he didn't attend church or anything like that. But considering that we'd go to the mall on my mother's birthday, I assumed that he just wanted to look nice, just in case. He would always manage to end up with doggerel sizes, despite the advice from sales representatives, recommending him to go with a tighter fit. I guess he anticipated his beer belly to grow over the years. It's too bad none of those outfits survived the fire; I'm pretty sure I could have used them in the future.

I remember walking around the mall, looking through the glass at the overpriced clothes that the mannequins would wear with bodily hubris. I tried to avoid the toy stores, in fear that I'd actually start desperately wanting something that I knew I would never have. And I remember specifically pacing outside the shops, not walking into any of them; to be able to touch the clothes and jewelry, but not be able to buy them just seemed wrong to me, sort of like giving a monkey a banana with unpeelable peels. Looking at the merchandise through the glass gave the experience a more realistic approach—the distance was there, and just enough so I would be interested without ever being deterred from the future prospect of walking in and buying whatever was on display. The jewelry stores especially caught my attention, with the beautiful diamonds shining from the bright lights of the mall. Most of the time, I would incessantly stare through the windows, my eyes gleaming with selfless desire. Of course, there were times when I was shooed away by impatient employees or taken aside by a caring adult, asking me if I needed help finding my mommy. I would lie, pointing to a nearby woman who wasn't standing too close to hear and say that my mother's right over there. Thankfully, this happened less frequently as I grew taller. Unfortunately, my growth only shortened the fuses of jewelry store owners, who complained that I either go in and buy a cheap locket for my girlfriend, or block the display of some other store elsewhere.

My mother loved jewelry of all kinds. Perhaps that's why I spent so much of my mall time standing in front of the jewelry store. Perhaps a little part of me thought that if I got her a pretty bracelet or a fancy ring, that she'd come back for me. Of course, it was all just wishful thinking, but I'm pretty sure the mere idea was what drove me to the jewelry store window. Hope is a powerful force, especially to a naive boy who has nowhere else to turn to.

There was one particular set of earrings that I remember gazing upon—that made me think, *Those are the ones that will bring her back*. The earrings were small gold orbs with diamonds, no bigger than specks of dust, molded right on the centers. They were simple in design, but somehow I knew they were my mother's type. The next year, they were gone from display, and their absence caused my heart to sink. I began to cry, which a woman mistook as a sign of me being lost. And I acted like a scared, lost child, because there was no way I would have been able to explain the true origin of my tears. My father bought nice clothes for himself as a way to cope with his missing wife, while I stared at diamonds through the jewelry storefront to comfort myself from the abandonment of my mother.

Just because my father isn't here anymore, doesn't mean I can't keep up tradition. Why not take a visit to the mall? It's not like I have anything better to do. I take the bus to the West Point Mall and take my time as I walk in through the revolving doors. It's not surprising that the majority of people shopping at this time are old people, retired from the work force with too much time on their hands. Most of the elderly shoppers aren't even buying anything. Instead, they're just occupying whatever sitting area they can, watching the handful of people scurry by. I've always visited this mall during the weekends, so there were hundreds of people walking around holding bags full of clothes bought and clothes to return. I guess during the weekdays around lunch hour, not many people have time to spoil themselves with new outfits.

The mall hasn't changed much since the last time I've been here. Sure, a shoe store would close down and reopen as a sports shop, but overall, the mall is pretty much the same. Lights come from all directions in order to display the colorful dresses of the new Spring and coming Summer fashion. The golden railings for the stairs gives off the tawdry imitation of a 1950's mansion a rich tycoon might buy—a rich tycoon with a lot of old people friends.

The jewelry store is located right next to a women's clothing store on the second floor. I pause for a second as I realize the store has changed names to Tiffany & Co (obviously having been bought out). It's a bit depressing, to see the store I've spent so much time staring into transform into one of the many multinational jewelry stores, and the fact that I can't remember what the shop was called before only makes the melancholy feel even heavier. I carefully step in front of Tiffany's and peer through the glass, taking in the sparkles of the jewelry that's considered "in" right now. A dragonfly shaped brooch covered with mini diamonds occupies the center surrounded by flower-shaped earrings at ridiculous prices. Tiffany's sure does take the seasons pretty seriously and literally. If I were to have come during winter, I'd bet that the main attraction would be a snowman brooch encompassed by snowflake-shaped earrings at equally ridiculous prices. I stand there, using my method of process of elimination, deciding which one would be the best to give to my mother—which one would underscore her distinguished features. Fifteen minutes fly by without me even noticing, my legs being able to handle my weight for far longer without a hint of strain.

"Excuse me, sir?"

I look to my left and see a woman in her mid thirties in a Tiffany's uniform.

"Yes?"

She gives me a cordial smile. "Do you need any help looking for something?" I draw blank for words as I notice her earrings—small gold orbs with tiny diamonds on the center—the exact same earrings that I've envisioned for my mother. "Perhaps you want to take a look inside?" she continues. I nod my head and follow her into the store, holding my breath as I take the first step inside.

She leads me to a display counter which she positions herself behind. The lights are even brighter in the store than outside in the general mall. I can see the rays bounce around, between diamond rings, through rubies and emeralds, and reflected off polished gold. It's almost like the lights are buffalo and the jewelry are Native Americans, with every part of the lights being used and absolutely nothing going to waste. Looking through the display window on the outside is only a small taste of what it's like on the inside. Inside, I could examine the jewelry for hours; in fact, it would probably take me days to fully satisfy my arising hunger.

"So, is there anything specific you're looking for? My name's Shauna, by the way." Her friendly smile is plastered onto her face like a doll.

"Oh, nothing in particular," I reply.

"Who are you buying for? Girlfriend? Sister? Mother?"

I pause. "Uh, girlfriend."

"Well, what's the occasion?"

"Her birthday is coming up soon. I was just thinking about getting her something small, but nice."

"First time shopping for jewelry, huh?" Shauna says searching through the display. "Don't worry, I'll make sure you get the perfect gift. Something that says, 'I care about you,' but nothing close to, 'I want to spend the rest of my life with you.'"

I give her a hesitant smile. "Yeah, exactly."

"I know just the thing," she says as she takes out a gold necklace from the case. "How's this? It's a 14K white gold necklace at a very low price. We can even get something engraved right here on the heart if you'd like."

"Oh, no, that's really not necessary."

"Is it out of your price range?"

"No, no, that's not it. I actually have quite a bit saved up from my part-time."

"All right then, something without the heart," says Shauna. "I completely understand, it's a bit childish, kind of over-the-top. But you know, this design has been unbelievably popular for the last couple of months."

I stare at her earrings as the memories of standing in the mall flood once again into my mind. Shauna notices and mistakenly assumes that I'm admiring her cleanly symmetrical face, the color of her cheeks flushing beet red. I quickly point to her ears and snap myself out of the nostalgic trance.

"I really like your earrings. They work well with your, uh, overall image."

"Oh, thank you very much." She turns away slightly as her face becomes even more bright. It's almost like she's playing the role of a schoolgirl, unfamiliar with how to react to the most basic of compliments. It's cute, in the most ordinary way possible.

"Are those small diamonds in there?"

"Yeah, they are. Here, let me get these off so you can see them up close."

She proceeds to take her earrings off and place them on the glass counter, blending them in with the surrounding merchandise. I examine them closely, surprised by how exactly similar they are to the ones I've ogled over many years ago.

"Do you have these for sale here?" I ask with little hope.

"I'm sorry, I don't think we do. But I'm sure we have something very similar around here." She slides down a couple of counters to where Tiffany's earrings are on display. I follow her across while carrying her earrings with me.

"How about these right here?" she says, pulling out a silver pair. "These are silver, so they're a bit cheaper, but they have the similar design with the small diamonds in the center. Or is the gold a mandatory preference?"

"Yeah, I'd actually much rather prefer gold ones. My girlfriend has these light brown eyes, kind of like yours, just as vivid."

"Oh, really?." Her face starts to glow red again.

I pick up an earring from each pair and compare them side-by-side in front of Shauna's eyes. "I really think the gold will bring out her eyes, you know what I mean?"

"I completely understand," she replies in the most sincere voice I've ever heard a sales representative use. "That's the main reason I bought those earrings. It's important to make sure your jewelry matches well with your color. You really take everything into consideration, don't you?" I merely smile in response. "Here, let me check the back. We were actually selling earrings similar to mine a couple weeks ago. They were gold with diamonds in them, but they were just larger and a bit flatter, so they weren't really little orbs. You might prefer those."

"I'd be happy to look at those if you still have them," I reply, and with that Shauna disappears behind the "Employees Only" door, leaving her earrings in my care.

The other employees are busy tending to other customers, some of whom are happily engaged couples eager to dish out over twenty percent of their yearly salary. No one is willing to pay any attention to an adolescent when one can take care of big buyers. I slowly count to ten, patiently waiting to see if Shauna pops out from behind the door. Each second chips away at my flimsy tower of scruples of what I'm about to do, like Jenga pieces being removed one by one until there isn't a playable piece left. I'm not going to continue pretending that I'm going to buy a pair of ugly earrings when the ones I've wanted for years are right in front of me. Casually, I grab Shauna's pair of earrings and walk towards the front door, leaving the silver ones behind. Right before I exit the store, I hear a, "thank you for shopping at Tiffany's." My shoulders jump ever so slightly, and without looking back, I scramble my way out of the mall. I'm pretty sure Shauna will realize any minute that I've stolen her earrings, which will alert security to hunt me down, so instead of waiting for the bus, I walk briskly down the street. I squeeze my hand, feeling the sharp poke of the earrings, and as if I've been shot with a dose of adrenaline, I burst into a sprint.

I've never felt so alive.

3

August, 2001.

"Next."

"Noel Ashman."

"Ashman, Ashman…oh, here you are sweetheart."

"Thank you," I say. I take the sheet of paper and scan it quickly, before handing it back to the young lady. "Excuse me, Miss—"

"*Mrs.* Fields," she says.

"Sorry. Mrs. Fields, I think you gave me the wrong schedule. My name's Noel. Noel Ashman."

"Oh, I'm sorry, Noel." She leafs through the stack again. "Here you are." I check the printout and give her a thumbs up.

"Enjoy your first day of high school, and have fun, Noel," she calls out as I walk away.

Her words linger with me for a while as I think how nice it

was for her to wish me, a complete stranger, a good first day. I weave through the lines until I find the one that is in front of a table labeled with the sign, "9th L-O." I spot Michael standing near the front of the line and call out to him to let him know we're waiting. When he waves back, I turn and enter the hallway to join Daniel.

Daniel has on a cumbersome light blue button-up shirt, which is tucked poorly into his oversized khakis. A brown belt holds up his pants, and he has on matching colored shoes, which are also a size or two too large for him. It's obvious Mrs. Brackman dressed her son utilizing her husband's wardrobe.

"Looks like Michael will be ready soon," I say.

"Okay," Daniel replies.

He has on these round-shaped spectacles, which combined with his loose-fitting outfit, reminds me of Harry Potter the moment before he's told what his true identity is. As if he can read my mind, Daniel removes his glasses and pretends to clean them with the parts of his shirt that have bunched up at his sides.

"So, what do you have for first period?" Daniel asks.

"Let's wait for Michael," I say, and I fold up my schedule and slip it into my jacket pocket.

I lean against the lockers and pretend that I'm pulling out an imaginary cigarette from a box, going through all the motions, even packing it before I light it with an old-fashioned strike-anywhere match. I don't smoke, yet (since I've promised myself I wouldn't until I turn 18), so all of my actions I've learned from watching actors in movies.

"Want one?" I hold out the pack to Daniel, and he throws up his hands and shakes his head. I grin at his silent denunciation and embarrassment as I take a long drag and exhale all of my troubles and newfound high school angst into the freshman hallway. For a brief moment, I try to forget where I am.

My minute of peace is disrupted when Michael jumps at us and wraps both of his bulky arms around our necks and shoulders.

"Hey, I'll have one," he says.

I take out my make-believe pack again, and he unlocks his arms from our necks and carefully pulls one out. I proceed to light it for him, this time with a Zippo lighter like how I've seen my dad do with his.

"Where's your backpack?" Michael asks me with a half-concerned look in his brows. He has already dropped the smoking facade and is now pulling out his schedule from his bag.

"Didn't think I'd need one," I lie, "it being the first day and all." I take another drag.

The truth is, buying a new bag has been the least of my worries. And besides, even if I wanted to buy one I couldn't even afford it since my father has recently decided to add to his neglectfulness by not giving out allowances anymore. And now that summer is over, my stint working as a full-time Happy Campers team leader is also over, so my mind's been preoccupied with finding a decent part-time job. If it's any consolation, I've been telling myself, the allowances were few and far between to begin with.

"And you," Michael turns his head to Daniel, "what's with that getup? Jeez, we're here for the first day of high school, not for a church picnic." He pauses to study Daniel's appearance in more detail. "Are those new glasses?"

Daniel takes off his glasses again and cleans them, but this time with his glasses cleaning cloth.

"They look like something a certain ten-year-old would wear," Michael says.

I add in my gruffest voice possible, "Harry—yer a wizard."

Michael and I laugh, and I too forget about my fake smoke. Daniel on the other hand shakes his head and holds out his schedule.

"We should really get to this," he says.

"Yeah okay," I say. "What've you guys got?"

"Today I have Intro to Physics, English, P.E., and Geometry, in that order," Michael says.

"I have English, World History, Intro to Physics, and Geometry," I say.

"Is your Geometry class with a Mrs. Stevenson?" Michael asks.

"Yeah."

"Nice, we got one!"

"How about you Daniel?" I ask.

"I have Honors Biology, Honors English, Algebra 2, and, Human Anatomy" he says.

Neither Michael nor I show any signs of surprise; we both know how seriously Daniel takes his studies, and how hard he tries (and struggles) to keep up with our more intelligent peers. But despite that fact, we have always managed to share some of the same classes since entering middle school, *and* he still found time to hang out with us outside of school, considering we were his only friends.

"Well, what about for Day B?" I ask.

"Unless you guys are in the Honors program or are taking

C++/Java, then there's probably nothing."

"What about P.E.?" I ask. "Maybe we can get the same period for that."

"Doubt it." Daniel says. "I was able to postpone it until next year."

We stand in silence for a good minute. The lines in the office and main hallway are now only a few students long. I lean to my right to check the time on a clock through the open office door. We still have ten minutes before first period.

"What the heck is C++/Java?" Michael asks.

"It's a CS, computer science, class," I answer for Daniel. "You know, programming."

"Oh," Michael says. He furrows his bushy brows, then suddenly shouts, "Why don't we all take that class together? Hey, Noel, you're in the regular elective program for one of your elective slots, right?" He leans over and glances at my sheet. "See, we could drop Mr. White's Business Management class, move some classes around, and join Daniel's CS class."

"All right, I wouldn't mind learning a thing or two about computers," I say. "Let's go see if someone from the office can change our schedules for us."

The three of us reenter the office and look for a free administrator who can help us. I notice the 9th grade A to C line is empty so I call out to Mrs. Fields and run up to the table, bumping into a few of my late classmates (some of whom I've never met, but most of whom I know of well). Daniel and Michael follow me to the table's edge.

"Mrs. Fields," I say, "Could you help us out? We want to change our schedules so we're all in the C++/Java class."

"Oh, sorry sweetheart, but I can't do that. I'm just filling in to help administration on the first day. Normally, I'm a substitute teacher you know. And, I was actually told to tell students that schedule changes can't be made today anyways, and that you have to attend your first two days of classes before you can even request a change."

"I see," I say, making an extra effort to sound disappointed. "Thanks anyways Mrs. Fields."

"Sorry about that. It's Noel, right?" she asks.

"That's right," I say.

"Oh good, I'm glad I got that right," she says. "And this is…" She's pointing at Daniel. "I want to say Danny."

Daniel nods and busies himself with cleaning his glasses again on his shirt ends, keeping his eyes down. Daniel has always been shy around girls, especially the pretty ones. So, when I turn to look at Mrs. Fields again, I'm surprised that I didn't notice earlier how beautiful she is, with her silky hair, shimmering eyes, and soft facial features.

"It's actually Daniel," I say. "And this is my other friend, Michael."

"Oh, I'm sorry, Daniel. It's just, you look more like a Danny." She turns to Michael. "It's nice to meet you, Michael."

"It's nice to meet you too, Miss," he says with one hand resting on the table. He has straightened his stance a bit and is easily more than half a foot taller than Mrs. Fields, maybe even a whole foot.

"*Mrs.* Fields," she corrects him, with a nervous laugh. "Well, even if you boys aren't able to work things out with your schedules, I'm sure you'll manage to stay friends. And who knows, maybe you'll make some new friends along the way."

"Sure, I guess anything can happen," I say. I glance at the clock again—it's almost 7:55. "We should get to class. Thanks again for your help Mrs. Fields."

As we leave the office, Michael turns and waves before we enter the adjacent hallway on the opposite side of the office. "Wow, I can't believe a looker like *that* works here," he says once we're alone in the hall.

"She's a substitute teacher," I remind him. "So we probably won't be seeing a whole lot of her."

"Maybe she'll go from being a sub to a full-time teacher," Michael says. "I'd take her class in a heartbeat. Wouldn't matter what the class is about."

"She's married," Daniel says.

"Didn't stop you from blushing all over her, *Danny*," I say.

"I actually like it," Daniel replies. "From now on, call me Danny." He then rushes out of the building, past the metal detectors to the science building. His shirt has completely fallen out of his pants and is flailing in the autumn wind.

"You know where your physics class is?" I ask Michael.

"No."

"Well, you should follow Danny then," I say.

"Right." Michael starts off after Danny.

"We'll meet up at lunch," I call after them both.

Danny is too far to hear me, but Michael acknowledges me with a wave. I throw my green scarf over my left shoulder and run up two flights of the main stairs to the English department. I made sure to wear this one today because it's easily my favorite.

The first thing Ms. Mielke has us do is stand to one side of the classroom as she calls role. After she calls a student's name, she asks whether or not she's pronounced the name correctly, such as in cases like Luca Lombardi (lOO-kaa lom-bahr-dee) and Nicole Qiu (ni-COAL chee-oo), or she asks if there is a preferred name, such as Alex for Alexander and Sam for Samantha, or she'd do both. You could tell she's nervous, attempting to draw out the role call for as long as she can in order to continue doing what she is comfortable with doing. If I had to guess, I'd say it's her first time teaching.

Afterwards, the student is instructed to sit in the next available seat, going across from the teacher's left to right. She tells us that this arrangement will help her learn our names faster.

Naturally, I was called first.

She's at the S's now. I've always enjoyed these moments, being already seated, watching the other kids call out "here" (and some of the more prissy ones go with "present"), then take their seats. I learn the most about my classmates in these few seconds than I do in the entire school year, especially considering how I'm not very chatty with people whom I've just met. There are certain factors to look for during these moments, in addition to their names and whether they prefer to call out "here" or "present." These include their clothes, their hair, their demeanor, their walk, and their backpacks.

I've known Nicole Qiu for several years now, she being Michael's date for a dance in 6th grade, so it's hard to judge her now based solely on these criteria, especially after hearing from Michael about her many eccentricities. Luca Lombardi, on the other hand, is a new face. He's sitting directly behind me at the moment with his feet resting on the back of my chair. He started off well by choosing "here," but someone with a name like Luca makes me think of the big lug in *The Godfather* (which, I guess isn't such a bad thing if you don't mind being a loyal idiot). And, like with most people, the name matches his look. His clothes are what you'd expect to find a teenager in: a custom printed tee with what looks like a wolf doing a backflip on the front and a lion doing the same on the back, faded jeans, and sneakers. His hair is long, but nicely trimmed, however it lacks the shine from any products, and therefore, isn't styled. So, he cares enough to tidy up his hair before the first day of school, but doesn't put in the exorbitant amount of time needed to style one's hair like some of the jocks and gays do. From the look of his eyes, he seems to possess a studious mien, and his voice was overly respectful towards Ms. Mielke when he was guiding her through the pronunciation of his name. When he walked towards his seat with a heavy gait, he stumbled, but I fault that to the fact that a bulky guy like him had to work his way through the narrow passage between the first and second rows of desks, and not that he's uneasy with being the center of attention. Finally, his backpack is a relatively new, green suede one, something I'm sure a fourteen-year-old couldn't possibly afford on his own. So, based on all of this, I already know all there is to know about Luca Lombardi.

After Ms. Mielke finishes with attendance, she proceeds to write her name on the whiteboard. "Hello class. As you may already know, my name is Ms. Mielke." She points to the "i" in her name with a marker. "The 'i' is pronounced as an 'e' since the name is German, while the second 'e' is pronounced as an 'a.' "

No one in the class says anything or makes any noise, and

Ms. Mielke quickly turns her attention back to the board, as if she's embarrassed that none of her students found the trivia of her name the least bit interesting. I on the other hand go over the pronunciation in my head: (MEEHL-ka).

"Anyways," she says, with what I think is a slight trace of an accent, "I will be your English teacher for the year." She writes 9th grade English on the board. "This is my first high school teaching position. I was a sixth grade English teacher in the city for two years before I decided to make the change."

Well, I got it partially right.

I can tell she has regained a little confidence because she puts the marker down and faces the class. She scans our faces before saying, "It's nice to meet you all. I hope you'll enjoy this class as much as I'll enjoy teaching it. Now, before I hand out the syllabus I want to do a little activity. It's an icebreaker I used to do with my sixth graders."

A few grumbles escape the mouths of my classmates, which steals away some of Ms. Mielke's newfound confidence. She picks up the marker again and starts writing on the board.

"Don't worry, it's not anything too unbearable," she reassures us. "All you have to do is turn to your neighbors and ask them anything you'd like. Try to make it about something interesting—bonus points for those who relate it to literature. For example, you could ask your neighbors who their favorite character is in literature or what their favorite book is. Then switch off and make sure to answer their questions." She writes these points down then turns back to us. "Have fun with it. And afterwards, I'll give you a chance to share some of your exchanges. Okay, you have five minutes."

Immediately the class is in an uproar as most people are

busy chatting away about their summer break. I turn to my right to complete the icebreaker assignment with Chelsea Browning, but she's already talking with some other plain-Jane about how she hooked up with a cute, random guy at a bonfire party. I sneak a look behind me to find Luca in a similar situation as I am in, and I do something I normally wouldn't do. I turn in my seat and pull my leg over to straddle the chair and make the first attempt to talk to someone I don't know.

"Hey, Luca," I say, "got anything for me?"

His face twitches upon hearing a stranger say his name, and he shakes his head as he sits back, obviously a little surprised that someone has taken the initiative to talk to him.

"Well, I got one for you," I say. "Ever seen *The Godfather*?"

He shakes his head again, but this time adds a simple "no."

"Really? Haven't you ever heard of Marlon Brando? Robert Duvall?" I pause as I try to remember the most important name that has managed to elude me. "You must know Al Pacino."

"Of course I know who Al Pacino is," he says. This time, I'm taken aback, by his assertiveness. "I just haven't seen the movies yet since they're rated R."

I try to hide a smile, but the image of someone like Luca being denied by his Italian parents from watching *The Godfather* because of its MPAA rating weakens my resolve. "That's a shame. I was going to ask you what you think about this one character. You know, the movies are based on a book, though I've heard it's a pretty horrible one. I'm planning on judging that for myself soon."

Luca goes back to not replying. I can't tell if I've somehow made him uncomfortable or if he's just shy. But then I re-

30

member that he's new to this school district, probably just moved here from New Jersey, and doesn't have any friends.

"I'm Noel by the way, Noel Ashman." I extend my hand, but he doesn't shake it. I'm not offended. I guess I've lingered far too long. I take the hint and decide to move on. It looks like Chelsea is about done with her summer anecdote anyways.

When Ms. Mielke is finally able to get the class's attention after five minutes of the icebreaker, she asks if anyone wants to share. When no one volunteers, she begins to call out names by random. Luckily, I'm not called on, because I have nothing to share; Luca insisted on remaining a loner in the school, and after Chelsea was done with her story, she went on to tell another. The rest of the period is used to go over the syllabus, word for word. I'm slightly disappointed to find that the year's reading list isn't a list at all, but instead one name: Shakespeare. This is going to be a long year.

At last, the bell rings after what seemed like an eternity.

When I make it out into the hallway I pull out my schedule from my jacket pocket to reacquaint myself with my next class. World History. I believe that's somewhere on the second floor of this main building.

I go back down the stairs, and at the bottom of the first flight, I run into Jamie. We share a brief hug (which she initiated).

"How was your break? Haven't seen you in a while." she says.

"Yeah. It was uneventful. So, good, I guess. Where are you off to?"

"I have Honors English next." Several students rush by us,

clutching their schedules. "We should get going, don't want to be late on the first day." She starts to run up the stairs.

"Oh, I think Danny has that class now too," I call after her. "Maybe you two will be in the same classroom."

Without stopping, she says, "You mean Daniel."

"No," I say. "It's Danny now."

4

August, 2006.

The wooden stairs creak with each step, warning residents of the potential arrival of a criminal or cop, depending on which side of the law they prefer. The bluish-gray carpet is covered with all sorts of stains and gives off a musky smell of old dust. I am tempted to hold my nose with my fingers, but in this neighborhood, I don't want to do anything that'll make me look like an easy target. I've heard that East New York is one of the most dangerous parts of the city, with muggings and murders occurring almost everyday. (That's what I've heard anyways.)

The resplendent light shines through the wall windows at the end of each flight of stairs, blinding me before I turn for the next set. Once I reach the third floor, I check the numbers on the doors, searching for apartment 312. I find the apartment towards the end of the hall where the carpet is noticeably fairer than the rest. The front of the door is barren, with only a rusty peephole masked into its woodwork. I check the number on the door again before I knock, not wanting to be greeted by some random junkie or thug. Silence on the other side compels me to knock once more, hoping that someone will eventually come to the door. The next door apartment opens followed by an elderly man wearing a worn-out sweater. He locks his door and takes a good look at me, as if sending me a message that his loft is not open for looting. I give door 312 another series of knocks.

"Give it up, kid, no one's home." I turn to see the old man eyeing me down while stuffing his keys into his front pocket. I ignore him and give the door another knock.

"What are you, deaf? I said no one's home." The man turns his back to me while muttering something to himself.

"Do you know when he'll be back?" I ask.

The old man turns back around, the edge of the light now barely grazing his shoulders, revealing the frazzled wool protruding irregularly about his sweater. "So you're looking for the grandson, huh? Figures."

"Yes I am. Do you know when he'll be back?" I ask again.

"I'll do you one better," he says as if doing me a huge favor. "He's at the grocery store on the corner of the street, right across from the deli. He's there for most of the day. Nice kid. Kind of quiet though. A bit too quiet if you ask me."

"Thank you, I've got to go." I rush past the old coot, holding my breath in case his sweater smells as bad as it looks. Inaudible mutterings join the creaking of the stairs, which shoos me down faster to the first floor and out of the building, back

34

onto the sunny sidewalk of East New York. The sudden heat on the back of my neck seems to evaporate the sweat crawling down from my head, instead of creating new droplets.

The grocery store only takes a couple of minutes to walk to, although I must admit my pacing is more like a brisk jog than a light walk. Piles of fruit (regrettably I cannot use the word fresh here) line up across the front of the store, basking in healthy rays of sunlight. I do my best waving away little gnats upon entering the store, only to be greeted by a gust of warm air finishing the job for me. The first thing I notice is my surprise at the organization of the layout, with the aisles all clearly labeled with signs hanging from the ceilings numbered one to twelve. The breakfast foods are all in one lane while the toiletries are on the complete opposite side of the store, a comfortable distance away from the organic foods. Orderly lines fill the checkout lanes with people rhythmically flowing through and departing with totes and bags full of groceries. It's beautiful, in a clockwork sort of way.

Just as I'm about to question a cashier, I spot my guy just a couple of lanes down from where I'm standing. Danny looks the exact same as he did roaming the halls of high school, although to be fair, not that much time has passed to allow him to improve on his appearance. His cheap glasses slides down his nose, riding the waves of sweat rolling down from his shiny forehead. Of course, the bulky uniform isn't helping with his look one bit. It's so pitiful to see that I almost turn around, deciding against my initial proposal. But really, now's a better time than any. If anything, his current position will reflect a positive light on what I have planned to offer him.

"Hey, Danny."

He continues to bag groceries, placing frozen pizzas and la-sagnas carefully into paper bags. The middle-aged woman swiping her card is obviously either single and can't cook, or is a mother wanting to take the easy way of feeding her children. And judging from the frozen kids' meals, I'd say she's taking it a bit too easy.

I let Danny finish double-bagging for Lady Microwave be-fore I try again to grab his attention. He takes off his glasses and wipes his face with his apron as the cashier closes their checkout lane. I stand there awkwardly, watching him transi-tion to his break as he lets out a long sigh of relief. I release my own sigh, the kind that dampens the moods of others around me—a kind of sigh that only those who have suffered (along with those who have lived long enough to know) can truly un-derstand. Danny turns around and jumps back upon catching sight of his high school buddy.

"Jesus Christ," he says while adjusting his glasses.

"Hey Danny."

"What are you doing here? And how did you find me?"

"Hey, relax man. You know what they say about people who are easily frightened. They can't hold on to a relationship. It's no wonder you've never had a girlfriend. You should really work on that." Danny just shakes his head. "Look, how I found you isn't important. Your family told me that you went to live with your grandmother to help her out in the city, and from there it was pretty easy to track you down."

"Well we've got to talk fast. I only have a couple of minutes before my break ends." He takes off his working gloves, which are redundant in his line of menial, light-lifting work. I take a quick look around and notice that the other baggers go without the accessory. "So what are you doing here?"

"What are *you* doing here?" I ask, already knowing some reason as to why.

Danny sighs again, similar to mine. "It's just like you said. I'm here to take care of my bubbie. She absolutely refuses to go to a home, and she won't move in with my family because she doesn't want to leave her 'community' behind. Also, she doesn't really get along with my dad. She's such a stubborn old woman."

"That doesn't seem right," I say. "I mean, I thought you had plans to study engineering or computer science at Johns Hopkins or whatever?"

"Yeah, well, my dad decided that it'd be better if I took care of my bubbie first and earn some money for myself. And besides," Danny says with a helpless grin, "my family doesn't have the money to send me to a private school right now, what with all of the medical bills."

"Oh wow, that sucks. I thought your family would have a secret stash hidden somewhere."

"You didn't come all the way to the city just to make fun of me, did you?"

"No, no, of course not," I say. "I have a proposition that's just perfect for you. Remember how I'd use to say how I was going to travel the world and rob banks from different countries?"

"Yeah, and?"

"Yeah, well, I was thinking. Why don't I just do it here? In the city that never sleeps."

"Do what?" Danny asks, missing the plainly drawn picture.

I pull him close and whisper loudly in his face. "Become

thieves."

"Are you out of your mind?" he says while shoving me away with his sweaty palms.

"Think about it, man. It's a get-rich-quick scheme. After just a couple of heists, you'll be able to pay for a nice college education and move on with your life. I mean, come on, do you really think you'll be able to save enough, bagging groceries everyday? This is what ex-cons do after they're released from prison. Haven't you read *Different Seasons*?"

"What?"

"You know, *Shawshank Redemption*?" Danny's shocked face is mixed with a swirl of confusion. "Forget it," I say.

"Shawshank or whatever, we'll end up just like them if we become criminals."

"Only if we get caught," I say. "And even if we do get caught, you'll just end up right back here where you started."

"After serving time with actual felons! Not to mention having a permanent criminal record for the rest of my life."

"Calm down, Danny. All of that doesn't matter because we won't get caught. Take a look at this," I say, revealing the earrings I stole from Tiffany's a year ago (or so). The diamonds shine magically, doing most of the convincing that I need.

"Where did you get those?" Danny asks.

"Where do you think?" I tell him. "All you need is just a little confidence. Now, I need a partner. And I shouldn't be telling you this, but I met a guy, Jeremy, and he knows all the places with easy pickings. With his information and your meticulousness and my bravery, we can make a pretty awesome team. Every jewelry store in New York City will be fresh oysters just waiting to be shucked open. Don't think of this as criminal work. Think of this as an escapade of really living, with the thrill pumping your heart and the risk opening your eyes to appreciate every single waking moment of your pathetic life."

Danny continues to shake his head in disbelief. "Jesus."

"Look, I came to you because you used to be a close friend, and you're the only person I know who'd be okay with the idea. Also, I know you can use an opportunity like this. And just to put you at ease with the whole ordeal, your job will primarily be the getaway. I'm the one who's really going to be living on the edge all the time, and I swear, if I ever get caught, your name will never crawl out of my mouth. You know you can trust me on that. And besides, I've got everything planned out for the next few years. I'm going to do everything I can to be one step ahead of the police to ensure that we won't get caught."

"What," Danny says in his flustered voice, "are you going to go to community college and become a cop yourself?"

"You know, that's not a bad idea," I say. "I do have a bit of money saved up from the insurance and all. Although my father didn't leave anything himself."

"Jesus Christ."

"You know, Danny, there's a diamond out there, even more precious than the Hope Diamond. No one knows where it is or who currently has it, but I know for certain that I'm going to be the one to bring it back into the light, where it can truly shine. You can be there, standing right next to me when I do, or you can watch me from afar, bagging milk and eggs for the rest of your prime years. Hey, maybe even for the rest of your life."

Danny looks down at his gloves that he's been fingering the whole time I've been talking. His face turns sour, as if I reviled him to receive permanent scars of self-pity and bewilderment of his current situation. Was I being a bit too harsh? Probably. After all, I'm in no better of a position than he's in. I might as well pick a lane and work alongside him. We can be the ultimate cashier and bagger duo, discussing last night's house party as we blatantly ignore customers and their fussy requests. If I didn't have so much damn pride, then maybe.

I write down my new number on a scrap of paper and hand it to Danny, and without looking back, I leave the grocery store, knowing that his next shift will only make my offer appear like the fair apple in the tree. Danny will come around, I know it. Despite his worrisome and submissive personality, he is never one to waste away in monotonous solitude.

I only last a couple of blocks out in the blazing sidewalk before I escape into a Chinese restaurant decorated with an obscure name. There are no diners in sight, which is pretty much a warning sign painted in bright red, but the air-conditioned interior convinces me to stay and try the place out. A middle-aged woman, who I assume to be Chinese, takes my order with a foreign accent and a generous smile, something I'm not accustomed to in these deprived parts. She thoughtfully recommends the eggplant in garlic sauce, which immediately alerts me to the restaurant's potential desperation of wanting to hurriedly expend its overdue supply of eggplant. However, not wanting to disappoint the woman and her affable aura, I agree to the eggplant dish with white rice, along with a cup of cool tea. She disappears into the back behind the decrepit curtains and yells in a startling volume, as if the hallway curtains are enough to abate her extrinsic dialect (though I know she really doesn't care if I can hear her or not). I attempt to zone out what sounds like an intense conversation as I take a look around, admiring the mini statues on the shelves and the moderately sized aquarium towards the back. Strangely, the aquarium contains multiple fake plants and even a mini treasure chest as decor, but no fish. I take a whiff above the water and recognize the familiar smell of fish food, followed by the extraneous scent of fried foods, specifically, French fries of sorts. When the woman comes back and brings me my tea, without thinking, I ask her what happened to the fish.

"They all dead, honey," she says with a simple flow, as if she answered the same question many times before. Her response leaves me uneasy, and I find myself gulping down the tea which tastes incredibly bitter.

She wipes a nearby table with a rag. "You part Asian, right?"

"Yes, I am," I reply, trying to be as friendly to her as she has been to me.

She folds up her rag and stares at me intently, picking up on my broad face and peculiar, mixed-gened eyes. And without the slightest hesitation, she tells me that I'm part Korean, as if her words can actually change who I really am. I guess you can call it confident ignorance, but with a more reasonable tone.

"Yes, I am," I say again with an attentive smile, not wanting her to think that she's offended me in any way, because she hasn't.

"So what you doing in this area?" she says, in an attempt to keep our bonding alive.

"I just met a friend who lives around here. Maybe you've seen him eat here before? He works at the grocery store down a couple of blocks. He's about my height, wears rectangular shaped glasses, and is completely white."

"Just a second, honey." She withdraws back behind the curtains and resumes what I imagine to be a swearing match with her co-worker or husband. I refrain from plugging my ears, and force myself to sit up straight and take in the raucous chatter. It's good to restrain yourself against your natural urges, once in a while; it increases your self-discipline. Or so I've heard.

A couple minutes later, the waitress reappears with a small bowl of soup and a plate of eggplant over steamed rice. The smell of hot food causes my stomach to grumble. "I'm sorry," she says, "we've never seen your friend here before."

"It's okay," I tell her as she lays out my food in front of me.

"Perhaps you should tell your friend to stop by sometime. Crab fried rice is very popular with Americans. A lot of customers get that to-go."

I almost tell her that Danny doesn't eat shellfish due to both his family customs and his deathly allergies, but it really isn't necessary to get into such fruitless detail. So, before even tasting a bite of my meal, I tell her that I'll definitely get my friend to try this place out in the near future.

The eggplant isn't too mushy, but the dish has an overwhelming amount of diced garlic sprinkled throughout. The spices are so sharp, I feel the inside of my nose being poked about. I do my best to swallow the garlic pieces without having to chew, not wanting to acquire a lingering garlic breath for the rest of the week. I've always wanted to try my hand at making

Chinese food, but I can never remember to buy the right cookware, specifically a wok for efficient stir frying purposes. I'm pretty sure, with the right ingredients, I can duplicate this eggplant with garlic sauce with my preferred amount of garlic. Although, if I were to cook Chinese food, would it still be considered authentic Chinese? I remember once eating at what was considered a Korean restaurant managed by Mexicans. They pretty much just pan fried low quality meat and served it on a large plate half covered with rice and pathetic imitations of kimchi. I wouldn't necessarily consider that Korean food, and not just because the dishes were cooked by non-Korean chefs. I guess that goes to answer my question, that as long as I do it right, then I can cook Chinese food and be able to call it Chinese.

My cell phone rings faintly in my pocket just as I'm about to finish the last bite of eggplant. I take my time, savoring the last chunk in my mouth and clearing my throat with a refill of chilled tea. After the fifth ring, I pick up without bothering to see the identity of the caller.

"Hello?"

"It's me," Danny says in a slightly robotic voice. "Count me in."

"Great," I reply. "But before all that, you've got to try out this Chinese restaurant I've just found. I hear the crab fried rice is pretty good."

5

March, 1997.

"This project comprises twenty-five percent of your final grades for both science *and* social studies, so make sure to do your research. I will be grading you based on the rubric on the very last page of this packet. And, this is important, this is due when you get back from spring break," Ms. Furner says as she waves her copy in her left hand, giving it three definitive shakes before releasing it and letting it fall onto her desk. An immediate cry of protest fills the room, and Ms. Furner sits and grins in response. I'm not sure what part of what she's just said is what we disapprove of. In fact, I'm sure we aren't really upset about any of it: the grading percentage, subjects, rubric, or due date. By this point in the school year, our wailings and grumbles have become a sort of friendly tradition, denoting the start of an assignment, pop quiz, or project. I know this is true because Ms. Furner is always fair.

"It's almost time for lunch," Ms. Furner continues, "so before we go I want you all to look over the instructions and let me know if you have any questions." A shuffling of papers follows her request. Not only is Ms. Furner always fair, she is also easily the most beloved 4th grade teacher at West Point Elementary School (most likely due to how fair she is). She is also the youngest teacher in the school district, which adds to her popularity with the students and their parents. Most of the other teachers are either married with grade school kids of their own or are somebody's grandparent. But Ms. Furner is neither married, nor has any kids, so her youthful appearance and mind are genuine and helpful to her career as a children's educator.

I flip aimlessly through the packet but can't bring myself to read any of the words. I'll have plenty of time to go over it later on the bus or at home. I turn around to check the clock—just four more minutes till lunchtime, my second favorite time of the day. I reach into my backpack and pull out my binder. I'm trying to find the printed lunch menu schedule. Yesterday was Thursday, so we had spaghetti and meatballs or cheese lasagna, and the day before that was Wednesday, so we had either sloppy joes or mac and cheese. I always choose sloppy joes and spaghetti when I have the chance since it's the only time I can enjoy such generous portions of meat (even if most of it is cheap ground beef). Also, the refrigerator at home is always empty and the freezer is stocked with microwavable dinners like lasagna and mac & cheese. Today is Friday, so we should be getting either chicken strips or pizza. I'm disappointed, because in addition to TV dinners, I've also been raised on chicken strips and countless slices of mushroom pizza.

I finally find the schedule. Despite already knowing what will be served today, I pull it out, but try to not let anyone else see it. (For some reason I feel ashamed for checking the menu so close to lunchtime.) I can't help but smile. March flew by and I totally forgot about the last Friday of the month special, shamelessly called, "Foreign Friday." Last month they prepared tofu teriyaki with brown rice and something that looked like green beans. The month before was chicken quesadilla with refried beans and cheese dipping on the side. It's good to know that there is more to food than just hamburgers and American-style pastas. I sit back and wonder aloud, "I wonder what the menu today will be."

"Is today." I turn to my left and find my desk-mate, face buried in the project packet, pencil in hand, feverishly under-lining and writing notes. "You meant to say 'is today' not 'to-day will be,' " she says with a matter-of-fact tone in her voice. She says this without looking up.

Jamie regularly does this sort of thing: corrects your speech, grammar, or pronunciation. You would think I'd be annoyed by it or even hate her for it, but it creates an opposite effect; I admire her for it, and I like to think we get along as a result. We've been desk partners since the beginning of the school year, since like most classrooms, seating arrangements are de-cided by last names in alphabetical order. Last year in Ms. Cousar's class, I was the first in my class, but this year, Miss. Anderson has dethroned me.

Like me, she is half, but you could almost never tell. Her dark hair and eyes are probably the only obvious physical characteristics she has acquired from her Korean mother. She flips a page and continues her careful reading and note taking. If I ever had an older sister, I wish it could have been Jamie. Although she's almost a whole year younger than I am, her smarts are easily two years ahead.

"Thanks," I say as sincerely as I can muster. "I wonder what the menu is today."

"And a better way to phrase the whole thought would be, 'I wonder what today's menu is' or simply 'I wonder what's for lunch, today,' in case you were wondering."

She always did this sort of thing too. Not only would she correct you, she'd also throw in a free lesson, trying to teach and improve you. At least, that's the way I see her voluntary remarks.

"Thanks again, *Noo-na*," I say half-jokingly. (From what I can remember, *Noo-na* means older sister in Korean.) I know she knows I mean it as a joke, but at the same time I have a small feeling she's caught on to the underlying sincerity of the word. She doesn't say anything back to tip this off; instead, it's her silence that seems to confirm, and even welcome this. I stare at her high, slender nose and deep-set eyes and prominent chin, and really, really wish she was my older sister. How great would it be to have an older sister who'd make me dinner, help me with my homework, and tuck me in at night? But then I think of my home, and how small and cold it is, and of all the grownup soda cans and bottles in the refrigerator and trash bags, and stop wishing for her sake.

"So does anyone have any questions?" Ms. Furner inquires from her seat behind the teacher's desk. Jamie's hand shoots up and Ms. Furner motions for her to speak.

Jamie stands, her face about five feet directly in front of Ms. Furner, and asks, "May the subject of the project be a group of people and not just a single person?" The pupils in her eyes light up like charcoal, and her brows fall into their ridges, giving off the impression of smoke.

"Well, it depends. What do you have in mind, Jamie?"

"Your instructions ask us to choose a person, living or dead, who has contributed to America's culture, but who has also made contributions to science. Well, I'd like the focus of my project to be on the Yup'ik peoples residing in Alaska."

"Are they even real? Sounds like some sort of weird game or yucky food," a boy named Jackie Ryder yells from the back of the room. Several of the kids seated around him snicker, but Jamie acts as if she doesn't hear them, and continues to meet Ms. Furner's eyes.

"Class, quiet *please*—Jackie, what have I told you about interrupting? It's not polite, and it can get you into trouble, okay?" Radclyffe, Smith, Taff, and the rest of the R's, S's, and T's go quiet, as Ryder slumps back into his chair. "Okay, Jamie, but have they contributed to America's culture?"

Jamie's eyes rekindle. "Oh yes, I should be able to make an easy case for that. And their lives have a huge impact on Arctic research in terms of natural history, marine biology, and tools technology. And, for the curiously ignorant few among us, the Yup'ik are Eskimos, indigenous to Alaska and eastern Russia. Their name can even be broken up, with *yuk* meaning 'person' and *-pik* meaning 'real.' So, yes, they are essentially, 'real people.' "

Now Jamie turns to face the rest of the class, and Jackie, unnerved, slumps even further into his chair and looks away, his eyes burned by her full flames.

"Ok, sure, that sounds fine. As long as you're sure you can meet the requirements, I'll allow it. Anyone else have any questions?" Jamie sits down, obviously content, but careful to not let it show. Other kids around me are putting things away and pulling out their lunch tickets or lunchboxes. It's nearly time to go, so Ms. Furner gives us one last reminder that the project is due the Friday after spring break and instructs us to line up outside the classroom and wait for her. I'm one of the first to dash out. The ones before me are my friends, Michael Lee and Daniel Brackman.

Our class is one of the first to arrive at the cafeteria, at least before Ms. Blake's and Mrs. Thompson's classes, so the line isn't very long. Students who brought lunch from home join Ms. Furner at our class's two tables in the middle of the building. Jamie is among them.

Michael, Daniel, and I stand with the majority of our class in line. Daniel and I slide our trays across the flat railings behind Michael's double trays. I like Michael and Daniel because they're like me—they love school lunch. We've been friends since the first week of school when we bonded over bloody sloppy joes (basically sloppy joes with a whole lot of ketchup mixed in) and spaghetti and fireballs (which are meatballs drowned in hot sauce). Others in our class call us the Red Devils because we like to douse our food in all sorts of condiments, and still enjoy eating it.

We're nearing the front of the line and I smell a familiar aroma of marinated meat, and I feel a weird sensation, like my heart is being swallowed whole by my stomach. I recognize the steep, seasoned smell from the days of living with my mom; although she cooked the meal only once or twice, the aroma would linger in the house for days, almost weeks. My mind continues to wander, and I see myself back in California, living with Susan, confused as to why I've been abandoned and why I'm being sent to New York. All I know is to blame my dad for how all of this has turned out.

"It's meat! Meat! Meat!" Michael turns and yells at us, and by circumstance, the rest of the line.

"Yeah, yeah, we got it Mike," Daniel says, his fingers firmly stuck in both ears. "I'm pretty sure everyone here smells the same thing you do."

"How can you be so sure?" Michael asks. "With a nose like yours I wasn't sure if the smell of meat got lost with the smell of freshly cut grass from outside."

"Ha, ha, yeah—that's a good one," Daniel replies. His face is expressionless as he quietly shakes his head for the remainder of the time we spend in line.

It turns out, today's Foreign Friday special is *bulgogi* with rice and kimchi, from Korea. The lunch ladies plop a scoop of white rice onto each of our trays and cover it with a respectable portion of *bulgogi*. The sight of so much meat on one plate brings my spirits back; it really is a treat to behold.

"Smells good, right?" Michael asks me.

"Yeah, I guess it does."

We reach the drinks and Daniel and I each pick up a small carton of milk while Michael grabs two miniature bottles of water. We complete our trays with spoons, forks, straws, and napkins, and hand our tickets to the man at the end of the counter before making our way to the table unoccupied by Ms.

Furner and most of the girls in our class.

As we've done since week one, we sit at the end of the table farthest from Ms. Furner and Jamie, but closest to Ms. Blake's second table where most of her class's boys sit. Michael has already started with the Red Devils tradition of adding sauces to his meal before I'm finished giving a nod of acknowledgement to the boys at the neighboring table and sit down. Today, it's a bit of mustard with a lot of Tabasco. Our culinary seasonings are always somewhat chosen with taste in mind (since we do have taste buds after all), but more often than not, they are chosen according to a theme. And it seems Michael has chosen as complimentary a combination as one can muster with *bulgogi* and American condiments. He has already decided on a zombie theme.

"See how the rice is colored brownish-red? I used Tabasco instead of ketchup because it looks more like dried blood. With ketchup, it'd look like blood is running everywhere, but zombies don't bleed like—"

"But they still have human bodies, with blood in them," Daniel says.

"Yeah, but by that point all the blood has drained out of them and is left on their skin and clothes. Haven't you seen any zombie movies? Jeez."

"No…I'm not allowed to watch anything with blood."

"Well, tell your parents that zombies don't have any blood," Michael says. "Anyways, as I was saying, the hot sauce is our dried blood, and the dab of mustard is for rotting flesh. So all of this meat hanging out of the body is slowly rotting off. I did a better job on this one"—he points to his tray on the right—"since I was careful not to break the mold of the rice."

Daniel and I lean over the table to inspect Michael's works. The details are quite impressive. Michael grins as he picks up his spoon and starts to chow down. It's his signal to us to hurry and follow his lead. So, we add a boatload of Tabasco sauce and a single squirt of mustard to each of our plates and pick up our spoons to complete the ritual. However, as soon as I go in for a spoonful, my chest starts to feel heavy again. Suddenly, I don't feel like carrying on with forcing Western influences in my wholly Korean (American) dish (even if it's for such a creative and logical theme), and I decide to give in to the feeling in my heart. I find an untainted spot in the steaming pile and spoon it out and taste it. The sweetness of the marinated mixture forces me to smile, but it is soon followed by a bitter aftertaste. And I don't know why, but my eyes begin to tear up.

"Hey, what's wrong, Noel?" Daniel asks me.

"Uh, I don't know, I'm fine. It's just really spicy is all," I say.

"Really?" Michael says. "I thought you eat this stuff all the time. I'm not even Korean and I eat kimchi all the time. My family goes to that one place on Main Street every week for the BBQ buffet."

Daniel wipes his mouth with a napkin and pulls out his glasses cleaning cloth and says, "That's because you practically look Korean."

"Nuh-uh, no I don't. And that's racist you know," Michael splutters. Sweat droplets are running down his flat nose and his glasses are also turning foggy. His face is painted red from the Tabasco sauce and chili pepper spices, and possibly a hint of anger.

"Oh, so now you know what racist means," Daniel mutters while cleaning his own glasses, but Michael doesn't hear him. "Hey, Noel," Daniel says, once he's put his cleaning cloth away, "why don't you take off your scarf? It'll help cool you down."

I decide to follow his advice if I want to hide the real reason for my puzzling tears. I pull at the free end at my front, but instead of loosening, it tightens around my neck. A tinge of frustration and suffocation surfaces on my face, and I can feel myself getting red from embarrassment. I reach over my shoulder to bring the opposite end from my back around, but realize it's stuck. It's held in both of Ms. Blake's boney hands.

"Ashman, didn't anyone ever tell you not to play with your food?" Ms. Blake rasps. She tugs, hard, and finally lets go. "That's a nasty habit I won't allow at this school!"

"Hey, what's your problem lady?" It's Michael coming to my defense, already standing behind the seat bench, making his way around the table. Ms. Blake scoffs at the sight of Michael's disdainful grimace, and brings her hands to her hips. They're now face to face with each other. Compared to Michael's full figure, Ms. Blake appears emaciated, even more so for her old age. I start to wonder if she has any children of her own, or if she has ever married, and having already decided she doesn't and hasn't, I feel sorry for her.

"Ms. Blake, what seems to be the problem here?" Like a mother duck, Ms. Furner has come to our rescue. Her hands on Michael's shoulders advise him back to his seat. Daniel on the other hand has remained seated, and continues to face forward, head shaking, not daring to involve himself in the rift.

"I caught this youngster here playing with his food. He should be ashamed of himself. The reason we have these Foreign Fridays are for kids like him. Doesn't he know—"

"You're wrong," Jamie says from the other table. She's on her feet. Embers return to her eyes. "Foreign Fridays are for people like you. People stuck in the past. People who are closed off from the rest of the world. People who have fear in their hearts and hate in their souls!"

Silence follows. And soon after, I hear a single retching sound, followed by the spattering of muddy fluids two seats over from Michael, where Jackie is sitting, and I'm thrown into the reality of how intolerant some of us actually are (in terms of the mind and the stomach). Ms. Furner is already by Jackie's side.

"I hope you're happy with yourself young lady—bullying this sweet, young man—making him feel uneasy to the point where he loses his lunch." Ms. Blake appears to have ignored the content of Jamie's recrimination, and turns back towards me. "It really is a shame that this youngster would disrespect the cooks who tirelessly made this food. It's even more of a shame"—Ms. Blake's voice rises to a shrill—"that this little gook would dishonor his so called countrymen by defiling this disgusting mesh!"

"Ms. Blake!" Ms. Furner rebukes.

Hate fills my body. I want to hit her as hard as I can, but I'm afraid I might break her in two. I'm not one to resort to violence anyways. But why would she insult me like this? Insult my Korean half? Insult my mom?

"Fuck...you," I say under my breath. I run for the exit of the cafeteria and look back once I reach the doors. No one has bothered to follow me: not Michael, not Daniel, not Jamie, not Ms. Furner, and not any of the boys from Ms. Blake's class. Instead, they all stare at Ms. Blake, who is shrieking and trembling like a madman.

I storm out of the building, burning with rage. I decide for the first time to skip the rest of the school day and have some fun. There's something I've been wanting to try anyways. "I need matches," I say to myself. "Where can I find some of those?"

6

January, 1999.

As usual, I am alone. The house is so empty and so quiet, that I can hear my ears ringing with silence. But I don't mind. I'm reading J. D. Salinger's *The Catcher in the Rye*, a book I probably shouldn't be reading for yet another couple of years, but my teacher, Ms. Finkland, encouraged me to take a stab at it. So far, it has proven itself a challenging, yet influential read. Holden Caulfield is a more interesting protagonist than any of the other characters I've read about in class. He isn't restrained by certain etiquettes and language that the more classic novels pertain to, with their proper dresses and their intolerances.

Not wanting to leave any unnecessary creases on the bind-ing, I flip the pages just enough so that the words are barely visible. The book is borrowed from my teacher, a first edition I might add, so I want to return it to her in better condition than

I've received it in (if that's even possible).

My hands cramp up, forcing me to take a break as I place the book gently on the living room coffee table. I wish it could be like this all the time, just me, reading peacefully by myself as the snow engulfs the surrounding lands outside, freezing the ponds to solid ice. And while the other kids go out ice skating, I remain comfortably within the imagination of my books. I only have five books in total though, one of them being a worn-out bible, so naturally, I borrow the rest from the school library. To be honest, I haven't really looked through the bible, having only glanced at the first couple of pages. After taking a copy home with me from a Sunday school session, I didn't really see the point in reading it. The mere presence of it within my collection is good enough for me.

I pick *The Catcher* back up, and as I gently turn a crisp page, I hear the front door slam open, jolting me from the couch onto the cold floor. I quickly slide the first edition book underneath the couch, not wanting anyone to ruin its mint cover.

"Noel! Get your ass over here *right* now."

I crawl over and hide under the dining room table with my legs folded at my chest. Down the hallway, I can hear the familiar, uneven footsteps of my father, with his snow boots still tightly strapped on. Wet prints of mud and snow seep into the carpet, which become permanent signatures of the household, similar to the holes created by the invisible nails holding up the absent pictures on the walls.

"Son," my father shouts in his deep, drunken voice, "come out here right now!" I pull even tighter, drawing myself in like a young armadillo, naked without its shell. "Don't make me come find you!" I pray to the heavens for forgiveness of whatever crime I've committed to receive such damaging love. What could I have done in my young life to deserve this?

"Get out of there, now!" My father is on all fours, reaching out to grab hold of my skinny body. I can smell the stench of booze reeking from his mouth, which causes me to gasp for air. With all my might, I attempt to crawl away from my father's large hands, weaving in and out of table legs and chairs. I feel a rough tug on my foot and let out a high-pitched yelp, loud enough to surprise even myself. I kick and struggle, hoping that somehow my sock will act like a lizard's tail and slide off, enabling my escape. But it is futile, and I know any more resistance will only backfire tenfold in the end, so I lay limp with tears flowing down my face, accepting my bitter fate. My father drags me out from underneath the table and proceeds to whip me relentlessly with his leather belt. With each blow, I cry out in immense pain and involuntarily taste the salty tears that trickle into my gaping mouth.

"Who—do—you—think—you're—running—from?" my father says in-between each lash. The sounds of the belt flying through the air start to drown out my pleading. And long after my feeble voice dies off, my father wears himself out and retreats back outside, probably to the company of more alcohol. I lay still on the dirty carpet, the lingering pain preventing me from moving a single inch in any direction. I stare up at the ceiling while thinking how I've been wrongly punished for a deed I probably did not commit. Father doesn't care though. As long as he beats someone, it doesn't matter to him at all.

I start to sit up, motivating myself to get to the phone and call for help. But really, what would that accomplish? I'll just be sent away to another family who'll maybe treat me even worse, probably not physically, but emotionally. It's too much of a gamble. I shouldn't. Yet, my legs fight the pain and allow me to stand up straight. I tread slowly towards the kitchen phone with each step resulting in a sharp sting on my back. I pick up the phone and press it gently to my ear. Silence. The usual buzzing dial tone is gone. I tap the numbers desperately, hoping for some kind of response. The only noise I hear is the empty clicking of the buttons. I check the wires, which are all plugged in. I drop the phone and let it bounce up and down from the swirly cord. I feel hopeless, alone. I follow Holden's example and curse.

"Fuck."

It's not the first time a household service has gone unpaid. Just last month, I had to endure pitch-black afternoons for days before my father was sober enough to even realize the electricity had gone out. It then took a couple of days for him to build up the initiative to sort out the problem. I never complain, though. It is easier for me to hide when all of the lights are out. In fact, during those times, it's almost as if I disappear from my father's cerebral vision as well. But with the lights gone, there's no way for me to escape into my stories, walk amongst the characters and breathe in the air in which they breathe. With the stories, it's almost as if I'm a part of something, and I'm preparing for my own fantastic adventure. I just hope my journey starts soon; there's nothing I'd like more than to leave this setting behind.

I reach under the sofa and pull out the book from its dusty shelter and blow off whatever dirt that has clasped onto the cover. A collective tear lands squarely on the art of the merry-go-round horse, which causes me to frantically wipe it away with the edge of my sleeve. The tear leaves behind a soft blotch, morphing the paper cover to concave outwards. I take the book upstairs, one steady step at a time, and place it between my desk and a large geography textbook. Hopefully the weight will flatten out the spot and make it unnoticeable. If not, I could always hold onto the book until Ms. Finkland forgets that I have it. I don't need another adult to be upset at me.

7

August, 2009.

"Woo, shit that's spicy—good, but spicy," I say before cooling my mouth with some non-alcoholic beer.

Josh chuckles, "That's not much of a review. I guess it's a good thing you didn't become a food critic. You would've most likely starved to death." He chortles again and picks up a chip with a hefty amount of grilled lamb and even more Sriracha sauce spewed on it. I watch him with great admiration as he finishes the piece without breaking so much as a sweat. When we were still in high school, I might have casually told Josh about my ambitions of becoming a world famous food critic or TV chef. It's not surprising that he'd remember this tidbit, considering his attentive nature combined with his superior memory.

"Hey, I can handle Tabasco sauce, but this stuff is like fire in a bottle," I say as I wipe away the moisture forming around my nose and forehead with my paper napkin. "Just ask Michael." Josh, with yet another generous portion of lava-on-a-chip in his hands, turns to Michael, but our chubby friend is too busy chewing and doesn't respond. Sweat beads occupy every pore of his flat, bulbous nose, and the fog on his glasses conceals his smiling eyes. Since graduating from high school, Michael has continued to grow in size: his stature easily surpassing six feet, which some would say is tall for an Asian man, and it is, but I'd say it's tall in general. He's managed to retain some of his baby fat, although I wouldn't exactly consider him overweight. Josh on the other hand has managed to stay more or less the same, maintaining his slim figure, though perhaps he's more staunch than he was a couple of years earlier.

After he has swallowed most of his food, Michael says, "I don't know...I remember you cried once when you used too much Tabasco back in elementary school." We all laugh. Jeanette, whom I've just met today, leans over to her right, and with her napkin, wipes Michael's red-painted face clean. She's a quiet girl, about to start her last year at the School of Visual Arts, studying communication design. She and Michael have been dating for the past two-and-a-half months, which I think might be a record for Michael. I credit it to the fact that she's not the typical lass Michael is usually attracted to (or attracts). For starters, she's not Caucasian (or white—whichever way you'd like to call it). Ever since leaving West Point, Michael has made a slow, yet steady, transition to pretty white girls, but it seems that stage is abruptly over (though it's obvious Michael is still sticking with the pretty criterion). If I had to guess—sitting directly across from Jeanette and noting her sharp chin, arched eyebrows, and the way the light reflects off of her light bronze skin—I'd have to say she's Vietnamese. Of course, I would know in an instant if she had just introduced herself with her full name (like I did), or if I just decided to ask what her last name is (unless she's adopted, or has an ambiguous Asian family name, like Lee or Chang), or if I'm bold enough to just ask what her ethnicity is. But, if I have to put my money on anything, which I rarely do, I'd say the chance that I'm right about her being a Nguyen is quite high.

When she's done being a model girlfriend, Michael thanks her and calls over the waitress by name. Tiffany rushes over, most likely setting a new personal best in her 10-meter dash, and takes Michael's order with a smile.

"Okay, a new plate of nachos and another round of drinks coming right up!" She pulls off a sort of jaunty half twirl, sending her natural blonde (almost white) ponytail into a swirl, as she races back towards the kitchen. Her fluid movements make it look like she's on a pair of roller skates.

"I hope you guys can handle some more," Michael says once Tiffany disappears behind the swinging doors, rubbing his hands together with gleeful anticipation.

"Don't worry about me," Josh says. "When I was growing up, my mom would use Bhut Jolokia, otherwise known as the Ghost Pepper, when making her summer curries and chutneys. I've read that that chili pepper is about four hundred times hotter than Tabasco sauce."

"Damn man, that's crazy," is all I can come up with, slightly embarrassed by my low spice-tolerance.

"Maybe we should order something else—something you can enjoy," Josh says as he grips my shoulder and gives me a friendly shake.

"Screw you. You may be blessed with spice-tolerating Indian blood, but I've got some Korean blood in me. And I don't know if you know, but Koreans eat some spicy shit too."

"So I remember," Josh says, most likely referring to the time when we first tried *tteokbokki* together. It was a long while back when I was hanging out exclusively with Korean foreign exchange students from my school, acting as their guide, and in exchange they saw it as their duty to fix my utter lack of knowledge of Korean culture by trying to teach me all there is to know about its etiquette, language, and beloved K-pop. I invited Josh to join us at a Korean late night eatery so I wouldn't be the only person there who couldn't speak Korean in a place that might as well have been taken right out of Seoul. I remember the spicy rice cakes dish was unbearably spicy at first, but became more delicious with each subsequent bite.

"That's for certain," Michael says. "Last week I had some soft tofu stew at a nearby place and made the mistake of asking for extra spicy. I think I lost two pounds in sweat by the time I'd finished it." We all laugh again. This isn't the first time the thought of Michael losing weight by eating has come up and it won't be the last.

"And another thing about Koreans," I add, thinking back again to the night with Josh and my Korean *chin-goos*. "They drink ridiculous amounts of alcohol like nobody's business. I bet with my Korean blood, combined with my European blood, I could outdrink you all."

"If you did drink that is," Josh points out.

"Yeah, if I did."

The real attraction that night wasn't the *tteokbokki*, but instead, was the Seoul Train Soju Bomb, and the resulting *so-mek* (soju mixed with Korean beer), which I was forced to taste. I haven't heard from any of my Korean buddies since graduation, probably because I was deemed too whitewashed, and hence, a lost cause, though it was most likely due to my killjoy sobriety. But, at least I have Girls' Generation and Wonder Girls to take away from the experience.

"Hold on," Michael chimes in, "what type of European mix are we talking about here? English and German? Irish and Swiss? Italian and Dutch? All of the above?" I take a second to think about this. I actually don't really know of what European descent my dad was. I only know that he was white American. And even if I did know, it doesn't make much sense to boost about being a white mutt, especially considering how I'm already a mutt of a different kind.

So I say: "Does it really matter? They all like to drink."

"Liking and drinking are two different things," Michael pushes.

"Okay, well, if you must know...German. I'm half Korean and half German." Everyone nods with recognition as their bottom lips pucker out with the seal of approval on their faces. I've given an acceptable answer.

I haven't seen Josh or Michael since the beginning of summer, but I can't say I was surprised when Michael invited us to his favorite late night place out of the blue. In fact, I was half expecting either Josh or him to call us together. I've been too busy making ends meet to initiate a reunion of sorts, but now that we'll be starting our training together in the police academy next week, I suppose we'll all be seeing each other on a more daily basis.

"And one last thing about Koreans," I say. "They love to smoke." I pull out a pack of smokes and offer them to the others. Jeanette politely refuses one, which I find strange, since everyone I've met since moving to the city over four years ago smokes a few cigs a day (to keep the withdrawal away), though it's usually closer to two packs a day. And, as usual, Josh also refuses. I know he'd never smoke, but I always make it a point to still offer him a cigarette, just to be polite.

"Noel, did you hear"—Michael starts to say as I light his cigarette—"about our old friend, Daniel Brackman? Apparently his mom died earlier this year from cancer—lung cancer." The last words fuse into the form of smoke as they exit his mouth.

I expend a moment to take a puff before answering. "No. That's too bad," I say, as I try to avoid making eye contact with him. "I know, as we get older, this kind of stuff is bound to happen sooner or later, but it still doesn't change the fact of how hard it is to lose a parent." I continue to try to hide my face in fear that someone can read past it.

"Yeah, I guess you would know." We fall silent for a while, enjoying our smokes and drinks, when Michael asks me, "Do you still keep in touch with him?"

"Who? Daniel? Or I guess, Danny? No, not really." Michael and Josh nod, neither of them clueing Jeanette in on the situation of broken friendships, although Michael probably will during their taxi ride home (if he hasn't already).

"I sort of miss the old Jew boy," Michael says, as Jeanette gives her boyfriend a judging look.

The four of us sit in silence. Jeez, (as Michael would say) when did our little celebration get so somber?

Michael takes a final puff of his cigarette—its end uncomfortably close to the filter—and puts it out. Michael is quick at everything: quick eater, quick smoker, and quick-tempered. I offer him another smoke, but he refuses, saying how he likes to pace himself during a meal (though I suspect the untimely death of Danny's mom and/or his girlfriend's disapproval is making him think twice). He then proposes we should find time to hang out with Danny together, "like old times," and I agree. Tiffany appears with our order—two beers, one non-alcoholic Guinness, a piña colada, and our nachos—which Michael thanks her for and immediately begins eating. The sight of his pleasure raises the mood of the table to its original gaiety. We perform a quick cheers, and I take a satisfying gulp, accidentally spilling a little beer on my shirt and scarf. I turn to flag down Tiffany and ask her for some more napkins for our table, but she's already out of sight.

Josh lends me his napkin to clean up and casually says: "Speaking of old, high school mates, I heard that Jamie Anderson will be attending Columbia Law School in the fall." He stops for a moment to take a bite of nachos. "April told me after my graduation ceremony. Apparently, the two of them are Skype buddies. I had no idea." Hearing Jamie's name causes me to mentally flinch, and I notice Jeanette has detected my brief distress. Josh on the other hand is uncharacteristically not as perceptive; my guess is that all of the alcohol has impaired the use of his third eye.

Michael abstains from the nachos long enough to say, "That's no surprise."

"Which part? Josh asks. He takes another bite. "That Jamie will be going to law school at Columbia or that she and April are still friends?"

"Both, I guess. Jamie was our class's valedictorian, and I'm sure she graduated at the top of her class in college as well. And, remember how she and April were inseparable in the weeks before prom until Jamie left for California? Come on, Josh, you should know. Weren't you and April an item back then?"

"Sort of." Josh grins. "Though, our relationship was probably closer to that of an older brother looking out for his younger sister. But we're just good friends now."

I don't like the direction the conversation is heading. Soon I'll be pressured into commenting on the epochal period of high school that I'd rather forget: the end of Jamie's and my friendship, high school graduation, and lastly, Penny Bennett. So, I attempt to derail the conversation before it gets any further. "Hey, when we're done here, how about a little karaoke? I know a place in K-Town that always has all of the new releases. It's one of my favorite places to go to when I find myself on the other side of the park."

"Sounds like fun," Jeanette says.

"Sure," Josh shrugs.

Michael on the other hand pretends he hasn't heard my suggestion and says, "Oh, and do you remember that pretty red head you took to prom? What was her name?" He signals towards my general direction, snapping his fingers in frustration—his face is starting to give off a tint of red.

I let out a sigh. "Penny. Her name was Penny Bennett." I say. "Yeah, she was nice."

"What ever happened to her, huh?"

"I don't know. I haven't heard from her since graduation."

I down the rest of my drink, welcoming the sweet aftertaste, and manage to signal Tiffany to bring me another.

"The one that got away, huh? Hey, did you pork her? Please tell me you did."

"Uhh…" This is bold, but not unusual coming from Michael.

"You know, I remember you always avoided telling me back in high school and college," Michael continues.

"Mikey, stop. Can't you see you've made him uncomfortable?" Jeanette half scolds.

I can tell Josh has finally caught on to my discomfort, and he apologizes for bringing it all up.

"No, it's ok. I don't mind talking about this stuff. It doesn't bother me," I say. "Though I'll be right back. Just have to visit the restroom. We'll talk more about this when I return."

I get up to leave Josh and Michael to continue their chat about the good ol' days, with Jeanette sitting idly by. As I'm making my way around the table and to the back of the bar, weaving past other small, mixed groups of young people that are around our age, I hear Michael's hearty laugh, and it instantly makes me feel better and glad that I've agreed to come out today—the torturous bit about Jamie and Penny notwithstanding. Something about the rawness of Michael's joy makes me appreciate my life and its limited virtues. During our short stint in junior college (and most likely after we dispersed to our own respective four-year-schools), Michael was never alone. Josh and I were amazed by his popularity, especially with the girls, as he was never, *not* in some sort of relationship. Every few weeks or so, he was at the campus café, linking arms with a new little damsel—some of whom I could swear were way out of his league. But now I know they were most likely attracted to the way he made them feel good about themselves, with his inspiring panda bear-like way. Of course, his indubitable confidence helped as well.

I have an inkling that things are slightly different with Jeanette. She doesn't seem like the kind of girl with low self-esteem—who needs someone like Michael to help her feel better about herself—though I don't really know her so I could be wrong. She seems like a nice enough girl, and I hope, for her own sake, she knows what she's doing. It'd be great if she's the last one in Michael's long line of cheap rejects, but only time will tell.

All of this pondering about Jeanette has gotten me thinking about Jamie, and I guess a little about Penny, but mostly about Jamie. Years ago, I found her phone number on her public Facebook profile and saved it into my mobile contacts so I wouldn't be caught off guard by an unknown caller id, in case she ever decided to give me a ring. When I reach the bathroom door I decide it wouldn't hurt to give her a call. It's been so long, and now that she's back in New York (or soon due to be), she might not mind meeting to catch up. I'm sure she'd be glad to know that I've managed to earn a B.A.

I am pleasantly surprised by the cleanliness of the bar's bathroom; and the ambrosial scent originating from the bowl of potpourri atop of the toilet is remarkably calming. It's certainly better than the communal washroom I'm forced to use at my studio apartment in the West Bronx, which is located only a few blocks from the memorable Botanical Gardens. I close the toilet lid and sit, mentally preparing myself. I think aloud, "Although I may be making this phone call from a bar, this can hardly be called drunk dialing since I'm not drunk...right?"

I select Jamie's 510 number and hit the call button. There's a minor delay before the ringing starts. *Ring...ring...ring... ring...* Maybe she has changed her number since I've last checked, but most likely not. And before the next ring, I start to panic. I haven't thought out what it is I'm going to say or how I'm going to say it. *Ring...* Maybe she doesn't even remember me anymore. *Ring...* This was a bad idea. But, before I can hang up, the ringing stops.

"Your call has been forwarded to an automated voice messaging system..."

Oh well, it was worth a try.

"*Jamie Anderson,* is not available..." But at the sound of her voice, hope swells within me. But hope of what?

"At the tone please record your message. To leave a call-back number, press five." I'm inspired now to right all wrongs, mend our friendship, and reconcile. If anyone's "the one that got away" it's Jamie.

"*Beep.*"

"Hey Jamie, it's Noel. Ashman. So, I heard that you'll be studying law here at Columbia. Congrats. Umm..." I pause for what seems like the better part of a minute. "I hope this isn't awkward, and I hope you haven't forgotten who I am. Well, I'm sorry for not staying in touch with you since. I'll be starting my police academy training here in New York City soon, so give me a call if you ever want to get together and catch up. Okay...bye."

After I hang up, I feel good about myself. I did something I would normally never do; I just had to be alone, in a bar bathroom to do it. I imagine all of the things I could achieve if this bathroom were to replace the one on my apartment floor.

I get up and lift the seat lid, since I really do need to go. I toss my cigarette butt into the toilet and light another, almost dropping my lucky Zippo in with it, then start to wizz. My sense of accomplishment and euphoria is extended and translated into the duration of my primal release. But the feeling is cut short by the sound of harsh yelling and screaming coming from the other side of the door, and I get a little annoyed at whoever is responsible for startling me midstream, and consequently, dousing the fire of my high spirits into cold, wet embers with their own noisy piss. I want to disregard the cacophony as the byproduct of a fleeting, boorish cheer by of a couple of inexperienced drunks at the bar, but the noise doesn't let up.

The moment of my ephemeral pleasure is soon long forgotten when I exit the bathroom and identify the source of the ruckus; about twenty-five feet away, two chairs are turned over at my group's table, one of them belonging to me and the other to Michael, who is standing with his back towards me, face-to-face, or rather, nose-to-nose with another man. Michael's fists are clenched so hard all of the blood in them is being pushed out, making them appear Casper-white, and I can almost see right through them. Josh is on his feet too, attempting to quell the situation, and I can tell he's trying his best because he's actually trying to squeeze himself in-between the two titans and push them apart, with one of his arms flailing up and down, most likely telling them to calm down. And, although Jeanette is still seated, she's the loudest one of them all, screaming for Michael and the other guy to stop. There are three other characters, a group of phonies, a good distance behind their friend, obstreperously jeering and egging them on to fight. The kids at the tables I passed earlier are all staring intently at the scene, and the bartender and a man in an apron hesitantly approach with assuaging movements, obviously hoping for a peaceful resolution. Strangely, the small bouncer who was manning the front door is nowhere to be seen. And lastly, Tiffany is standing idly next to the table on the opposite side of the room, with a pitcher of beer in one hand and four beer mugs grasped in the other. Her eyes are wide open and refuse to blink—it's obvious that she's about to witness her first bar fight and isn't sure what she should do.

Apparently, that makes two of us. I want to join in and help appease the conflict, but I can't seem to bring myself to move. Over the years of growing up, whenever I saw violence (or sensed its vicious approach), my body's natural response has always been to freeze up and stay out of sight, no matter how guilty I felt or actually was. Not getting involved has saved me from a number of beatings, although not all of them. I was hoping to eventually overcome my cowardly habit, especially since physical altercations are to be expected in my future line of work.

Somehow, Josh manages to place himself in-between Michael and Jimmy (whose name I've managed to catch from Jeanette's repeated pleas for the two to stop), but his intrusion is met with a swift blow to the face. Jimmy, accidentally or not, elbows Josh during the pre-scuffle, sending him straight to the ground. And in a flash, Michael responds with a quick swing to the side of Jimmy's head, landing him next to poor Kapoor on the floor. A collective gasp escapes from the spectators, and the fight is over as soon as it began, with Michael as the last man standing.

Jeanette runs past Michael to join Jimmy's side as Michael helps Josh up and back into his chair, then takes his own. The three stooges have vanished by now, leaving Jeanette to help Jimmy up and support him on her own. The bartender and cook jump in to help, but she holds out her palm to them. She says something to Michael, but he waves her off and doesn't turn around. I'm guessing she's saying her final farewells because Josh reaches over and hands Jeanette her purse, and she walks out of the bar with Jimmy stumbling at her side. At the exit, Jimmy turns around, and something resembling a grin, but possibly a scowl (it's hard to tell with his face already starting to swell up) occupies his face. I look around for Tiffany to see how she has processed the event, only to catch a glimpse of her entering the kitchen empty handed, which cues me to follow her lead and get back to business.

I start my slow trod back to the table and pick up my chair and sit as if nothing has happened. Michael has resumed vigorously eating and Josh joins in at a leisurely pace. I ignore the food and stick to finishing my smoke. The three of us sit in silence for a minute until Tiffany shoots out of the kitchen with my beer and two packages.

"Here's your drink, sorry it took so long," she says. I take it and thank her.

"Also, here are some bags of frozen carrots. I thought you guys might need them. One for you. And one for you," she says as she hands one to each of my friends. They both nod in thanks and apply the carrots to their respective wounds.

As Josh finishes a chip, I notice splotches of Sriracha sauce above his upper lip and point it out to him.

"Oh no," Tiffany says, "that's not Sriracha sauce. I think it might be blood. Hold on, I'll bring you some napkins." She runs off again, this time opting out on the twirl, and I think to myself how a girl like that must have some nicely toned legs; it's too bad pants are part of the uniform here.

When she returns she's all out of breath, so I offer her Jeanette's seat. Most of the other patrons have left by now, probably scared off by the fight, which leaves us, two other tables, and some old men by the bar. I figure she has some time to take a break now. She hands Josh some napkins and he puts down the frozen carrots and uses the napkins to plug his nose. My cigarette goes out, so I light another and offer what's left of the pack to everyone else. Michael doesn't hesitate to take one. I hand him my lucky lighter as I hold out the pack to Josh, who acts upon my courteous habit by surprisingly taking one as well. I rotate my arm to the left for Tiffany, and smile when she takes the last one.

After the lighter makes its way around, Josh lifts his beer, so we all follow suit, with Tiffany picking up an untouched glass of water. "To good friends," he says in a nasally voice. "Old and new."

We all drink. Michael finishes his beer and goes straight back to the nachos. Tiffany offers to get him another, but he tells her he's good for the time being. In any other establishment we would have been kicked out—not offered more drinks—but I guess Michael holds a lot of weight here as a loyal patron.

"Okay," Tiffany says, "but when you feel like another, just let me know—it'll be on the house." She inhales and slowly feathers smoke out of her nostrils, creating pairs of tiny smoke rings—something I haven't tried doing since I bought my first pack.

"So," Josh says, "how are you feeling, Michael?" He takes a small puff of his cigarette and starts to cough uncontrollably. Tiffany and I try to stifle our laughter, but we're unsuccessful. Josh does a good job at not appearing embarrassed.

"I'm fine," Michael blusters. His thick panda-brows are knitted as he slides his bag of carrots off his right hand. It's probably smart not to bring up Jeanette or what has just transpired, but it's actually Michael who does so. "I knew it wasn't meant to be. Something about her felt off, like she was just waiting for a reason to break things off." His voice softens. "I'm sorry you got in the middle of it—literally."

"I'm fine," Josh says. By now, the napkin plugs in his nose are completely soaked in a crimson red color. Tiffany suggests he replace them, which he does.

"I'm glad you invited us out here though," Josh continues. "I mean, who knew a place with a name like Five Eagles Bar would have such tasty roasted lamb nachos. Each bite has a perfect spread of crisp texture, meaty flavor, and of course, a hint of spice." He gives me a look of validation, to which I roll my eyes. His amusement is reflected in the warmth of the yellow lights.

"I'm surprised Michael's never brought you guys here before," Tiffany says. "He talks about you two all the time."

"I do not," Michael says.

"You do to." Tiffany gives him a light jab on his shoulder.

One of the remaining tables asks for the check, which has Tiffany back on her feet. Before she leaves, however, she says, "Well, I had fun chatting with you guys, even if it was only for a couple of minutes. Thanks for the smoke." She twirls off, but not before wiping her hands on her apron and giving Michael a quick bowed hug.

When she's out of earshot I say to Michael, "You should ask her out."

"Maybe I will," he says.

I sit back, strangely satisfied with the way the night has turned out. I take a long drag and attempt to blow smoke rings, when I'm jolted up by a sudden revelation.

"Oh shit," I say.

"What is it?" Josh asks.

"Oh...nothing." I take a swig of my Guinness. I just remembered I forgot to leave my number.

8

August, 1993.

Today is a special day because it's my first day of school. Mom woke me up early to get ready. She's already in her working uniform and she's wearing a brightly colored bow tie. Her black hair is tied back and a pretty red flower is holding it in place. She kneels down to help me put on the same clothes I wore for the past week, and when she does, I can read her name off her shirt pin—Mary Song. I learned over three years ago how to read and write my own name, Noel Song, and since then, I've been learning lots of new words every day from Susan. Each summer, mom made sure to buy me plenty of new books to read with Susan during the day. Susan says I'm gifted and that I'm a lot smarter than the other kids she babysits for. I'm not sure that's true though because I think she's just being nice. She is a very nice person.

Of the books we read, *The Giving Tree* is my favorite since it reminds me of myself: how my mom and Susan play with me, and help me when I need help or get into trouble. It's like they're my apple tree. It would be great if I could end up like that little boy, living a happy, long life with mommy and Susan.

Now summer is over again and the air is cooler, but it isn't cold. It never gets too cold here. Mom finishes helping me get dressed and tells me to bring my schoolbag to the kitchen. It's a brown one she bought last week. I wanted a different color, but she said there was nothing else left. It's ok though, since I know she tried.

"Honey, we don't have time, so I'm going to need you to eat breakfast on the bus," she says as I enter the kitchen. I watch her work on the counter and pull out a juice pouch from the fridge. From the way she closes the fridge door I can tell she's in a hurry.

"Are we late?" I ask.

"Yes, that's why I need you to grab your things and put on your shoes. Mommy's almost done packing your lunch."

So I put on my bag and slip into my shoes and wait for her by the door.

"You're such a good boy," she tells me a minute later as she opens my bag and puts my lunchbox in it. "I put extra chocolate candies inside for you to share with your new friends, okay?"

I nod. She comes around to my front and straightens my hair with her hands and licks her finger before cleaning my eyes.

"And this week's a lot colder than last week so I want you to wear a scarf." She wraps one of her own around my neck.

The ends almost reach the ground and I point this out to her, but she says it'll have to do for now and that she'll buy one for me soon.

She runs back to the kitchen to grab our breakfast off the pan—toast with jam—and rushes us outside. We have to walk four blocks to reach the bus stop for my school, and as we speed walk, I can see a group of kids and grown-ups at the end of the street. There are even some big kids without their parents who are probably in middle school or even high school.

When we get to the stop, mom says hello to some of the parents and some of the parents say hello back to her and me. It's been a long time since I've been around so many people, so I hide behind mom's legs.

"He's very shy," mom explains.

"Is this his first day of school?" one of the adults asks.

"Yeah, well, it'll be his first time around kids his own age ever since preschool."

"Oh, how old is he?"

"He just turned seven last month. There were just some complications that made it hard for him to attend kindergarten."

I can hear the bus pull up to the curb, and without replying, the man smiles at us and turns to his own child. Mom kneels in front of me. "Okay, remember to listen to Ms. Butler and do as she says. Don't give her any trouble." She and the man catch each other's eyes, and they smile again. "And also make sure to get along with your classmates. But most importantly, have fun sweetie, okay? Promise me."

"Okay...I promise." We link our pinkies and touch our thumbs. I feel bad though because I don't plan on making any friends. I'd much rather read books at home with Susan and mom. I don't tell her this though because I know it'll make her upset and sad.

"Susan will be here to pick you up after school."

The line in front of the bus door is almost gone so mom tells me to get on. She hands me my toast and waves goodbye. I run to the bus and climb the stairs as the door shuts behind me. The bus driver lady smiles at me and points her finger towards the end of the bus. I start walking down, looking at the floor because I'm scared of having to talk to anyone. There are already so many people on and I don't know if I'll be able to find an empty seat.

The bus still hasn't moved yet. I don't know why. I reach the end and run into a boy's legs, so I turn around and walk back towards the front of the bus. I feel the bus spring up and a woman says, "Hey, can someone find the kid a seat already? Move your backpacks off the seats and make room for him, will ya?" No one listens to her so she says, "Kid, come up here and sit right here next to this young man." The bus driver lady is pointing to a seat a few rows behind her own chair where a big kid is sitting by the window. He pulls his bag off the seat and I hop on. The lady sits too, and the bus wobbles again like a seesaw and starts to move. Kids on the other side of the bus are waving goodbye, and I know mom is probably waving back. I want to join in, get mom to notice me, and somehow convince her to take Susan's place and be there waiting for me when I get back. But I know, no matter what I do, she will always have someplace more important to be.

During the ride I don't talk to anyone. I just eat my toast, taking one nibble at a time. When I finish, I clean my fingers and bite my nails. The boy next to me has been listening to music for the whole trip. He smells like the matches mom uses to light the candles in our home.

The bus makes only one stop before it reaches the school about thirty minutes later. I'm happy because I know things could have been worse.

The bus stops in front of the school and I stand to follow the rest of the kids. The older boy pushes me a little to get out, but he doesn't really hurt me. The bus driver lady smiles at me as I make my way down the steps. When both of my feet are on the ground I step away from the bus door and look around. The building doesn't look familiar. It looks different from when I came here with Susan during opening-day last week to meet Ms. Butler and find her classroom. Susan told me to enter through the big doors and turn left and walk all the way down the hall until I see Ms. Butler's classroom. But I don't see any big doors. I'm afraid. Kids are running into the building and the one next to it. I have to ask for help but I don't know how. I'm crying now. I'm going to be standing here all day crying until it's time to go home. I won't learn anything new, and mom will be disappointed.

"Hey, are you okay? Are you lost?"

I look up and see two older girls walking towards me. By now there's only a few other kids left outside. They come closer, and the same one who just spoke kneels next to me while the other girl checks her watch.

"Emma, we're gonna be late."

"Wait a sec, don't you see this kid here needs our help?" She turns her attention back to me and asks, "Who's your teacher?"

She reminds me of mom, even though her eyes are blue and her hair is yellow. I think it's the niceness in her voice and the flower in her hair.

"Ms. Butler," I say. This is the first time I've talked to someone, other than mom and Susan, since we've moved here.

"Isn't she a first grade teacher?" asks the other girl with brown hair.

"Yeah." The yellow-haired girl turns back to me and says, "Don't worry, we'll take you there. What's your name?"

"Noel."

"Okay Noel. Just follow us, okay?"

I nod. She takes my hand and leads me into the building, the other girl following close behind.

We turn right and then left at the end of the hall. Yellow hair points to a classroom two doors down and tells me that that one is Ms. Butler's. I say thank you, but I want her to know I really mean it. So I pull my hand out of hers and take off my bag and reach in for my lunchbox. I open it and find a sandwich, a bag of chips, the Capri Sun, and four pieces of chocolate. I hand her two of the chocolates, one for her and one for her friend. Now I have two left, one for me and one for a friend of my own. She smiles at me and I run to the class-room door. Before I go in, I turn around to wave goodbye, but she and her friend are already running away, down the hall.

9

July, 2010.

As soon as I exit the elevator I hear a familiar, yet strangely stilted voice beckon me, "Ashman, over here." With a quick look around I recognize its owner and start my march over to him as the elevator doors shut behind me with a loud clank. Today's my first day on the job, so I'm relieved, having been spared the embarrassment of looking like a little boy who has lost sight of his mom in a crowded Mall of America on a Saturday afternoon. In my current scenario, my fictitious mom, Sergeant Special Assignment Alexander, has managed to find me before I've started to cry and draw the attention of the (mall) cops.

When I get close enough, he stretches out his hand and I hastily take it. His hand is surprisingly dry and coarse, but also quite warm. (It doesn't shock me that a man like Sergeant

Alexander skimps on the hand lotion.) To top it off, the sheer strength of his grip makes me think of how my own hand is disappearing into a dark quicksand. I've met the Sergeant only once before, a few days before graduating from the academy, when I was approached by him during the graduation rehearsal. He was very reticent about his motive, but seeing how I'd graduated near the top of my class, I knew he was trying to recruit me to his precinct. As tradition has it, those who graduate at the top of their class get to choose their precincts, while everyone else is assigned to patrol precincts on a "most needed basis."

"I'd like you to meet someone," Sergeant Alexander says, and without turning his head or breaking eye contact he calls out, "Matthews."

A short man in blue rushes over and performs a quick, sloppy salute. Despite his thinning hair, he looks only a few years older than I. He then turns to me with an outstretched hand and introduces himself as "Police Officer Richard Matthews" and I introduce myself as just "Noel Ashman." P.O. Matthews's hand is so smooth, I wonder if I'm shaking a wax hand, but the surprisingly firm grip tells me it's real.

"Matthews will be your field training officer during your Field Training and Evaluation Program. If you have any questions, just ask him," Sergeant Alexander says before walking off. Matthews and I both watch the Sergeant disappear into the open office.

"Well, on behalf of the Sarge, welcome to the Fifty-third Precinct. Did you have any problems with administration? I see that they've already issued you your gun."

"Yes sir, though I—"

"Please, *please*," Officer Matthews begins to say as he frantically waves his hands in front of him, "just call me Dick. Save your sirs for the chain of command." He throws his thumb over his shoulder, pointing in the direction of the office doors. "You were saying?"

"Um, yes…Dick, it's just that, it's sort of dumb, but I can't seem to get the holster to stop creaking whenever I move."

Dick titters, and I don't know why but at that moment I feel a little bad for him. Maybe it's his short stance or his unsolicited practice of saluting or his premature balding head or his insistence for me to call him Dick, but I feel sorry for him. So, I decide to treat him like an old friend.

"The leather is just stiff is all," Dick says. He slaps his own tattered holster a couple of times and says, "Don't worry about it, it'll eventually get broken in. How about your off-duty gun? Did you decide to go with the Glock, one of the Smith & Wessons, or the SIG Sauer?"

"None, actually."

Dick stares at me like I just came out of a mental institution. "Huh," he says to himself with his hands on his hips. "When I first laid eyes on you I had a feeling you weren't a typical rookie. You know, most new officers can't wait to get their off-duty gun."

"I would rather be responsible for just this one," I tell him. And hopefully, I won't ever have to use it.

"To each his own I guess," he says with a shrug. "Come on, we still have some time before the morning briefing. Let me show you around."

Dick leads me through the glass doors to the workstations which reminds me of a brokerage firm's floor, wide and open, and stops next to the first desk we come across. "This will be your desk," he says. "And I actually sit right next to you, so you'll have access to me all day for whenever you need help." He gives me a straight smile and a thumbs-up before sitting at his own desk. "Give me a sec here to check some emails. Don't get too comfortable though. We'll be up and about again soon." He pushes a small bowl across the divide onto my desk. "Go ahead and help yourself to some chocolate in the meantime."

I take one piece and slip it into my pocket before sitting at my new desk. The thing is hardly three feet long, and the small backrest on the chair makes it more of a stool on wheels than anything. Immediately, I notice all of the foot traffic passing me by—a number of people have already bumped into the edge of my desk during just the first minute I've sat here, but none of them apologize or even seem fazed—and there's an uncomfortable breeze that hits my face every two seconds whenever someone opens the glass doors. I peer over the single monitor on my desk towards the end of the room and notice Sergeant Alexander is seated closest to the briefing room, which is adjacent to one of the Lieutenant's private office. He is reprimanding two junior officers, one of whom is visibly trembling. The other is blue in the face. I hope I never end up in that situation.

I turn my attention back to my desk and try to figure out if my computer is on sleep mode or if it is off. I end up on my hands and knees to find the power button below my desk. When I press it, I hear the fan turn on and the CPU beeps as if it is cursing me for waking it up from its slumber. At least my station comes with a working computer.

"Almost done, Noel," Dick says.

"Okay, no problem," I respond.

"How'd you like the chocolate? My sister sent them to me from Zurich. You can't get them from around here."

"Oh. It was really good."

Dick gives me a thumbs up and turns his attention back to his emails. I take another look around the floor in an attempt to subside my nerves, making note of statistics such as how many desks there are; how many of them are occupied by officers; what the female to male ratio is; what the racial mix is like; and trying to determine which of the plain clothed individuals are detectives and which are visitors (though the presence of shoulder holsters prove to be a dead giveaway).

"Alrighty," Dick says, standing up. "We'll make a quick stop at the kitchen, then I'll introduce you to some of the guys."

I nod and follow him down a hallway. My holster creaks with every right step I take.

"So, why'd you decide to become a cop?"

I clear my throat before responding. "Well, it was either this or becoming a fireman," I say. "There was more reason for me to pursue a career in law enforcement, so I went with that."

"Fireman, huh."

"Yeah, like Guy Montag," I joke.

Dick gives me a confused look as we make a final right turn into a high-end kitchen. There are two sinks, two refrigerators (granted one is significantly smaller than the other), and two coffee machines brewing fresh coffee with post-its on them, one labeled with the time 7:20 and the other with 7:35. There are also two tables set up in the back against the wall, with the first occupied by three officers, while the second is occupied by a lone man in plainclothes.

"Well, it looks like most of the guys are here. Let's get some coffee and join them," Dick says.

As he is handing me a mug inscribed with the words "World's Greatest Dad" it slips out of his hands before I can get a firm grip on it. Luckily, I'm able to catch it with my other hand, preventing the floor from being littered with ceramic shards. After Dick bestows a quick commendation, we each pour our own coffee from different pots. Before I get the chance to add cream and sugar, Dick says, "Come on, let's not keep the guys waiting."

Dick continues to use the word "guys" despite the fact that the breakfast club consists of three men and one woman, which is a fair representation of the ratio I've concluded with on the office floor.

"Hey, morning guys," Dick addresses the bunch. They're all enjoying their coffees, huddled around a large box of doughnuts. The sight puts my last stroke of new-job jitters to rest. "I want you all to meet one of the Fifty-third Precinct's newest officers, Noel Ashman. I'm going to be his *FTO* during his *FTEP*." He pronounces each letter distinctively and proudly.

The closest officer introduces himself. "Nice to meet you, Noel. I'm Sergeant Dan Akamatsu. You can just call me Dan."

"Joseph Schmidt," the officer across from Dan says. "Everyone calls me Joe."

"Welcome Noel, dear, I'm Pam, more formally known as, Sergeant Pam Palmer," the female officer says, reaching over Joe.

"And the gentleman at the other table," Dick tells me, "is

Detective Lieutenant Bradley Br—,"

"It's Lieutenant Commander Detective Squad Brown, head of the Major Case Squad," Brown interrupts. He ignores my outstretched hand as he continues to say, "So you're one of our newbies. Noel was it? Well, I'd love to stay and chat and get to know you, but I have more important things to do. Excuse me ladies."

Wow, what a dick I think to myself.

Sergeant Palmer seems to sense my disgust. "Don't worry your pretty little head about Detective Lieutenant Brown. None of us do. In fact, Dan and I have learned to avoid dealing with him by simply staying away from investigative work. Soon enough, you'll learn that as long as you stay out of his way, he'll stay out of yours."

"Take a seat you two and help yourselves to some doughnuts," Dan says. Dick takes the empty seat next to Dan, and I slide over the stool, formerly occupied by Brown, and sit at the end of the table. "So, what's it like being in uniform?" Dan asks me.

"Feels good," I answer. And it really does. "If you were to tell me six years ago that I'd be making the transition from wearing a fast food employee getup to wearing the uniform of New York's Finest, I wouldn't believe you. But I somehow managed my way through the academy, and here I am."

"Oh, you did more than manage your way. From what I heard, you ranked fourth in your class of nearly three hundred. That's quite a feat!" Dick says.

"Wow, congratulations," Dan says. I respond with a quick thank you in an attempt to mask my modesty.

"So, just how old are you, son?" Joe asks

"Twenty-three, though I'll be turning twenty-four at the end of the month."

"Sort of a late bloomer then," Joe says as he finishes his jelly doughnut and picks up another.

"Well, I finished a four-year criminal justice degree before enrolling in the academy, which I guess is unusual these days."

"Oh, that's like Dan and Pam," Dick interjects.

Joe grunts. "I'll never understand why people would waste time and money to complete a four-year program to become a cop when a two-year program is just as good. Heck, nowadays they let you start right out of high school."

"Um, it was just important for my friends and I to—"

"Sweetie, you don't have to explain yourself to this bitter old man," Pam says. "He's just upset that young'uns like you and I are given higher pay grades and faster promotions."

"I'm actually comfortable right where I am, thank you," Joe retorts. "And look who's talking. You're not so young yourself."

"I wouldn't exactly call thirty-nine old," Pam says.

"Almost the big four-oh," Dan mutters.

"Don't make me go four-*eight*-oh on your pretty little butt," Pam whispers as she takes a sip of coffee.

The men all erupt in laughter, while Pam is hiding a smirk in her coffee mug. I join in on what I can only guess is an inside joke, and pick up a doughnut that I hope is cream filled. Dick has already finished his first sprinkled doughnut and like the rest of the table, is working on his second.

"So, what's four-eight-oh?" I ask.

"You don't know what four-eight-oh is, son? What's the point to all that schooling?" Joe sputters, sending sprinklets of coffee across the table.

A young lady with baby blue eyes pokes her head into the kitchen and interrupts with a message for my FTO in a drowsy manner: "Officer Matthews, the Sarge wants to see you before the briefing." I'm guessing she's an intern or support staff.

Dick asks the "guys" to watch over me until he gets back, to which Pam replies, "We won't let the little chick out of our sight." Dick rushes out with his mug in one hand and his half-eaten doughnut in the other.

As soon as he disappears Pam says, "You know it's his first time being an FTO." I can't tell if she's telling me or if she's making an offhand comment, because she's still facing the exit, so I just nod. "Knowing how he is," she continues, "I'd say he's a nervous wreck right now. I mean, he has a hard enough time taking care of himself." Pam turns to me. "But I'm sure you're a good kid and you'll make things easy for him, right?"

"Of course," I say.

"Good."

"So, Noel, do you know any of the other rookies from the academy who've joined you at our precinct?" Dan asks.

"Sure, I know *of* them, but I don't really know them. Most of them performed really well in trainings and exams, so it doesn't surprise me that they've chosen this precinct. I mean, it was either here or Midtown Manhattan."

"What about any friends you've made in the academy? Where did they end up?" Joe asks.

"One of them was actually assigned to a closeby precinct in the East Bronx. The other, unfortunately, was sent to Staten Island."

"Ouch," Dan says. "Well, assignments aren't permanent.

After a few years of hard work, he can transfer."

"I hope so," I say, though I know Michael's chances are bleak, considering the number of black marks he has received in the academy for his volatile behavior. I remember Josh trying to raise his spirits when we heard about the assignments by joking that maybe dumping Tiffany and seducing a police chief's or commissioner's daughter might help.

"Well, boys, it's about time we head over to the briefing room," Pam says. "Noel, you can just follow us there, okay sweetie?"

"Hey son, take this doughnut box with you and share it with the rest of the officers at the briefing, will ya?" Joe asks of me.

When we leave the kitchen, the office is practically empty. All of the hustle and bustle ten minutes earlier has died down. A few officers are seated, but I don't see Dick at his desk.

"Kid, in here," Joe directs me into the briefing room. It's a large room, which reminds me of my high school's band room. "You're welcomed to sit wherever you'd like, but it's probably best to wait for Dick."

Joe joins Dan and Pam as they greet some other cops who have saved them seats. I overhear them talking about an arrest Pam has made last week: "I heard you had to bring out the old billy club on this guy," one of the officers says. "That's Pamm-Pamm for ya," says another.

The room is packed with approximately fifty personnel and the noise is getting unbearably loud. The whole scene makes me nervous again, so I turn around and start to cogitate on how I can somehow sneak in a cigarette break, when I bump into Dick. A couple of doughnuts fall out onto the floor, but thankfully I've drank most of my coffee to spill any of it.

"Hey, where are you off to?"

"I was just about to go looking for you," I stutter. I kneel to pick up the escaped deep-fried treats, and throw them into a nearby trashcan.

"There's no need to be nervous," he says. "Listen, you see that guy over there?" Dick has his hand on my shoulder and is pointing at a familiar figure in the front of the room.

"You mean Sergeant Alexander?" I say.

"Yup. You know, he also had a first day."

And remarkably, I feel confident again, and I can see Dick is proud to see the spirit return to my eyes. "No kidding," I say with a smile.

"Come on, let's go see if there're some seats left."

We end up standing in the back. I hand off the doughnut box and watch it make its way around the edges of the room. It doesn't even make it to the middle before someone chucks the empty box onto the floor. When it hits the ground all of the chatter stops, and for a second I have a funny thought of a *The Far Side* comic with an image of an officer, kneeling next to the doughnut box that now has a police cap on, and jelly, spilling out of its cracks, with a caption that reads, "A moment of silence for our fallen comrade." Now that I'm a paid NYPD officer, if anything will put me at ease, it's a picture of a cop and his doughnuts.

It takes me a few seconds to realize that the sudden silence is due to Sergeant Alexander stepping up to the podium. "Good morning, ladies and gentlemen. Seeing how it is now eight o' clock, I'd like to get the briefing started. But, before I hand it off to Lieutenant Hendricks to go over today's agenda,

I'd like to remind everybody to properly wear your uniform. I don't care how hot it gets out there, your uniform reflects not only on you as a police officer, but also on the NYPD as a respected law enforcing department. Citizens need to feel comfortable enough to approach you for help on the streets, and they won't be doing that if you don't look the part. This is your only warning."

And with that, Sergeant Alexander returns to his seat, allowing a white-shirted man, who is most likely Lieutenant Hendricks, to take the podium.

"Thank you Sergeant. So, for those of you whom I haven't had the chance to meet yet, I'm the precinct's Field Operations Lieutenant. As you all may know, we have a number of new recruits here with us today. They're some of the best graduates the academy's had this year, which is why Captain Ramirez has joined us today to help welcome them to the precinct." The Lieutenant gives a deferential nod to the Captain before continuing. "So I'll try to keep this short and sweet. Each new recruit has already been assigned an FTO, but just because you haven't been appointed as an FTO doesn't preclude you from acting as a mentor and helping guide our recruits throughout their probationary period. Your job is to make them feel welcome. If it helps, just think back to the times when you first started out as officers.

"Next on the agenda. The holiday weekend is coming up, which means more events, more crowds, and more traffic. We'll be running the same drill we go through every day, but with more checkpoints and patrols leading up to the weekend, starting today. Schedules have already been set, although details are still being worked out as to how many of our officers we'll be needing to lend to neighboring districts. As for the day of, a lucky few will be stationed at select events, in uniform, until the last firework has been shot over the Hudson. The unlucky ones will be on routine patrol.

"Non-life threatening investigations by the Major Case Squad will be taking a backseat until this is all over. Any cases of priority will be determined and lead by Detective Lieutenant Commander Brown. Now, I think it's time for Captain Ramirez to give his speech. Captain."

A brief applause fills the room again as the two men shake hands and Captain Ramirez takes the podium. "Thank you, Lieutenant. I too will try to keep this speech succinct and to the point. Are all of the probationary officers present?"

"Yes sir, I believe so," Lieutenant Hendricks says.

Sergeant Alexander stands and shouts in a peremptory manner, "All recruits, on your feet!"

Since I'm already standing I decide to step forward, and I notice a few familiar faces do the same. It's strange how I didn't sense their presence until now.

"Thank you, Sergeant," the Captain says. "I'm pleased to announce that we have five new officers who'll soon be calling the Fifty-third precinct their second home. I'm even more pleased by the diverse turnout."

I take a quick look around and recognize the rest of the four newbies.

"I would like to personally welcome Noel Ashman…"

Although I wasn't expecting my name to be called out, I'm used to being first on the list. So, out of habit, I call out, "Here."

Thankfully, the Captain ignores me and continues with the

names, "…Thomas Banner…"

The one time I did talk with Thomas, I remember him being a prick and sort of oafish. It's actually kind of surprising to see him here.

"…Julie Hernandes…"

Smart, but an ass-kisser if I ever did see one. I guess the intelligent ones usually are.

"…Louie Nunez…"

I don't really know much about Louie. It's safe to say he kept to himself.

"…and last but not least, Megan Wheeler…"

Attractive, in an athletic sort of way. She outperformed most of the men in terms of the number of push-ups and sit-ups one could do per minute (easily performing 45 and 60 respectively), and could easily bench 130.

"On behalf of Police Chief Theron Daniels and our own Deputy Inspector Salinger, I welcome you to the first day of your lifelong career. I, along with Lieutenant Hendricks, Sergeant Alexander, and the rest of the ranked officers, expect your best every day, and I also expect you to leave everyone you meet with dignity and respect. As you know, a lot of people wanted to be where you are standing today. Don't forget that, and you'll be fine."

After another round of applause, the briefing is over and everyone starts filing out as soon as we're dismissed. I get caught in the departing wave, which is fine since I can just meet Dick at our desks.

As I exit the briefing room the same girl who stopped by the kitchen earlier approaches me in a nonchalant manner. From up close I can see all of her freckles and notice her soft, auburn hair.

"Are you Officer Ashman?" she asks in her languid fashion.

"Yes I am. It's nice to meet you…" I search for her name on her blue clip-on id, "Emma Church." It turns out she's one of the administrative assistants.

She gives me a half-smile and says, "I have your photo id for you. Don't lose it. I mean, losing your badge is a lot worse—there'd be endless paperwork and a penalty of as much as ten days' pay—but losing this can be just as bad." She hands me the card and I take a few seconds to study it.

A picture of me, grinning in uniform, is plastered onto a red background. Right below that are the words "Police Officer Ashman Noel T., Shield Number 347378."

"Well, if it wasn't official before, it is now," I say.

"Well, good for you," says Emma. I can't tell if she's being sincere or not.

"So, how's it like working here?" I ask her as I slip the card into my pocket. "What do you normally do around here?"

"Filing, scheduling, and errands. I've actually got to get the Sergeant some flowers. It's his wife's birthday today and he usually doesn't have time to do things like that himself."

"Oh, really? What kind of flowers did he ask for?"

Emma raises her eyebrows. "Mostly just roses."

"Classic choice," I say. "Can't go wrong with plain red roses."

Emma slowly nods her head in agreement. "Sure."

I nod back, and for a moment we're both nodding in sync.

"Chocolate?"

Her nods evolve into shakes.

"By the way, what's your favorite flower?" I ask.

"Huh?"

"What's your favorite flower?"

Emma crosses her arms. "Why?"

"It's just a question I like to ask people, you know, to get to know them a bit better. Kind of like asking what your favorite color is or what you like to do for fun."

"I don't know," she replies with her defenses still up. "Hydrangeas, I guess."

I can't help but develop a smile. "Good choice."

10

February, 2011.

I really despise meetings with Jeremy, but they are utterly necessary in order to continue my line of work. Another thing I despise is riding the damn taxi. If you look any bit like a Japanese tourist, then taxi drivers try to take advantage of that. Your eyes are a fraction slanted? They take you down the opposite direction for several blocks before you realize their deceitful intentions. Your skin is a tint of yellow? Expect to be driven the long way around through unnecessary detours. Funny thing is, most taxi drivers are considered foreigners themselves. I guess taxi drivers, especially those in New York, are oblivious to the saying, "Treat others the way you want to be treated." I know drivers have to put up with hell on a daily basis, driving around passionate lovers, impatient businessmen, and even offensive delinquents. But I don't have the amnesty to be treated like a foreigner by a foreigner—especially like a Japanese tourist.

You know, the Japanese say that a woman's hands are too warm to make sushi. Frankly, I think the Japanese have no idea what they're talking about. From what I [think I] remember, my mother's hands were as cold as the winter air is today, without the slightest hint of blood pulsing through her veins. The only times I saw her at ease, was when she cooked dinner in front of the stove and the artificial flames resonated heat throughout her tired soul. She especially enjoyed cooking with her stainless pan, with her hands on the hilt just inches away from the fire. It was the only way she tolerated the winter seasons.

The winter air is more than just cold; it is a bitter chill that punishes you for keeping still, trapping those who refuse to make occasional contact with their frigid jeans against their naked knees and thighs. So to avoid punishment, I constantly move my legs and end up walking down the narrow stairs into the subway with my hands tucked firmly in my coat pockets. Danny trails right behind me, with his boots gently making contact with the slushy steps.

It smells like shit down here. You'd think that the great mixing pot of the world would produce a richer, deeper fragrance, with over a third of its population being foreign-born from all over the world, including countries like China, Jamaica, Colombia, and Germany. But it turns out the spices from various regions blend into a big pile of shit, similar to how mixing all sorts of paint colors form a distasteful brown. Not even fontinella cheese from the Italians or soybean paste from the Koreans can override the stench underneath the great city of New York.

"Ugh, Jesus it smells bad," Danny points out the obvious with his mittens barely covering his large nose.

"You'd think you'd be use to it by now," I reply as I take off my dark purple beanie. The subway is always warmer than on the surface. I guess you can say down here, the stink replaces the cold, usurping the title of the greater evil.

"You know why the subway never improves?" Danny asks. I shrug in response, not wanting to open my mouth and let the malodor seep onto my tongue. "It's because they never close it down. The subways are always going to be filthy unless they close them down, section by section, and renovate each and every station. But they can't close the subway down, because this is New York City for Christ sake—the city that never sleeps!" Danny's address reminds me briefly of the religious preachers in the streets standing on their recycled boxes.

"It's a real catch-22 situation," I say with a sigh.

Danny appears clueless with both of his mittens back over his nose and mouth. "What's that?"

"*Catch-22*, the great American novel?" Through his thick, borderline Coke-bottle glasses, Danny's eyes magnify his continued ignorance. "Forget it."

The train screeches into the station, turning heads in its direction. The compartment windows are tinted a light brown shade, signifying the dank quality of air. Someone could use the windows as canvases to draw on with their fingers, but who would want to touch such filth?

"Looks like we got a dirty one," Danny says as he walks up to the opening doors.

"Aren't they all?" I reply from the corner of my mouth. We

both give off a soft chuckle while Danny shakes his head in small increments.

After 15 minutes of riding the grimy subway and walking across slippery sidewalks covered with puddles, we reach our destination—a bar in downtown Manhattan called The Docks. It's a joint Danny and I visit often, despite the mediocre food. The place is, however, oblivious to tourists, which creates an authentic atmosphere only regulars can fully appreciate. Classical music bounces off the walls embroidered with unknown paintings supposedly from the Age of Enlightenment, all replicas of course. However, The Docks is in no way considered a fancy place with cocktails going for $15 a piece. At most, the drinks cost around half that price but still taste two times better. And the best part is, there's no wall of people around the counters, fishing for the attention of the bartenders.

Danny and I grab our usual seats on the edge of the counter, the side furthest from the chill leaking through the door. Rita, a familiar barmaid who has been working at The Docks for the better part of the year, greets us from behind the bar. Like most bartenders, Rita is fairly young, probably no more than 22-years-old. I've never asked her how old she is, because that is usually a question a man asks a woman he's interested in. I'm not saying Rita is undesirable; on the contrary, she is fairly pleasant to look at. Her face is attractively small, which pronounces her big, brown eyes that match her dark brown hair almost perfectly. Her ears are large, but not in a Dumbo kind of way—more like her blood possess some elvish lineage. It is mainly due to her Middle-earth appearance that I imagine my visits to The Docks like entering straight into a Tolkien fantasy novel. Her raggedy dress helps, of course.

"Hello Rita," I say. Danny just smiles at her while looking hesitantly away.

"So, what can I get for you guys? The usual?"

"You know what, I'll have something slightly different today." I rest my head in the palm of my right hand. "I feel like something a bit sweeter than usual."

"How about a Shirley Temple?" Rita leans against the counter with her large eyes pulling in my gaze. "Our cherries have just enough sweetness to bring out that zing. You'll probably be ordering it from here on out. It's popular with the ladies."

"I guess I'll venture out a bit." My lips rise faintly on both sides. Danny is off staring at the paintings across the room. "Hey, what do you want Danny? Rita's waiting." He looks down at his hands and turns to me as he begins to mumble a few syllables. "Just get him his usual Gelt Chaser," I say in his stead. As I watch Rita start to make our drinks, I wonder how she is able to live her life as she does. You couldn't tell from her plain accent, but Rita is a British exchange student attending law school at Columbia. She is different from many young bartenders who have chosen their profession by choice (although it doesn't seem like a preferable one). That's not to say that she hates her night job; she is actually pretty jovial for the most part during her shifts, unless, of course, she's a hell of a good actress. I can see why Danny is so attracted to her that he is constantly left speechless when she's around. Rita is pretty, smart, and funny—the whole package, really. Also, you know she'll be raking it in once she becomes a successful lawyer. Sometimes, Danny is just too easy to read.

Once Rita is busy making our drinks, I nudge Danny to

snap him out of his daze.

"Why do you have to be such a fucking embarrassment when Rita's here?" I whisper. Danny briefly chokes upon hearing my words.

"I just..." he says, "I can't help it, all right? She's just so amazing with her cute voice and her big brains."

"Oh yeah, that brain," I say. "Mmm mmm!"

"God, you know what I mean."

"You know, you could just ask her out. Take her to a movie or something."

"I can't."

"Well, why not?"

"Because, why in the world would a girl like her go out with a guy like me?" Danny's voice starts to rise, causing me put out my hands to calm him down.

"No need to get upset. Just trying to give you some advice."

"Sorry, but I always assume you're being facetious, especially when it comes to my issues."

"Don't get all sissy on me now," I say. Danny silently shakes his head in response.

We sit quietly until our drinks are served. I tepidly sip my non-alcoholic beverage through a straw as Danny takes a large gulp of his cocktail. Other customers trickle in, demanding the attention of Rita as she turns her back to our view. I take my time, taking a sip every minute or so, not wanting to leave the cherry alone in an empty cup. The drink is so sweet, I can feel a bump form on the tip of my tongue—or at least I can imagine it.

"If it isn't Ashman and Brackman."

I turn around already knowing who I'm going to see. An

African American man of average height wearing a cleanly pressed dress shirt under a tan blazer stands a mere foot away from where I'm sitting. With a generous smile, his cleaner than white teeth contrast sharply with the dark around his chapped lips. He reaches out for a handshake, to which I comply, unsure of whether to end the gesture formally or informally.

"We got Ashman and Brackman here. Now, where is Superman at?" He laughs loudly at his own joke. I roll my eyes as I take a long sip of my Shirley Temple. Being a teetotaler definitely has its drawbacks.

"Hey Jeremy," says Danny as he shakes the newcomer's hand. "You know, too bad your last name isn't Freeman. Then you could join our superhero team. We could always use a Black guy."

Jeremy takes a step back away from Danny while giving him an insulted look with his mouth skewed open. "Are you trying to make a comment about slavery? You think just because I'm a Black man, my superpower would be me being free? Is that what you're implying?" He crosses his arms as if asking for some sort of explanation.

"No, what? I mean, come on, I didn't mean anything like that. Morgan Freeman's last name is Freeman, right?" Danny struggles to find words and looks to me with pleading eyes.

"Nah, I'm just messing with you, man." Jeremy lets out his roaring laugh as Danny chuckles pitifully with relief.

"So, did you bring what I asked you for?" I say, wanting to keep the meeting as brief as possible. Extroverts like Jeremy really take a lot out of me simply from just listening to them talk. Some conversations with him seem incessant, like a door-to-door salesman who loves to hear himself go on about irrelevant details. He would have made a better salesman, no doubt about it.

"Let me get a drink first," he says while signaling down Rita. "I haven't had a good drink since the last time I saw you guys."

"Please, no need to remind me," I say.

As Jeremy orders his drink, I take out a reed I finished late last night with a blue silk thread usually used for heirloom clothing. I stroke the wrapped silk with my fingertips, imagining it to belong to the dress of a young princess—the cane, smooth like the skin on her shoulder. And for a brief moment, I'm transported away from this bar perturbed by its own varied themes, to an olden castle in a distant land, undressing the fair princess of a freshly ripen age. The silk is woven tightly about her skinny body, amplifying the curves which illuminate her physique. And as I am about to pull down her dress from behind, I can't help but instead, wrap my arms around her, holding her tightly as I would a delicate branch. She just stands there, with her dress even more firmly on than before, while exhaling slowly through her thin lips. I breathe in calmly through mine.

"You still play with dolls, Ashman?" My daydream falls apart as I'm warped back to the classic pub of Middle-earth.

"It's a reed, you idiot." I notice the harshness of my tone as soon as I mutter the words.

"Jeez, I'm sorry. Somebody obviously has a reed up his ass." Jeremy lets out a hearty laugh.

"The files, Jeremy, just had over the damn files," I say. "We don't meet with you to hear your antics."

"All right, I hear you." Jeremy takes out a folder from his

leather suitcase and places it on the bar table. He then downs his drink in one shot, and turns to leave.

"Thanks for the drink, superhero." The door jingles with his exit.

"Why do you always have to be so mean to him?" asks Danny with disapproval.

"Why do you always have to try to please him? Freeman? Really?"

"I'm just trying to be friendly with the guy," Danny says while adjusting his glasses. Today, he is wearing the oval frames, the ones he thinks he looks best in. "We're working with the guy, so we should probably have a good relationship with him."

"No. Jeremy works for us. We pay him to gather information, not to be good buddies with him. Hell Danny, you know this."

"Well, it doesn't hurt to have some sort of bond with him, you know, just in case things go wrong?" Danny is being cautious, as usual.

"If things go wrong," I say while watching Rita laugh with the other patrons, "he'll be the first one to fall, I assure you that."

"Jesus, that doesn't sound good."

"What? It means I have him fucking under control. If you want to get to know him, then do it on your own time. I just think your time can be better spent trying to get to know some other people." With the straw in my mouth, I nudge my head towards Rita's direction. "Unless, of course, I have your preference all wrong."

"You always have a way with words," Danny says with his

head shaking more than ever.

"Good words need no explanation."

"So, are we going to take a look inside the folder or what?"

"I haven't even had time to finish my drink here. Why don't you relax? We'll take a look at it once we leave." Danny takes the last sip of his cocktail, and I can tell from the way he leans back in his chair that he wants another. So without thinking, I call over Rita.

"Sorry, you guys, I've been a bit busier this evening than usual. New customers always need extra explanations."

"It's no problem, Rita, just been missing your company, that's all." She smiles a lot more naturally than she usually does. "If you can get Danny here another glass, that'd be great."

"What about you? Would you like another?" she says signaling to the remainder of my drink.

"No, I think I'm good, thanks."

"Is it too sweet for you?"

"Yeah, just a little bit. But it still tastes pretty good." I stroke the silk reed as I ease myself into a friendly smile.

Once Rita carries off Danny's empty cup, I drink what's left of my mixed ginger ale, leaving the maraschino cherry untouched at the bottom amongst bits of ice. I never understood the appeal of cocktail cherries. With all the chemicals used to preserve, bleach, and color them, they can hardly be called cherries at all. Who are they trying to fool with the red food dye and the plastic fruit appearance? Certainly not me, that's for sure. I'm not one for eating especially healthy, but a maraschino cherry is about one of the last things I'd consider putting into my body.

"Are you going to eat that?" Danny asks while pointing at the red berry.

"Go on ahead."

Danny flicks the cherry into his mouth and wraps the stem neatly in his napkin, leaving my cup barren with melting ice. Thank goodness he didn't put the stem back into my cup. I guess you could say it's a pet peeve of mine to leave trash out in plain sight.

11

April, 2011.

The room appears pitch black, with only the light from the streets filtering in through the windows. A sliver of the moon hangs in the sky, alone in the absence of the surrounding stars. It makes sense to go out for a midnight walk under a full moon, but under a miniscule slice? Forget about it.

Then why am I out on the streets next to a jewelry store? Because like the moon, I am alone. And what better time to take a walk when there is little chance of running into someone?

I casually walk up to the door and take out a rusty golden key from my jacket pocket. The grooves are slightly worn down, yet, retain their original mountain range shape. Time to put my faith in Danny. I know he's been able to disable anti-burglary devices before, but you can never be completely sure with all the backup systems that credulous store owners install nowadays. As long as relentless salesmen are involved, there's no way you can just purchase a basic package. Salespeople have to eat too, after all.

I prepare myself to run at a moment's notice as I insert the key and turn it slowly, sensing the metal scraping together from the tip of my fingers and resonating throughout my entire body. I hear a click followed by absolute silence. Looks like the Jew pulled through. I walk into the store like the king from sleeping beauty, without worry or moral. Ironically, the store is called Talia's, named after its owner. You really can't make this kind of stuff up.

And without Talia knowing, I rape her store, stuffing jewels and diamonds into my duffle bag with little grace. The amount of jewelry I collect could keep a warlord's wife and his 12 mistresses happy for a very long time, as long as he doesn't present his gifts all at once. Woman need to be constantly reminded that they're appreciated.

I jump at the sound of static. "What's taking so long?"

"What the hell, Danny?" I whisper angrily into the walkie-talkie. "This better be a fucking emergency."

"You're suppose to call me Dismas, remember? You're Gestas and I'm Dismas. You have to use our code names."

"I don't give a shit about codenames, Danny."

"Stop saying my name out loud," he quickly replies.

"Look," I whisper back, "if we don't have a problem, then I'm going to turn this thing off and get back to work."

"Jesus, okay, just hurry up already," pipes Danny with a hint of urgency in his voice. "I'm getting a bad feeling over here."

"The next time I hear your voice, your bad feeling better have some evidence to back it up," I tell him. I turn my walkie-talkie off and slip it back into my bag. It's so typical of Danny to panic when he's not even doing the dangerous work. So fucking typical.

I rob the place fairly clean, knowing that I'll never have the opportunity to break into Talia's again. Only a fool would rob the same place twice and thus, return to the scene of the crime. I don't care if Talia's ends up with twin diamonds as big as my fists, I am never coming back here again. Hell, it's just bad form.

I take out a reed with coral silk (perfected over hours of meticulous carving) from my pants pocket and place it neatly in display where an enormous diamond ring use to sit. I crafted the reed several weeks ago and held onto it for such an occasion. Despite never using it for its practical purpose of playing the oboe, I still made sure to pay as much attention to detail as I usually would when making my reeds of superior quality. I'm sure someone will appreciate the design and care I put into making my calling card. And everybody knows, a good calling card is necessary for every criminal wanting to become infamous. At least that's how it's portrayed in popular fiction. Besides, where's the fun in committing a crime and not receiving the proper credit for it?

Leaving behind my reed among cheap metals and silver jewelry, I walk out of the store as confidently as I walked in. My duffle bag hangs heavily on my shoulder with my guilt contributing to none of its weight whatsoever. I guess you could say over the years, I've grown immune to feeling guilty after swiping so many things that weren't mine. I can breathe as easily as I can walk out of a bodega with an unpaid pack of chips in my hands. It is a gift, a natural talent. And I'm not one for letting such a talent go to waste.

I turn my walkie-talkie back on and instruct Danny to get the van ready.

"Why weren't you responding before?" he asks.

"Like I said before," I reply, "I turned off my walkie-talkie so I wouldn't have to hear you whine the whole time."

"Yeah, well, there's been a small problem." I roll my eyes knowing that Danny is probably overreacting to nothing. "A cop just arrested a guy for indecent exposure a block away from where I was waiting."

"Okay, so?"

"So?" I can sense Danny's frustration from the erratic sounds of his breathing. "There was a freaking cop car less than a block away from me!"

"Yeah, and is the cop car still there?"

"I don't know." Of course he doesn't know.

"So what the hell do you want me to do, Danny?"

"Dismas! Call me Dismas!"

"Okay, look, calm down, Jew boy," I tell him as I take off my fake mustache and empty frames. "You know, the cops arresting someone else is a good distraction for us to get away unnoticed. So, just tell me where the hell you are right now, and I will be there as fast as I can."

"I'm near Hundred Seventy-ninth and Washington."

"All right, just stay the fuck still."

"Just hurry up," Danny pleas. The walkie-talkie becomes silent in my stiff hand. This whole heist was far too easy from the start. Not that having police in the area was going to make it any harder—after all, no one knows the jewelry store has been robbed yet. The police probably won't be notified until the morning anyways, when a store employee checks in and notices all the extreme valuables are gone. That's what happens when you don't put your merchandise into a vault overnight. It only shows how new Talia is to the business. The inexperienced ones are always the easiest to steal from.

I walk briskly down Washington Street with my bag tucked under my right arm. The last thing I need right now is to have the jingle of the jewels attract unwanted attention. I spot the van about twenty yards down near the corner, when Danny leans over from the driver seat and pushes open the passenger door.

"Hurry up and get in!" he yells at me. His baseball cap is pulled much farther down over his face than it should be. I can barely see his crooked nose stick out from underneath. I get in the van and tell Danny to chill out as I carefully place my bag under my seat along with the walkie-talkie. I then take out a cigarette as Danny drives the car down the road.

"Hey, don't smoke in here," Danny cries out. "You know I don't like secondhand smoke."

"Calm down, I haven't even lit it yet," I say as I take out my lighter with my initials embroidered on both sides. "And you know, I think I deserve a goddamn smoke, don't you?" Danny grows silent, trying his best to shift his concentration away from my cigarette and onto the streets ahead. I'm considerate enough to open the car window on my side and puff out smoke towards the cool winds of understanding. Ever since Danny's mother died of lung cancer about two years ago, he's developed a short fuse when it comes to the people smoking around him. It doesn't help his paranoia that his mother never smoked a day in her life.

"So," Danny says anxiously, "got any good loot from this haul?"

"Got a bunch, Dismas," I reply, trying to get even more under his skin. "The cuts on some of the diamonds are almost close to perfect."

Danny shakes his head slightly back and forth like he always does when he starts to get agitated. "Oh, so *now* you use the code names, when it doesn't even matter anymore."

"Relax," I tell him. "I think we should be fucking celebrating right now instead of sulking. After all, we have about 90k in this bag right here, maybe even a hundred." This is our first major heist—the rest were of much smaller in scale. I've been careful not to draw the attention of the law as Danny and I perfected the craft slowly over the years, gaining confidence robbing pawn shops and small antique stores with the help of Jeremy's consultations. But now, we're ready to join the big leagues and make our presence known.

Danny takes a deep breath and gives a faint nod. "You're right—no—you're right, I'm sorry. Jesus, I always do this, don't I? I always focus on the negative when the positive is staring me right in the face."

"Come on, don't be so hard on yourself. Nothing you can do about it really, it's in your blood after all."

"Hmph, you think you're funny?" Danny starts to shake his head.

"It's also in your blood to feel fucking happy when you get your hands on a whole bunch of gold," I continue on, ignoring Danny's interjection. He lets out a friendly scoff and pulls back his baseball cap.

"You got that right, Gestas!" A big smile is plastered right under his huge nose, revealing his surprisingly straight set of teeth. You could say, disregarding his huge nose and funky glasses, Danny is an okay looking guy. At least, his mother probably thought so.

I spot a Halal cart on the side of the street without the usual lines deterring me from grabbing a bite. I tell Danny to pull over to which he complies and instantly asks for a chicken plate. Most people prefer the chicken, but I find the chicken to be pretty plain and dry. I get a lamb plate myself and ask for extra hot sauce (if you're not sweating bullets, then you're not enjoying the meal properly). We devour the rice and meat drenched with white sauce in the comfort of the van. Five minutes later, only the aluminum plates are left, and my tongue is left burning with fiery ecstasy. There's a certain gratifying feeling of enjoying the dirt cheap pleasures of life after experiencing a delicate thrill. It really doesn't get any better than this.

"By the way," I say, "what's up with the code names?"

Danny looks at me as if I just asked a stupid question, despite what teachers constantly reminded us back in grade school. "Kind of obvious, if you ask me," he says while wiping his hands with a paper napkin. "What if there's a hidden camera that picks up sound? We don't want our real names being recorded as evidence."

"No, no, I know that, doofus. I mean, the actual names that you've chosen—Gestas and Dismas."

"Oh, that. Well, those are the names of the two thieves who were crucified alongside Jesus Christ."

"Can you elaborate?" I say. "I didn't exactly read the Bible, cover to cover, while I was growing up."

"Well, neither did I. My family is Jewish, remember? I grew up reading the *Tanakh*, which is considered the Hebrew Bible."

"Okay, so, who exactly are Gestas and Dismas?"

"If I remember correctly, Gestas was considered the impenitent thief while Dismas was called the penitent thief. Gestas mocked Jesus Christ while Dismas asked for forgiveness. I think Gestas was on Jesus's right and Dismas was on his left." Danny pauses as he stretches out both arms, imitating the well-known pose. "Or was it the other way around?"

"I don't think that matters all that much," I say. "So, why am I the bad thief and you're the good one?"

"What do you mean bad and good? Bad as in bad at stealing?"

"No, I mean bad as in *impenitent*."

Danny appears as though he's carefully thinking about what he should say. "Well, I mean, you don't really seem sorry about stealing. It's like your conscience isn't affected by shame or regret. It's almost as if you're happier when you steal."

"So, how about you? Who's the one who had a stupid smile on his face when I brought back a bag full of jewelry."

"I know, I know," Danny says nodding in agreement. "But that's not what I'm talking about."

"What are you talking about, then?"

"I mean, yeah, I'm happy about a successful heist, but I still feel bad for the people that we steal from. They've got families to feed, while we're just stealing for our own selfish reasons. I can't sleep peacefully knowing that I've caused financial suffering to innocent people. It's a bit too heartless."

"Wow," I say, "I didn't know you had such an indignation

towards what we do."

Danny shakes his head. "You know what I mean."

"Yeah, I do. You're pretty much saying that you feel guilty about pilfering other people's valuables, while I simply embrace it, sin and all."

"Well, yeah."

To be honest, I'm hardly upset about the negative impression I've gained from my colleague. It's actually sort of a compliment, to have others make note of my fortitude, which has gotten me this far in life. Only the strong survive after all. I can imagine plenty of thieves falling apart from the overwhelming cry of their good conscience, which should be neatly silenced away in the bottom of their minds in a dog carrier (or a cat carrier if their conscience is more aloof). I just hope Danny will gain control over his conscience before he starts paying it too much attention—overindulging it with catnip and unrequited love.

"You know, Danny, it's okay to feel shameful about what we're doing. I'm pretty sure your family raised you differently with all your Jew morals. But don't let your emotions about all this eat you up. If you can't handle it, then you should probably just quit. It'll be better for me to go solo now, than have you cause problems for me later on."

"Wow, I didn't know you had such little faith in me," Danny replies.

"Says the guy who accuses me of being cold blooded."

"Not cold blooded, just apathetic towards others."

"It's like you don't even know me," I say.

"Sometimes, you make me wish I didn't."

"Danny, let's face it, if you didn't know me, then you

wouldn't know anybody. Except, of course, your Jewish family. I bet you love those bar mitzvahs, those little parties where people actually recognize you."

"This is exactly what I'm talking about," Danny says, shaking his head right on cue.

"You know I'm just joking. Come on, let's go get some drinks. I'll buy.

"Good."

"You really make it too easy."

12

March, 1995.

My teacher always tells me that the reed is the most important part of the oboe. But it's so small, like a little pinky finger. How can a little pinky finger be so important? The only thing my pinky is good for is doing pinky swears, and those promises never really work out.

But today, Paul keeps his promise of showing me how to make a reed after the lesson. He's a pretty nice guy, even though he's in the Army, like my father was. He's younger than my father, but is bald, so he always wears a cap to keep his head warm. He wore his uniform to a lesson once before, and he had an army hat on instead. I think the army hat looks worse than his regular cap, without a doubt.

Before being in the Army, Paul played in an orchestra somewhere in Europe. He always says that one day he's going to go back to Europe to play in an orchestra again. But right now, the Army needs him more than the orchestra does. He's really good at playing the oboe, and I hope someday I can play just like him.

"This is from a cane," he says as he takes out a small piece from his brown sack.

"It looks like a piece of wood," I say.

"It's kind of like wood, I guess," he replies. "More like bamboo, you know."

"So pandas eat these?" I ask excitedly. I think about how I can feed the pandas at the zoo by making reeds for them.

"No, I don't think so," Paul replies, and my dream of feeding the pandas with yummy reeds slowly disappears. "And this," Paul takes out a metal machine that looks like a hole-puncher. "This is a gouger. Now, first thing we do is clip this here, and then place the piece in the slot here and shave it, nice and easy." He slides the machine back and forth. Thin wood chips come off.

"It's kind of like sharpening a pencil!"

"Yeah, it kind of is, I guess," agrees Paul.

"I wanna try," I say. Paul stops for a bit, thinks about it, then moves the machine in front of me.

"All right here, just move this knob back and forth like this, see?" I grab the knob and copy Paul's motions. "All right, not too much now. We have to do the other side too, you know." Paul flips over the piece and lets me shave the whole side myself. "And the reason we do this, is so the reed has an even diameter on the inside."

"Okay."

"Some people soak it in water for a few minutes in-between

steps, but we'll just skip that for now."

"Uh-huh."

"Now," he says, taking the piece in one hand with a small metal knife in the other, "we have to bend it in half, like this, after measuring it, of course." He bends the piece using the knife. "And after that, we have to cut off the edges." He then uses the same knife to cut the sides off, little by little. I just watch, because I know he probably won't let me try even if I ask.

After cutting off a bit of the sides, he puts the piece on a metal pencil thing that holds it as he continues to slice off the sides. He becomes really quiet. I think he's forgotten that I'm here.

"What are you doing now?" I ask loudly. He jumps a bit.

"Oh, sorry, now I'm shaping it, see?" he says as he shows me the reed up close. "And now, we connect the reed to a staple." He shows me a small brown tube thing and connects it with the thin bamboo piece. "Oh, but before we do this, we put the staple on a mandrel." He then takes out a roll of string from his bag and ties it to the table. He wraps the string around and around the connection. He's quiet again.

"What else do you have in your bag?" I ask.

"Huh? Oh yeah, just a bunch of reed equipment. I have a lot of different colored thread rolls too."

"Why did you use the red one?"

"Oh, no particular reason. It was just the first one I grabbed."

"But blue's my favorite color, though."

Paul stops working for a second. "I'm sorry, I'll use a blue thread next time."

"It's okay, I'll use the blue one myself. Although, I like black as well." I don't think he hears me, because he is quiet again. It feels like forever as I watch him wrap the red string around and around, tying little knots.

"Now, comes the most difficult, but most satisfying part," says Paul. "Well, at least for me." He is smiling, just like I do when I hear a funny joke. "We have to scrape the reed, get the bark off of the tip, and get the shape just right." He starts scraping it with a small metal knife. "The tip should have a very faint 'V' shape." I just keep watching him carve the bamboo. "And now, we can cut the tip open." He cuts off a tiny part at the top and sighs with relief. He then puts the reed in his mouth and makes a funny sound."

"That sounds just like me when I play!"

"No," he says, "you sound better than this."

"Thanks."

"There's still a lot more shaping that I have to do with this one, but I think you get the general idea."

"Does it always take this long to make one?" I ask Paul.

"Most of the time, it takes much longer than this," he tells me softly. "But you know, it's worth it, because the only perfect reed is the one you make for yourself. Everyone makes reeds a bit differently. So naturally, no two reeds are the same—even the ones you make yourself are always going to be slightly different from one another." He waves the new reed in the air. "This one right here, this is one of a kind."

"Whoa."

"With the oboe, it all comes down to the reed. You have to always practice making them, because an oboist is only as good as how well he makes his reeds." Paul hands me the red stringed reed. "You know, I've been making these things for years now, but I still have a lot to learn. That's why I think it'll be good for you to start practicing now."

"How many have you made so far?" I ask.

"Thousands, I guess."

"Why do you have to make so many?"

"Because," Paul replies, "reeds only last for about seven hours of playing time. They don't last that long. And because they only last for a short while, each has to be made to be better than the last. That way, eventually one day, you'll end up with the perfect reed." He smiles again. "For now, study that reed I just made and remember the steps I followed to make it. I sort of rushed through that one though."

"Okay, I will!"

"Also, don't forget the breathing exercises. You can use that reed there if you want. Remember, use one long breath and tongue each note. Don't breathe after every note."

"Okay."

"And don't forget to practice those scales. Make sure to start with B-flat."

"Okay."

"All right then, I'll see you next week. Don't practice too hard though." He smiles again and packs up his bag.

"Don't worry, I won't," I lie. I wish another week will fly by quickly so I can be back in this music room, learning how to play the oboe. There is really no where else I can practice without feeling like I'm being a bother. My father always tells me that I don't sound very good and that I need to practice some more to get better, but he doesn't like me practicing at home. Most of the time, I practice in my room when he's not home. I like it best when I'm alone.

As I walk home on the side of the street, I imagine how great it would be if father was out for the rest of the night. Then I can practice all I want, as loud as I want. After all, the best time to practice is when the lesson is still fresh in my mind.

I hold up the red reed against the horizon of the setting sun. The string with its layers fades into the red and orange colors of the sky. It is definitely one of a kind, just like a sunset; there are 365 sunsets every year, and each one is slightly different from the rest. Some have more red than others. Some have more clouds. Some are clear and focused, and others are hidden from view. Some are remembered and some are forgotten. Today's sunset—today's is one I'll remember. Today's is one I'll never forget.

13

April, 2011.

"Where were we supposed to go again?" Thomas asks as he slows the cruiser to check out a lady in a resplendent red dress. He lifts his aviators and produces a low cat call. Fortunately, she doesn't hear his wolf whistle, or wisely chooses not to acknowledge it.

"Hundred Seventy-ninth and Washington," I reply as I rub my eyes. "Right now we're on East Hundred Eightieth street, so we just need to turn left onto Washington when we get to it. We're running late so you should—"

"Man, I tell ya, there's nothing I wouldn't do to spend a night with that sweet piece," Thomas says as his eyes slowly return to the road. "And the things I'd actually do to that ass."

I shake my head and take a sip of my coffee. It's both our days off, yet here I am, spending it with the last person I'd ever imagine I would. We've been called in for a special assignment that is part of integrating the junior officers into the system. I was told it would only take up a part of the morning.

I shake my head again (something I've been doing a lot lately in Thomas's presence) and say, "Did you even hear what I said, huh, Tommy-boy?"

"Hey, I told you not to call me that," he says. "The next time you do, you'll be hearing from my pops."

Whenever things don't go quite the way he wants them to, Thomas never fails to mention his father, Jerry Banner, or as most of NYPD knows him as, Deputy Commissioner of Training. I've found however, that these are just empty threats. And, even if Thomas were to run to his daddy about a little name calling, I doubt the Deputy Commissioner would embarrass himself, and his son, by doing anything about it. So, I continue my banter, unimpeded.

"Whatever you say, Tommy-boy."

Thomas's face gets a little flushed and a vein on his forehead stands out, but he pretends like he didn't hear me. For the most part, Thomas is harmless. His large frame and the abundance of hair on his arms and chest give the illusion of a tough guy from East Brooklyn, when he really grew up with his family in Upper East Side Manhattan. Back at the precinct, the senior officers have taken the liberty of creating nicknames for all of the junior officers. Apparently, it's part of the precinct's tradition to be given one after successfully completing the FTEP and becoming a full-fledged police officer. Thomas's nickname is Teddy, short for teddy bear, but I, along with the rest of the junior officers, have elected to give him a nickname of our own, something not quite as cute as a stuffed animal.

After a minute of silence, Thomas asks, "So, where do we have to go again?"

"Just take a left onto Washington when you see it," I say.

"Damn, I hate making left turns."

"Don't worry. Washington is a one-way street so it'll be like taking a right."

"Oh, right on man." This infinitesimal news has spontaneously lifted his mood to its original cheer.

We make the turn onto Washington, and after a couple of blocks, reach the 179th intersection. Three cop cars are already parked on the packed streets, so I instruct Thomas to double-park next to the cruiser closest to the rear.

"Time to solve some crime man," Thomas says as he pockets his shades and jumps out of the car, leaving behind his keys.

I sigh, but also can't help smile as I pull the keys out of the ignition. After spending the past four months partnered with ol' Tommy-boy, I've come to realize that he's not so much of a prick than he is just plain stupid. His facetious behavior can easily be chalked up (or down) to his low IQ.

I fix my tie before exiting. When I catch up to Thomas, I recognize the rest of the officers who're already present. Detective Lieutenant Brown is standing with his arms crossed, surrounded by the rest of the junior officers, with Sergeant Alexander watching close-by. Sergeant Supervisor Detective Squad Stephen, whom I've never formally met, but who I know is always by Brown's side, is also present.

"Officer Ashman, could you walk any slower?" Brown says.

"Yeah, hurry up Noel. You don't want to keep the detectives waiting," Julie says with a smirk. She then murmurs something to Brown, and the two share a laugh, probably at my expense.

I decide to sprint the rest of the way there, and stand between Louie and Sergeant Alexander.

"Now that we have everyone here," Brown says, "let me remind you that I only agreed to take up Lieutenant Hendricks request to acquaint you all on how investigations work within the Major Case Squad only if I have everyone's full cooperation. The next time something like this happens you can forget about these special shadowing sessions."

Julie shoots me a dirty look full of her usual scorn. If I had to guess, she was the one who put this whole idea into Hendricks's head, like how Leonardo DiCaprio did to Cillian Murphy in *Inception*. There's no other junior officer (besides myself) as eager as she is to eventually get promoted to detective.

The Detective Lieutenant continues with his briefing: "As you can see, the jewelry store is called Talia's, and is a fairly new establishment. Detective Sergeant Stephen and I have already contacted the owner, who's told us that her manager called her around 9:30 am as soon as he arrived and noticed a number of their most valuable merchandise was missing. We're talking about a net total slightly north of 85k people."

Thomas lets out a high-pitched whistle.

"Nevertheless, since the value of the stolen property does not exceed 100k, that makes this a low profile case, which is why I've cordially invited all of you here. When asked why she doesn't lock up her goods overnight, the owner told us that she hasn't gotten around to purchasing a proper vault, which in other words means the owner's a cheap bastard who had what's coming to her. But, if it weren't for miserly knuckle-heads like her, we'd have nothing better to do but twiddle our thumbs back at the station. Anyways, from what I was told, insurance should cover most of it—lucky son of a bitch."

Sergeant Alexander promptly clears his throat and says, "Sir, if you could hold off on the foul language and wrap things up here."

"Sure thing," Brown says with no sign of resentment. "So, we have our crime scene technicians on their way with an ETA now of approximately fifteen minutes. During that time you're all free to study the scene, but be extra careful not to touch anything. You may also question the store manager if you'd like. Let me know if you find anything unusual. Okay, scatter."

And with that, Julie dashes into the store and immediately strikes up a conversation with the manager. Thomas and Louie stop in front of the glass door and pretend to inspect it for any signs of forced entry, when in actuality they're really talking about last night's game. Thanks to baseball, the two Yankees fans have formed an unusual friendship during our short stint in the precinct. Thomas found out early on that the secret to getting Louie to talk, is just mentioning baseball; when you do that, you have a hard time shutting him up. Sergeant Alexander is on his phone, and the two detectives have returned to their car, which leave me with Megan "White Serena" Wheeler (coined after Serena Williams, because of how strikingly similar Megan's build is with the superstar tennis player's).

Megan is easily my favorite class peer, and the way I see it, it would make perfect sense to swap partners with Louie and take a break from Thomas. But, I don't get a say, and for some reason, our superiors are happy with how the way things have ended up.

"Ashman, how're you today?" Megan asks.

"Hey Wheeler, I'm good. I just wish I was as excited as Julie is to be here."

"Tell me about. I'd rather be out there making arrests and letting my fists do the talking," she says, pounding her left paw into the open palm of her right hand.

"Well, we might as well go inside and take a look." We walk by Thomas and Louie who are both yammering about some game-changing play in the 5th inning. I hold open the door. "Ladies first."

Megan pulls off the most over-the-top curtsey imaginable before going inside. When I follow her in, the first thing I notice are the posters of female celebrities on the walls; the smiling faces of Beyoncé, Selena Gomez, and Jamie Chung hover over the ravaged displays, which only hours before contained jewelry that they each supposedly wore before. Aside from the posters, there's nothing much that differentiates this jewelry store from any of the others I've been to; the bright lights in the display counters, the shiny metals, and the abundance of cheap lockets can all be found at your local mall's Tiffany & Co. I can't help but let out a small laugh at this thought.

Julie is still busy interrogating the poor manager, who has by now taken a seat and is holding his head in his hands. With every word he speaks, Julie is scribbling it down in her notepad.

"Look at the thing go," I say. "It's almost as if it's her mission to make the lives of others more miserable than her own."

Megan doesn't say anything back. When I turn to see what's gotten her attention, I see her peering into the far right counter.

"Hey Wheeler, I didn't know you were interested in this stuff," I say. "Hell, I don't think I ever remember seeing you wear any sort of jewelry or fashion accessory, except for that hideous yellow rubber wristband." She doesn't answer me immediately, so I'm afraid I've hurt her feelings. Of course she's interested, I think to myself, she's a girl after all.

"Ashman, shut up and come take a look at this," she says, still staring into the glass.

As I walk over, she points distinctively into the glass counter, narrowly missing the sharp, broken edges. "What do you think that is?"

"Where?"

"Right there, towards the back."

"I'm not sure," I lie. Of course I know it's an oboe reed. The sight of it causes my heart to race, and I have a sudden urge to push my body out of the broken store and jump in front of the oncoming traffic. But I stand my ground, as the fiery intensity wanes from my utter acceptance of the reed's concrete presence.

"It looks like some sort of whistle," Megan says as she turns around. "Excuse me, Mr. Manager. What's supposed to be here?"

The manager jumps up and rushes over to us, obviously overeager at the opportunity to terminate his Q&A session with Julie.

"Oh yes, this is where our Manhattan Mini Diamond engagement ring used to sit—named by the owner. Of course, it wasn't actually cut from one of the famed Manhattan Diamonds, but it was still amongst our most valuable pieces. The diamond itself was a 3.54 carat, very good cut, near colorless, with very small inclusions, and was valued at twenty thousand dollars."

Someone lets out a whistle. I turn and find Thomas and Louie standing behind us.

"Oh shut up, little Tommy-boy," Megan says.

"Hey, you'll be hearing from my pops," Thomas says, but Megan waves him off.

"So, what do you suppose *that* is then?" she asks the manager.

"Hmm, I don't recognize it," he replies.

"It's a reed," Louie says, "and by the looks of it, a very well-crafted, handmade one at that. You know, they're used with woodwind instruments."

"How'd you know that?" I ask, slightly taken aback by Louie's chattiness.

"I used to play the bassoon in high—"

"Oh my god, it could be the culprit's calling card!" Julie yells from excitement. "I'll go tell the detectives." She runs out the door like an obsequious waiter fetching the chef who is about to receive a compliment.

"Let's take it out and take a closer look," says Thomas.

"Let's not," Megan says. "If it is some sort of calling card, then we don't want to tamper with it. Though, I must admit, the color of that wound up thread at the end of it is very pretty—sort of reminds me of the color of a dress my mom would wear to church on Easter."

I steal a glimpse at the reed again and understand what Megan meant. It's a very warm color that even I can image my mom wearing to church. Although, my family was never one to celebrate the resurrection of Jesus Christ, and hiding colored eggs in the backyard.

"We should check the rest of the displays and see if we can find anything else," Megan says. "You two, start on that side. Ashman and I will start here."

And with that, the four of us are bending over, peering into the glass cases, looking for something that doesn't belong. Even the store manager joins in. But of course, we don't find anything else. Julie returns with Brown and Stephen, and she shows them the reed.

"Who found it?" Brown asks.

Despite the fact that Julie doesn't get along with Megan (and the rest of the us), she surprisingly answers, "Wheeler did, sir." I guess even Julie can be magnanimous when it counts.

"Good work, Officer Wheeler," Brown says. And I guess even Detective Lieutenant Brown can be high-minded too. "Detective Sergeant Stephen and I will take it from here. You are all dismissed."

"Thank you, sir, for the opportunity," Julie squeezes in before we're shuttled out by Stephen.

When we're on the pavement, Sergeant Alexander meets us with his trademark expression of stern obedience. "I just had a long conversation with Lieutenant Hendricks. He filled me in on a possible gridlock situation caused by a collision off the Cross Bronx Expressway on Webster and wants a squad to manage traffic. The area patrol is already at the scene, but they need help. Ashman and Banner, you two return to the station and go on home. Nunez and Wheeler, you two follow Hernandes and me."

"Have fun," I say to Megan out of the corner of my mouth.

She gives me a light, single-handed shove that throws me off balance.

Two cruisers drive off before Thomas and I return to our own, leaving the detectives' car side-by-side ours. I hand Thomas the keys and he starts the car, performing an illegal U-turn before driving off in the opposite direction our comrades left in. He then brings the radio microphone to his mouth, pushes the button, and says, "Dispatch, this is two-Adam-thirty-two, now ten-eight."

I turn to him and say, "No, you idiot. We're not in service. We're returning the patrol car to the station and enjoying the day off."

"Oh, right," he says. He picks up the radio again. "So, what do I tell them?"

"Ten-seven."

He pushes the button and says, "Disregard that, I meant ten-seven."

I leave Thomas to concentrate on the road and enjoy the occasional eye candy, while I close my eyes and lean back. We spend the rest of the trip in silence. I feel exhausted after such an exciting and interesting morning that I start to look forward to spending the rest of the day relaxing at home.

As soon as Thomas pulls into the station lot he runs off, saying something about a date he has later on. After the drive, I'm practically sleep walking, so I don't want to make any effort to say bye to him, but I tell him to have fun and wish him luck, since after all, he's not that bad of a guy.

I decide to change out of my uniform and into my civilian attire. I know being a cop is a 24/7 job, but I want to be able to take the subway home without being asked for help at each stop. I've already made the mistake of riding the train in uniform once before, and having to endure looks of misguided admiration, fright, and hatred.

I remember leaving a jacket on the chair of my desk, but I decide to not go for it since I want to avoid running into Dick. Over the past ten months, Dick has been nothing but friendly and helpful, and I've made sure to treat him with extra kindness and respect. But, my venerable actions backfired on me when Dick started thinking we were close, *close* friends, and followed me after his shifts ended, inviting himself, for dinner or drinks. At first, I didn't mind so much, since I was new and thought he was looking out for me as my FTO, and frankly I could learn a thing or two from him afterhours. But, he never wanted to talk about work during our hang outs, only about stuff like how he misses the Bush administration, and the girls he's been lucky enough to get dumped by, and how lonely he gets at home. The more I got to know him personally, the more depressing he seemed. Six months later, when my initial probationary training was over and we became peers, he didn't let up, and I didn't see any reason to continue the farce. Of course, I've never told him that I no longer need him to be my mother bird and that he should give me space to fly freely— that's something I don't have to heart for, and frankly, I'm afraid he wouldn't be able to take it. If I did tell him something akin to that, he'd probably end up doing something drastic. A depressed man with a gun is the most dangerous kind I know of.

My one saving grace these past few months has been Joe's retirement. Ever since Joe was forced to retire after his first heart attack, Dick's desk has been moved to Joe's old desk, which is clear on the other side of the office. Otherwise, I would never be able to avoid Dick in the mornings.

I sneak into the locker room for a quick in and out change. The entire room is empty, which is no surprise considering how it's bordering on lunchtime. I throw on some dirty sweats, running sneakers, and a hoodie, and turn to leave with a smile on my face, thinking I'm scot-free. But, during my rush to get changed, I failed to hear someone walk in and end up nearly bumping right into the intruder.

"Hey, Noel, how's your week been?"

I let out a deep sigh of relief as Dan gives me a funny look.

"From the looks of it, you're hiding from someone, aren't you?" he asks. "Let me guess, it's Pam, right? Everyone's new training coordinator. I know she's been giving you a hard time with your reports, but you know she only does so because she cares. To tell you the truth, I'm also trying to hide from her too. Every Friday she insists on eating at that god-awful sushi place on Hundred Eighty-eighth. She says it's the only place that makes curry just the way she likes it, not too spicy, and with enough beef *katsu* on top. I was hoping this time she'd give up on trying to find me and go on by herself."

I laugh. Dan and Pam may be in their early forties now, but if I were to ever tell Michael stories about them, he'd probably think that I was talking about a couple of school children who are obsessed with cooties. "Well, this *is* the best place to hide from her."

Our secret meeting is interrupted by an officer named Eddie Curran, a young guy in his early thirties who, like Julie, loves to please others, but unlike Julie, is completely selfless.

"Lieutenant Palmer wanted me to tell you to come out to the front doors," Eddie says to Dan.

"What about him?" Dan asks, pointing at me.

"She didn't say anything about Ashman, sir." Eddie leaves immediately after, most likely to tell Pam that the task has been carried out.

"Come on, Noel. Let's go."

I want to excuse myself, but I would just be abandoning him, so I follow him out of the locker room. At least I'm still headed in the right direction: out of the station. I'll just get a quick bite and rest right after lunch. We past by the storage room, the staff lounge, and finally the office floor. Like in the locker room, the office is practically empty. But, I'm still afraid of running into Dick, knowing how he likes to pop in and out of the kitchen. So as soon as I spot a visitor going into the elevator, I call out for him to hold it due to my desperation. When we get close enough, I shout my thanks, and Dan and I file quickly into the compartment and find an additional person already present.

"Oh, Hello," I say.

"Oh, Officer Ashman and Sergeant Akamatsu. Which floor?" Emma asks.

"Ground," I answer, and seeing how the ground floor button has already been selected, she listlessly pushes the close door button as the doors clank close.

"Hey, where are you off to Emma?" Dan asks.

"Just going to get some lunch," she says as she pulls up her mini purse over her shoulders. The thin leather strap digs into the side of her neck. She must be carrying around fishing weights in that purse of hers.

"You should join us. We were just about to meet with Pam and enjoy some delicious sushi at the place on Hundred Eighty-eighth," Dan says.

"Sorry, I can't. Meeting my boyfriend," she replies.

"Well, does he like curry? If so, you should bring him along. They make some of the best *katsu karē* in the area."

"No, he can't eat spicy foods."

The elevator doors open and we let Emma and the stranger exit first.

"Ok, well, maybe next time then," Dan says.

Emma gives us a half-smile and walks off out the front doors. I know why Dan was trying so hard to get Emma to join us. The same day I started working here, I asked Emma out, without knowing she was already in a long-term relationship. I thought what the hell, and just went for it. Somehow, despite the fact we were alone in the kitchen, most of the precinct heard about it.

"Whatever you're trying to do won't work," I say.

"Well, it was worth a shot," says Dan. "There's no other way of knowing if she's available or not. Of course, you *could* always ask again." He laughs. Enough time has passed since my embarrassment that I do too.

Pam is waiting with her arms crossed and her back leaning on the open door. "What took you so long?" she asks Dan. "I want to get there before it starts getting crowded." She notices me beside Dan and says, "Hi sweetie."

"Sorry, Noel and I were just talking about the times when he first started here."

"No kidding, I just saw Ms. Church pass right by me. Looked like she was in an awful hurry."

"Yeah, she's on her way to get lunch," I say.

"With her boyfriend," Dan adds.

Pam gets a concerned look on her face and says to me, "Aww, I hope you're okay with that, my little Loverboy."

Dan and Pam both giggle, but this time I don't join in. I try to avoid showing any acknowledgment of my lousy nickname.

"Well, I should go. You two enjoy your lunch," I say, as I start to walk off.

"Oh, I'm sorry dear," Pam says. "At least it's not as bad as the nicknames for your friends. Let's see, there's Girl Scout for that little brown-noser, and A-Rod for the baseball enthusiast..." She trails off for a moment then claps her hands together, producing a deafening crack. "You know what? How about we all go someplace you want to eat?"

"That's a great idea," Dan says, dragging me back.

"Well, to be honest," I say, "I could go for something simple—like a hotdog." There aren't many foods that I can enjoy quite like a hotdog; you can add chili, onions, relish, ketchup, or just enjoy it with Dijon mustard. It seems like the perfect meal to take my mind off of today's event. "I'll treat. I recently received a nice bonus, plus I want to congratulate you, Pam, for making Lieutenant."

"To the Shake Shack!" Dan says, and the three of us step out into the blistering sun.

14

April, 2005.

It's the last Friday of the month—which means it's field trip day. I've been looking forward to this day since Punxsutawney Phil cursed us with six more weeks of winter. Not only do I have a legitimate reason to miss Mr. Prescott's class, but I also get to hang out with Jamie all day. Lately, our friendship seems to be one-sided. Back in junior high, we used to see each other almost everyday in class, but now that we're in high school, I don't share any classes with her. She's always been years ahead of everyone else in our class, but never actually skipped a grade. Instead, she's challenged herself with advanced placement classes, starting with AP Calculus and AP Physics in her sophomore year. We're in our senior year now, and she's busy finishing up AP classes I never even knew existed, like AP Microeconomics and AP Human Geography. Me on the other hand, I'm taking the bare minimum courses to graduate, and struggling with them, not because I'm dumb or anything, but because I don't care enough to try. But, I'm also enrolled in my first AP class, psychology, which, surprisingly, I'm doing very well in. We're learning about impulse control disorders, such as kleptomania, and these experiments scientists used to do in the past, in the sixties and seventies, dealing with social and psychological effects on people's minds when subjected to extreme pain or hostile conditions. I thought about taking AP Literature, but the teacher, Mr. McCloskey, is an idiot who limits the seats to his course only to those who are extremely smart or who are good ass-kissers. So, I decided to stick with regular English Lit with Ms. Clarke. I took her English Language class last year, so she already knows what kind of student I am, which is a huge plus. Once, she told me that I'm wasting my potential, that I could end up doing great things in the literary field (or with my life in general) if I wanted to. But I assured her that I don't really have much to offer, only a lot to gain. I thank her for her interest, and I think she understands how much I appreciate what the classics have done for me.

After school, Jamie partakes in countless extracurricular activities: soccer, MUN, NHS, varsity strings, swimming, student council president, and the garden club. So, I figured the only way I'd get to see her is if I joined a club, and the only one I could manage (or get into) was the garden club. I had no interest in gardening when I started over three years ago, and I still don't. But it's the only way we get to catch up.

The garden club meets twice a month, half an hour before first period, in Mr. White's classroom. Mr. White is the school's business and marketing teacher, and he teaches a number of other electives, such as photography. Needless to say, his classes follow a workbook, and therefore, aren't taught, but supervised. But, he's not completely redundant to the school—like with his Business Management classes, Mr. White supervises the garden club.

We're not the sort of club that grows food in the school's backyard plots, and we don't preach the importance of the word "organic" to other students. Our club's mission is to beautify the school. We also deliver flowers to nursing homes and sponsor the occasional youth poetry contest.

So, twice a month during zero period, thirteen of West Point High's students meet in Mr. White's classroom to form the most anomalistic bunch that can ever be produced by an interest activity.

In any case, I'm one of them, and I'm running late. It's 7:36 am, and I've already missed the school bus. I have 24 minutes to make a 30 minute walk to catch the field trip bus. Before I leave though, I decide to prepare a quick breakfast since I probably won't get the chance to eat again until after school. I curse as I turn on the stovetop, pull out a moldy slice of bread, and throw it on a pan. "Shit, shit. Why today of all days?" The image of my dad, passed out in his room from his nightly drinking session, surfaces in my mind. "That useless old drunk," I say to myself. I grab the half toasted bread off the hot pan and wrap a scarf around my neck. But, before I sprint out the door, I notice one of dad's lighter fluid cans sitting on the countertop—right where he left it from last night. I pick it up and flip open the nozzle and take a whiff. "The sweet, sweet smell of gasoline."

I'm relieved when I spot a bus still parked in front of the school. I wouldn't be able to forgive myself if I missed it. Everyone is already seated, and I find out they haven't left yet because they've been waiting for me. "Oh shoot, sorry everyone!" I say as I climb the steps, practically out of breath. Most of the faces are ignoring me, but I feel obliged to give an excuse: "Uh, I overslept, you know." It's a lie. I never oversleep. I've been an early riser for as long as I can remember; there's only so much that can be done after dark.

"It's fine Noel," Mr. White says . "We all know how difficult it is for you to show up on time…or sometimes, at all."

It's obvious he's referring to my spotty attendance record, but at least it's not as bad as the records of the school's past dropouts and most of the current delinquents. A kid named Stevie snickers, so I give him a smile and a half-hidden middle finger. When he notices he turns away and looks hurt. I would feel bad if it was any other person, but this is Stevie, the prick.

"Oh, and Noel, your permission slip please?" I hand over my slip with my father's forged signature sitting on the printed line. I normally don't need permission from my father since, legally, I'm an adult, but there's still a liability issue according to school policy. I don't plan on forgery to become a habit, but it's hard to say. I probably won't have to resort to it for very much longer anyways. I meant to ask him for his permission, but it's nearly impossible to engage with him about anything and escape unscathed. In any case, I don't need anything from him, much less, permission.

I start to make my way towards the end of the bus when my eyes meet with Danny, my old grade school friend. I was able to get both him and Michael to join the garden club with me, seeing that they both had ample free time. But, thanks to Michael's truculent nature, a rift finally occurred and Michael left the club after having a fight with Danny over some girl, whose name I no longer even remember. (The girl in question has since moved away.) That was a few years ago now. For some reason, Danny has chosen to stick with the club, even after I've remained close with Michael. Despite our falling-out, I give Danny a slight nod and he returns the gesture. I stop at an empty pair of seats, which happens to be adjacent to where Jamie is sitting. She's taken the window seat.

"Hey *Noo-na*, what's up?" She doesn't answer me, but she also doesn't tell me to go away, so I sit down across from her.

I hear Mr. White inform the bus driver up front: "Okay, that's everyone. We can leave now."

I turn my attention back towards Jamie, "Sorry I'm late. I didn't mean to be."

She looks up at me from her book. It looks like it's something for Mr. McCloskey's class, but I can't be sure. With Jamie, there's a fine line between work and pleasure. She says something back to me in Korean.

"I'm not sure what you just said," I say, "but I think it's about how much you've missed me." I laugh at my own arrogance. She doesn't find it as funny.

"Why do you keep calling me *Noo-na*?" she asks. "You do know that I was born a year later than you. So if anything, you're my *Oppa*."

"Well, I thought that was our thing, you know, friendly banter."

"Well, seeing as you can't speak any Korean, maybe you should drop it altogether."

"Hey, that's not very fair," I say. I think about the old family videos we have hiding back home: boxes full of videocassettes showcasing me when I was two to three years old, speaking Korean more fluently than I probably ever will again.

We both sit in silence for a while. It's somewhere close to a two hour trip to the Botanical Garden, and I don't want to start the day in such an awkward state with Jamie, so I get up, cross the aisle, and take the seat next to her.

"So, what are you reading?"

She turns the book over to show me the cover. "It's *Frankenstein.*"

"Oh cool, I didn't know there's a book about him."

"Of course there is. It was written by Mary Shelley and published in 1818."

"Frankenstein was created by a woman?" Jamie narrows her pretty, dark eyes and gives me a menacing look. "Sorry, I didn't mean it like that. I just didn't know."

"There's a lot you don't know. You should really read more." She turns her attention back to *Frankenstein.* Wow, I'm less interesting than an ugly, dead (or alive?) guy that isn't even real. Well, I guess I could see that.

"I read a lot, you know," I tell her. "Well, when I can. I used too at least. I just didn't know Frankenstein originated from a novel. I thought he was created by the same people who started Halloween, you know, like with witches and goblins...and zombies..." I loosen my scarf, letting it hang on my neck as more of a fashion statement than anything else really. "I do know about Dr. Jekyll and Mr. Hyde though, and how they come from a novella written by Robert Louis Stevenson." I'm hoping this factoid is enough for her to forget how thick-headed I can be sometimes.

"Hmm, yeah I heard. Ms. Clarke has y'all reading *The Strange Case of Dr. Jekyll and Mr. Hyde.*" When Jamie gets a little annoyed her speech starts to imitate her parents' accents, which were picked up when her mother and father attended high school in Dallas. (Her father was actually born and raised a Texan, but her mother was born in Seoul. Jamie was born here—well in Upstate New York.) When she gets really annoyed, and edging on surly, she'll start to use double modals like, "I might should have you expelled," which she said to poor Andrew Hackford when she caught him smoking in the bathroom back in the 8th grade. Of course she didn't since that's not the kind of person she is; instead, she pestered him until three days later, poor Andrew told one of the school counselors himself what he had done. As it turned out, he was given a warning and two weeks of detention, with no suspension (I'm guessing due to his honesty). To top that off, as far as I know, poor Andrew never touched a cigarette again until his family moved away when he was midway through his high school career. So, I guess in some fucked up way, Jamie saved his life in the long run from lung cancer. I haven't heard her talk in such a way since, but she does occasionally pronounce certain words curiously, such as "idea" with an "r" sound at the end. I think she gets that solely from her mother, although I have heard that it is pronounced that way in the UK and in some parts of Canada, but who can be sure. One thing I can be sure of though is that out of the eight years I've known Jamie, I haven't heard her swear once.

"Were you also going to tell me how Stevenson burnt his first draft and rewrote the story in only a few days?" she says.

"Uh no, didn't know about that."

"Mm-hmm."

"Sorry, I didn't know you'd get riled up about these things," I say, even though I know something else is eating at her. I'm used to Jamie's cool, detached mien, but her attitude today is different.

She lets out a long sigh. "It's not you…. It's that red head transfer who's come to snatch my valedictorian title," she says, still reading.

"You mean Penny Bennett, right? Come on, you know there's no one else out there who's taken as many AP classes as you have and still managed to get all A's. Isn't she in a few non-AP classes, like regular U.S. history? I'm sure there's no way she'll beat you."

"Don't be too sure. My mom heard from one of the counselors that Penny's GPA trails mine by less than one-tenth of a point, which means it's possible for me to lose if I don't keep my grades up. I'm convinced she cheated somehow. Maybe one of her parents works in the school system."

I wonder if the problem really lies with the grades. From what I can speculate, a new girl with a pretty face (and breasts) like Penny's is bound to make a few enemies. Our bus has only just reached the interstate entrance, which leaves us with about an hour and forty-five minutes left of one-on-one time. I decide to change the subject since talking about monsters and their disturbed masters and shapely rivals isn't going to help patch up our surprisingly precarious friendship.

"So…" I say. "I heard you got accepted to Berkeley. Congrats."

She puts the book down, I'm guessing because she's no

149

longer able to ignore my presence any longer. But, I notice her eyes are wide now and they're shining like they did when she gave her speech at the student council president election back in Fall. I guess college is her next challenge and ambition—the next ultimate hurdle in her race for perfection.

"Yup, thanks. I'm really happy because it's one of my first choices. Of course, I got accepted to a few places around here as well, but I really want to explore the west coast."

"Yeah, I bet."

"Hey, where was it that you lived before you came here to live with your dad?"

Jamie and I have discussed my life in California plenty of times before, but I decide it can't hurt to do so once more.

"LA. Compton to be more exact, but I think the whole area is considered part of the LA metropolis. I remember it being really warm all the time. How close is Berkeley to LA anyways?"

"Like four hundred miles away. Berkeley is in the SF Bay Area."

"Oh, then I'm not sure if the weather will be similar or not."

"Probably not."

Well, it's come to this; the quality of our conversation has finally been reduced to a discussion about the weather, in a state on the opposite side of the country. But I guess the timing couldn't be any better, considering how we'll never see each other again after two months time anyways. We had a good run as desk-partners.

"So, any idea what you'll be doing with your life?" Her question interrupts my thoughts, and I'm more fazed by the compassion and concern in her voice than by the question it-self.

"Uh...I don't know. I haven't really thought about it. I'm been so busy with work and doing just enough to barely pass my classes. I don't know, maybe I'll go to community college once I've saved enough."

"Hmm, yeah, that's actually not a bad idea. I mean, it's probably too late for you to turn things around in high school, but once you get into community college and work really, *really* hard, then maybe you can transfer to a good school. Like NYU."

"Like NYU, huh."

"Yeah, or maybe even Columbia. Nothing's impossible you know." Yeah, that's true for you at least, I think to myself.

"Hey, are you going to prom?" Jamie asks. This time I'm startled by the question itself. In addition to never witnessing Jamie utter any sort of expletives in the eight years I've known her, I've also never seen her attend any school dance, much less show any interest in them. In fact, I can recall her use the words "grotesque" and "superfluous" when describing the homecomings, Sadie Hawkins, and winter balls of the past.

"You know I have no interest in those things," I say, accompanied by a nervous laugh. I've actually attended a few, some with dates, and others with friends, but I'm trying to tell if Jamie remembers any of that.

"Well, I was asked you know—by Dave."

"Wait, Dave as in David Garretson in the garden club? The Dave who's sitting at the front of this bus right over there?"

"Yeah, he asked me last week on Wednesday after the meeting, and I told him I'll give him my answer on the field trip." I'm not convinced, and Jamie sees the doubt on my face and says, "Don't believe me? Ask April. She was there when he asked me."

I guess there's no reason for her to make this up. It's not even that big of a deal. And, it does explain why someone as busy as Jamie would miss an entire day of school just to look at some flowers. Jamie may be super smart, and as a result, a bit intimidating to most boys, but she's still attractive. It was only a matter of time before someone grew a pair and gave her a shot. So I tell her, "You should go."

She grins and says, "Yeah, but I'm not sure if I want to go with Dave. I mean, he's nice, and handsome, but he's sort of a loner." Her words are in a slightly higher, unusually innocent pitch.

"Jeez, I didn't know you were the type of person who'd judge someone like that." I pull myself up to see over the seat in front of us and take a peek in Dave's direction. He's in his usual attire, smart casual: a nice pair of pants, clean shirt, light blue plaid blazer, and a new looking pair of loafers. The white pocket square is a nice touch I'd say for today's Spring outing. He may be a loner but the kid sure does have style. "But, you're right; he's a good looking guy." I turn to Jamie and say, "I'm sure Mr. and Mrs. Anderson would be proud to know that their only daughter actually likes boys, and is in fact, not an emotionless robot." As soon as the words leave my mouth I want to take them back. I don't know why I thought such an insensitive comment would be at all funny. I suddenly feel like I'm trapped in an out-of-body experience, witnessing myself having just uttered the words that will finally end my friendship with Jamie, who I thought knows nothing more beyond the world of textbooks, studying, and extracurricular activities.

Jamie looks like she's about to cry, and I can tell she's trying really hard to stop herself from letting any unsought tears fall. When the volume of water in her eyes seems to no longer be growing, she says, "Noel, why are you so stupid? You know, you might oughta go to prom with Penny, since you two are obviously so close." The perfect pitch in her voice is gone.

In an attempt to pacify the situation I say, "Why do you even bring Penny up? I hardly know her. I've only noticed her in a few of my classes. Look, I'm sorry. I didn't mean to get you so upset. That wasn't right for me to say. I only realized after I said it how wrong it sounded."

But, it's already too late. Jamie picks up her stuff and pushes my legs aside to slide by me into the aisle. Before heading off to join Dave, she turns to me and says, "*Kkeo-jyeo.*" I know enough Korean (well, enough profane words) to know she just told me to "fuck off."

"Shit," I say to myself. It might have been in Korean, but there's always a first time for everything.

It's 9:47 am when the bus rolls into the Garden's parking lot. Mr. White ushers us out of the bus, and once we're all standing on the pavement he reminds the driver to meet us back here at 1:55, so those of us who need a ride home from school can catch one of the extracurricular buses at four. Jamie and Dave are busy chatting at the front of the group. I try not to stare at them, but I can't help but notice Jamie showing off her pearly whites a few too many times. She's faking her smiles, I can tell because when she does, she shows too much redness of her upper gum. I decide to ignore them for the time being, and if I can, for the rest of the trip.

The Garden doesn't open till ten, but the admissions person, a woman with long silver hair, has agreed to count our tickets and bodies now to save us some time. Our tickets were paid for by a fundraiser our club organized over the Presidents' Day weekend. We sold all sorts of flowers—daffodils, tulips, and lilies—which we raised in the plots behind the main school building. In all, we made $215 selling our potted plants to mostly parents, teachers, and occasional friendly passersby. It didn't cover the entire cost of the trip, so Mr. White actually paid the difference out of his own pocket. He may not know it, but I'm very grateful. I know teachers barely make enough for themselves, so I find his dedication to us impressive and sort of chivalrous, like he's our Disney prince—though on second thought, gracious is probably the better word to use here since it creates a less creepy image. As I've told Jamie before, any money I make from my job in food services, I save, so without Mr. White, I wouldn't have been able to partake in this trip.

I pass the time pushing the edge of the skin on my fingernails into neater curved lines, a habit usually followed by me biting my nails, but I don't. I'm pretty good at refraining from doing so in public. When it's time, the silver-haired lady lets us in, telling each of us to, "Enjoy your visit." On the other side of the entrance Mr. White motions for us to gather around him.

"Okay," he says, "let's go over the schedule and rules of the trip. First off, please be respectful of the Garden and to its employees. I don't want to have to hear from someone that one of you broke one of the ground's rules. Secondly, I know each of you is a responsible young adult, which is why you are all allowed to explore the Garden on your own or in your own groups, though you are welcomed to stay with me as well. Which brings me to my last two points. For lunch, I want everyone to meet me at the picnic area near the café at noon, so I can check up on you. You can find it on the map near the visitor center. The last thing to remember is that our bus leaves at one fifty-five." His eyes find mine for a brief moment. "I'll remind all of you again at lunch. Give me a call if you run into any trouble. Ok, that's it. Have fun."

Our already small group breaks into even smaller ones: kids like Stevie, with no real friends within the club, stick with Mr. White; my old friend Danny and his new buddies constitute the next largest group; Jamie and Dave walk off as a pair; which leaves me and April Green and Josh Kapoor.

"Hey Ashman, come join us. We won't bite," April says, imitating a cat with her claws out. "Though we may give you a good scratch."

"April, stop," Josh chuckles. "You'll scare him away."

Besides Jamie (and Danny, before he and I parted ways), April and Josh are the only other members of the club with whom I get along well with and would consider friends. Now with Jamie gone too, I have no choice but to be embraced by their open claws.

"Thanks guys," I say as I follow them. "I hope you don't mind."

"Nah, it's fine with me," Josh replies. "Besides, it looks like you're in need of a couple of new best friends." He smiles and gives me a pat on the back. I've always admired Josh for his ability to comfort others. He has a sensitive side that I lack, which amazes me, knowing how insensitive some ignorant

155

classmates can be towards him.

April skips in the lead. If I had to guess, I'd say she's still keeping up her act as a cat, something she does when she's in high spirits, which seems to me like all the time. The first time I talked to her, I mentioned how it was weird someone could have a color for their last name. She just shrugged her paws and pointed out how strange my own family name is—how it makes me sound like a person made of ash. I laughed, not knowing what to say since it was the first time I ever thought of my name in such literal terms.

Unlike me and almost half of the club, April isn't a founding member, or more easily put, one of the seniors; she's only just joined this year as a sophomore. She also knows Michael, not through the club since he left before she joined, but from a few of their shared classes. It's actually because of Michael that I've gotten to know April (and by default, Josh) so well.

April leads us towards a tram stop while it appears the other groups have already diverged into nearby exhibits. "Hey Ashman, so what happened between you and Jamie?" she asks, no longer frolicking around. I shrug and she shrugs back. We wait for the next tram in silence.

It arrives a few minutes later and the three of us get on. April sits in the middle with her pink backpack on her lap. The cool breeze is soothing. I close my eyes and want to forget where I am and imagine myself in the back of a convertible, driving listlessly across the country with my new company.

"Hey Ashman, what's your favorite flower?" April asks.

Without opening my eyes I think of the first flower that comes to my mind. "Lilies."

"Mine's hydrangeas. They remind me of colorful and bright

pom-poms. I just want to shake them to no end." April waves her hands in the air as if she's performing one of Mrs. Robert's cheerleading routines.

"Hey, watch it Green," I say, but she ignores me and continues to attempt to motivate the team and entertain the audience of her imagination with her swinging arms. I assume she'll stop once I cease paying attention to her, but she doesn't, so I decide to continue the conversation April has started. "Josh, what about you?" I ask him. "What's your favorite flower?"

Josh crosses his arms and tilts his head back in thought. I can tell he's glad I asked him from the way he's trying to hide his smile. "Hmm, well Noel, I think the sunflower is my favorite. I don't need to say why, do I?"

"No," I laugh. "I'm not trying to get you to write me an essay on sunflowers."

"Grrrrreat!" April yells. She's stopped flailing her arms, which I'm thankful for, but now my ears are ringing. With April, if it's not one thing, it's another. "Let's make sure we find each of these flowers before we leave today."

"Gosh Green, you're awfully commanding today."

"Well, it's only fair I'm in charge, since it is still April. You're entitled to certain privileges when you're named after the month you're born in. It's only fair!"

"Understood, Captain Green," I say, rubbing my ears.

It's nearly noon now, and over the course of just a couple of hours we saw hundreds of different kinds of plants and flowers. April even managed to find where the lilies, hydrangeas, and sunflowers are grown, achieving today's goal. Of course, she wanted to take it a step further and locate every type of flower we've worked with back at our school. If it wasn't for Josh reminding April about the lunchtime role call, we would have been on the opposite side of the grounds, instead of just six yards from the entrance of the café.

Mr. White and approximately half the club are already seated at a few of the picnic tables. There's also several other large groups enjoying their lunch, and I've noticed the garden has become a lot more crowded since the morning. As we walk towards the group, I notice the only ones missing are Jamie and Dave. My stomach starts to feel a little uneasy, but it's probably only because I'm hungry. After all, I've only had one toast to eat for the entire morning. However, the worst has yet to come, since I don't have anything to eat for lunch and no money to buy anything with.

April runs ahead, and I can see her talking to Mr. White, pointing back at us. Before Josh and I get the chance to reach the tables, April runs back.

"Come on," she says, as she skips past us, in the direction we just came from.

"Hey, Green, where are we going now?" I ask. "Don't we need to join the others?"

"Nope. I told Mr. White that we're going to eat at the café. Come on!"

Josh and I follow her to the café's entrance, but before I go in, I turn to do a quick headcount of the club; still only nine— the two lovebirds are still missing.

The café is a rather small establishment and is situated almost four feet below the ground. I almost fall down the steps when I walk in practically backwards. Luckily, my two companions don't witness my stumble, although some of the preexisting patrons do.

April and Josh walk up to the counter, while I grab a two-person table farthest from the door and steal an extra chair from a neighboring table. I don't have to wait long since most of the food items are pre-made sandwiches, salads, and wraps. Josh comes back first with a *panino* and *Nature's* lemon iced tea.

He says, "Thanks, Noel, for getting us a table. You can go ahead and get your food now."

"Oh, I don't think I'm going to eat anything. I had somewhat of a big breakfast," I tell him.

"Are you sure?" Josh asks with narrow eyes. "You might have fooled April back at the Rock Garden by telling her that the grumbling sounds were coming from the waterfall"—he twists the cap off his tea—"but you didn't fool me."

I enjoy a brief chuckle. I forgot how keen Josh can be at times. Once, he volunteered to take my place for watering duty because he somehow caught on that I'd be late to work otherwise. It's as if his superpower is the ability to observe everything around him without having anyone notice him doing so.

"I knew you'd see through me somehow. I didn't have time to pack a lunch, and I'm out of cash at the moment. But, don't worry about me, I'll get myself fed once I'm at work."

Josh pretends he doesn't hear me and gets up and goes back to the counter. After talking with the cashier, he comes back with a paper plate and a small cup of water. He places the plate and cup in front of me, then takes half of his *panino* and slides it over onto the plate.

"Thanks Josh," I say, "but I can't take your food."

I'm about to push the plate away from myself, but Josh reacts too quickly, and holds the plate in place. "As if I'm going to eat anything while you're starving in front of me," he says. "Just enjoy it."

My eyes start to water as a growing warmth sails throughout my body. I pick up the cup of water and take a sip in an attempt to hide my tears from Josh, but something tells me he's already seen them. The cool feeling of water rushing down my esophagus and into my empty stomach works to calm my emotions.

"I'll pay you back," I say.

Josh smiles. "If it'll make you feel better, but don't worry about it." He takes a sip of his own drink. "I hope you like ham."

April finally arrives with her tray of what looks like Caesar salad, a cup of vegetable soup, and a juice bottle. Before she takes her seat though, she takes a second to glance at our table, and I can tell she's trying to make sense of what has just transpired. It looks as though she's grasped the situation because as soon as she sits down, she tosses me her pack of saltine crackers. Of course, I thank her for it, to which she replies with an uncharacteristic nod, and starts eating. Josh and I follow her lead and pick up our respective half of the ham panini. It's one of the most delicious things I've eaten in a while; nowadays, my diet consists of leftovers from work, cheap burgers and fried foods, and whatever's lying around at home.

I finish the panini in fewer than four bites, and sit in slight embarrassment over how quickly I've cleaned my plate. The saltine crackers are still sealed in their wrapping, and I decide to leave them unopened for a while longer—at least until Josh and April are about done with their meals.

"So." April breaks the silence. "I was wondering, what do

you want to be when you grow up, Noel?" She doesn't look up, as she continues to scoop what turns out to be lentil soup. It's a very unusual question for April to be asking.

"Well," I say, "You guys may not know this about me, but I love food. I'm hoping to someday become a respectable chef. Maybe own my own restaurant. Do you think my current job at Val's Burgers will help with that?"

I can see Josh is about to reply, but April cuts him off. For some reason, she's back to her cheery self. "I want to be a popstar," she says. She stands suddenly, almost knocking over her chair, and wields her juice bottle like a mic.

I turn to Josh, whose eyes are smiling, and ask him the same question: "So, Josh, what are your plans down the road?"

Still smiling, he says, "I haven't really thought a lot about it. My parents want me to become a doctor like my cousins, but I'm not too sure. I mean, I like helping people, but I'm sort of waiting for a something else to turn up."

"Maybe you could become a teacher," I say. "Or you could become a counselor, or—"

"Or a good guy, like a police officer," April says.

"Yeah, a police officer sounds nice," Josh says.

April finally pulls in her chair and sits back down. "Though, you can't be too nice, otherwise the bad guys will walk all over you."

Josh and I laugh, and as if waiting for the opportune moment, Mr. White pokes his head in to tell us to meet him and the rest of the club outside. He says we're going to see a special exhibit together. It's strange to see Mr. White so engrossed in anything that could be said to be a teaching experience. I pocket the pack of crackers to save for later and tell Josh and

April that I'll meet them outside with everyone else. It's not that I'm tired of being the third wheel; in fact, I could tell they were trying hard to make me feel welcomed, or at least Josh was—April was too busy being herself. I just want to give them some time alone, even if it's only for a minute.

My eyes are blinded by the sun the moment I exit the café; it's also a lot warmer outside of the den. As I'm making my way towards the pack, I take off my scarf, bundle it up, and hold it in one hand.

"Where's April and Josh?" Mr. White asks me.

"They're finishing up their lunch," I say. "They should be out soon."

A few moments later, April emerges from the café with a vanilla ice cream cone, with Josh trailing behind her, carrying both of their bags. As soon as they're close enough, Mr. White has us gather around him.

"Okay, group. We have about an hour and a half left before we have to head back to the school, so I thought it'd be better to stay together until then. Besides, there's a particular exhibit that I want to make sure all of you get to see." Mr. White starts walking off and motions for us to follow him. "We're heading towards the Haupt Conservatory, which houses the Victorian glasshouse where we'll witness the blooming of a titan arum. I was told it'd be ready after noon. It's really a once in a lifetime opportunity."

"Wait," April cries, "What about Jamie?"

"Oh, I gave her and David permission to eat their lunch at the Perennial Garden, which is all the way on the other side of the grounds. They've already been informed to meet us at the glasshouse."

Of course he let her, knowing how she could be trusted.

As I trudge along, I inadvertently walk alongside Danny, who today, is sporting one of those frameless glasses. From the look on his face, it's apparent that he's had better days. His nose is runny and his eyes are red, and although not swollen, are slightly enlarged (though that may be due to the illusion created by the new intensity of his lenses).

"Allergies," I say, almost in the form of a question.

"Yeah," Danny replies.

We continue to walk in silence, listening to the chatter of others pick up sporadically around us.

"So," Danny says, "how was your time with Josh and April?"

"Oh, you know. They're both really friendly, and nice. We went and saw practically every plant in here."

"That's good."

"Yup."

Danny takes out a pack of tissues from his pocket and carefully wipes his eyes and blows his nose. He then places the used tissue in his other pocket and sniffles before saying, "I had no idea it was going to be this bad. If I had known, I would've passed on this field trip."

"No kidding," I say. "I didn't know you had seasonal allergies in the first place."

"Neither did I," he says, wiping his nose once more with a new tissue.

It's been a while since I've had a one-on-one chat with Danny. I've missed Michael poking fun at his physical and emotional insecurities, and Danny sarcastically telling him how funny his remarks are. It was all I could do to not fill in for

Michael by saying something about Danny's new glasses or his big runny nose.

"Okay, everyone, we're here," Mr. White says. He holds the door open and ushers us in.

"Oh god," someone inside says. "What's that smell?"

I'm a bit puzzled by the exclamation, having yet to enter the building, but in the following moments I understand the degree of disgust in the person's voice.

"It smells like something's rotting," another student says.

"That's because it *is* the smell of rotting flesh," Stevie says. He turns to the rest of the members and explains. "This is the titan arum, a flowering plant with the largest unbranched flower head in the world!"

"That's right, Stephen" Mr. White chimes in. "It's also known as the corpse flower. The stink attracts carrion-eating beetles and flesh flies that are supposed to pollinate it. The dark red, almost burgundy color adds to the illusion that it's a piece of meat…"

I nudge Danny and say, "You're lucky your big nose is stuffed with snot. You probably can't smell a thing."

"Right," he says, rolling his eyes.

"…it's endemic to the rainforests of Sumatra, Indonesia, and can reach over ten feet in height," Mr. White continues. "It looks like this one is about five and a half feet tall. Actually, the most interesting thing about the titan arum, other than its size and smell, is the fact that it blooms like this only once every two to ten years. And, it usually blooms in the afternoon and stays open for only twelve to forty-eight hours. It's one of those rare flowers that 'dies' as soon as it blooms."

Everyone tries to get a closer look at the gigantic tropical megaphone, with an equally large banana growing out of it. I, on the other hand, decide to ignore it (and the crowd), and go off to the side to read the exhibit display:

"Titan arum (*Amorphophallus titanium*)...Native to tropical forests in Sumatra...four- to nine-foot-tall...blah, blah, blah...nicknamed 'Baby'...The first documented flowerings in the United States were at the New York Botanical Garden in 1937 and 1939. This flowering inspired the designation of the titan arum as the official flower of the Bronx in 1939..."

Wow, they must have been so proud.

"...only to be replaced in 2000 by the day lily."

Well, nothing last forever I suppose. I take out the crackers from my pocket and pop open the wrapping.

15

September, 2014.

"You know those famous paintings in museums, like *Mona Lisa* and *Starry Night*? You think the ones out on display are the real ones?"

"I don't know, Danny," I reply. "I suppose so."

"They can't be. I mean, they're right out there, exposed—naked on a wall, like a stripper on a stage. Some don't even have a glass cover for Christ sake! All it takes is for one crazy person to ruin a priceless piece of art and it's gone forever."

"Kind of like a human life and those crazy murderers," I say as I throw bits of pretzel near a flock of pigeons.

"Yeah, exactly!" Danny's voice startles the pigeons away from my ample offering.

"Why the sudden interest in paintings? Those really aren't our area of expertise."

"I don't know," says Danny while looking off into the distance. "It'd be nice to have a one-of-a-kind painting hanging on my living room wall. Imagine having the *Mona Lisa* hanging across from your sofa, and you're the only one to appreciate the treasure, the famous stare. That would be something."

"Yeah, sorry, not really a fan. I prefer woman with real bodies, not paintings of them. But whatever floats your boat."

"You know that's not what I meant," says Danny, shaking his head.

A large flock of pigeons is now gathering around the pretzel crumbs. Each of the birds has its own precise pecking ritual. I imagine myself as a king and the pigeons as the peasants, bowing to my grand presence and thanking me for my graciousness distribution of crumbs. Their continued bowing pleases me, so I rip off another large chuck and toss it into the mass. A dark brown pigeon, slightly larger than the rest, forces himself onto the piece and does its best to gobble up as much as it can before the others join in.

"I really do need a painting though," says Danny. "I've got a blank spot on my wall and it makes me feel empty just looking at it everyday."

"How about hanging up a picture instead?"

"You mean like a photo?"

"Yeah," I say, already regretting bringing up the idea.

"I don't know," says Danny. "I don't really have any good photos of my family. And I don't think I would want to hang one up even if I did."

"Who would?" I mutter. I take out a cigarette and light it quickly. Before I even exhale the first puff of smoke, Danny shifts a foot away from me on the bench.

The last of the pretzel is pecked off from the cement ground, resulting in the peasants to scramble for generosity elsewhere. So fickle is the mind of a peasant, but really, I can't blame them for wanting to merely survive; they really don't care who their king is as long as they can acquire food for their bellies.

I get off the bench and start to walk towards the lake. During this time of the year, the surrounding trees are full of green, which carries on in the wind. The scent of green connects people with nature, encouraging them to take boat rides and walk along the shore, watching the various birds that inhabit this isolated ecosystem. But I despise the smell of green that acts like a drug, putting people under its influence of obligation; hence the smoking to ward off its repression. The cigarette is my incense that shrouds and protects me like a frail boy in his artificial bubble.

The ducks swim in harmony with the boats, unnerved even when a paddle gets too close. They know that the lake is theirs during the warmer seasons, despite this particular lake being man-made. People are no more than guests who pay for their visitations with slices of bread. Bring a whole loaf and you can even take a dip in the water. But from the murky green color, I would highly advise against that. Not all green is good, you know.

I turn around to see Danny, still sitting on the bench as a speck in the distance. Like a twelve-year-old child, I have wandered off, away from my guardian. And like a parent, I see Danny the speck wave for me to return to his worrisome company. Me being able to distinguish his wave compels me to walk even further to the point where he is consumed wholly by the bench—or rather, becomes one with its wooden arches.

In the corner of my eye, I spot a familiar arch of a woman's body. She is bent over, tucking in the shirt of a little boy no older than five. Her long, red hair flowing effortlessly down her side prompts a name bundled safely in my mind—Penny Bennett, the pretty girl from high school who shared three of my classes, including band. While Penny and I weren't friends per se, we were close acquaintances, socializing during breaks and working on group projects together (with her usually doing most of the work).

It's strange to see an old classmate take a walk with her child. I'm still as irresponsible as ever, but there's Penny, strolling in the park with her son's hand held tightly in her own. She's one of the many who choose to speed through life, opting to rush on the moving walkways that you normally find in airports rather than take the regular pacing of her own two legs. Seriously, what's the hurry? The twenties are supposedly the best years you'll ever get—or so I've heard.

As I put out my cigarette, I notice the absence of a ring on any of her fingers. This should be interesting.

"Penny Bennett?" I ask standing still like a statue with a half-smile on my face.

Confused recognition translates from her inscrutable look. "Do I know you?"

"We went to high school together." A pause follows as I give her the decency to remember me before I tell her myself. "Come on, it wasn't that long ago. I mean, it hasn't even been ten years yet." I let out one of my most convincing fake laughs.

"Wait, yeah, I know you. Ashmen, right?"

"Ashman, yeah. How have you been?"

169

"I've been really good," she says. The boy tugs on her arm.

"Is this your son?"

"Yeah, his name is Charles. I was just taking him to see the ducks."

"Well you've come to the best place for that."

"Don't tell me you come here to see the ducks too," she says while brushing back her hair. "I don't remember you being so involved with nature."

"Yeah well, the truth is I come here for the pretzels. That cart right over there has the best pretzels in all of New York City. Ol' Ralph is obviously doing something right."

"Really? You come all the way here for the pretzels?" Charles tugs on his mother's arm again. "What is it, baby?"

"I want to see the ducks."

"Okay, but don't touch the water. Mama's going to be right here watching you."

"And you came all the way here to see ducks," I say as the kid scurries off towards the edge of the lake. His blue overalls gleam next to the sparkling water.

A tender grin grows on Penny's lips. "What can I say? Charles is my life now."

I don't know what else *to* say, so I just nod my head as I watch her son jump up and down at the sight of the aquatic birds. Penny watches her son in silence as well, and for a brief moment, I feel like I'm on a family outing during a sunny Saturday afternoon. There's a certain fragility that comes with a such a moment; the moment is fleeting, but the memory lasts forever, withstanding all the bad feuds that arise while growing up. Bits and pieces are chipped with each lash and blow, but the memory is still there until you deem it too painful to recall—too painful to know that there was such a time when your smile was innocent and real. Little Charles had best remember these moments well—the times he spends with his mother—because he will surely need scapegoats to take the hits for him when he faces life's realities.

"So what are you doing in New York City?" Penny asks, breaking the silence. She never could stand prolonged absence of conversation. Listening was always one of her favorite things to do, even if it was a bad joke told by a horny freshman.

"I'm a...I got a job here."

"Oh."

It's strange. Even during high school, I was never one to chatter, but Penny was always fine being around me. I'm guessing it was because I wasn't one of the many douchebags desperately chasing after her. I've heard girls like it when guys play a little hard to get themselves, although that was never my intention.

"How about you? Do you live here in the city?" I ask, making sure to keep the conversation alive.

"Yeah, I got an apartment up in the Bronx," she says. "It's just Charles and me."

At first, I'm a little taken aback by how blunt she is about her living situation, but then again, who cares if other people know that she's raising a child without a partner. It's not like that's so uncommon these days.

"Single parent, huh? Must be pretty rough."

"Yeah well," she says with a deep breath, "it's worth it."

"A motherly thing to say."

"I bet you never expected me to be a single mother."

"I can't say the thought's ever crossed my mind." A pause follows once again. "But you know, for a single parent, you look great. And your kid looks likes he's being taken care of pretty well. I mean, it's a lot better than what I can say about how my father handled me."

"Thanks, that's really nice of you to say." Her eyes light up as she lets out a smile like she used to back during high school. The innocence is lost, but the attractive features are all still there. I promptly look away, not wanting to get lost within her perfectly symmetrical beauty.

"Mama, mama! Come look!"

"What is it, baby?" Penny joins her son at the edge of the lake. I follow slowly behind her, keeping an appropriate distance.

"The baby duck right there. He's lost."

"Oh, it's okay, sweetie. The mommy duck is going to come back for him. See? She's right over there with the other ducklings."

As Penny is busy caring for her son, I slip away back from where I came, as if the whole meeting never happened. It's rude, I know, but I'm sure Penny will understand. I was never one to linger. Besides, kids tend to remember the strangest details, unlike adults, and I don't want to get in the way of little Charles's happy memory.

Right as I turn away from the lake, I make out a faint shadow of a stork descending ever so quietly.

I return to the bench where Danny is sitting just as I've left him, alone despite the multitude of people walking about. His pitiful image has done well in driving away others from my empty seat.

"Hey, was that Penny Bennett you were talking with over there?" he asks with his hands hovering over his eyes.

"Yeah, it was," I reply. "You saw that from here?"

Danny points to his glasses, which now reflect the unobstructed sunlight. "I've got super-vision, don't you know?"

"Of course you do."

"And was that a kid with her?"

"Yeah."

"Hers?"

"Her nephew," I say. For some reason, it doesn't feel right to talk about Penny's life, especially with someone like Danny, who doesn't know in the least bit how to be happy.

"Wow, she looks just as good as she did during high school." His hands are back over his eyes, but this time, in the shape of binoculars.

I light up another cigarette as I take my original seat. "Cut it out, Danny. You're starting to act like a pedophile, staring at the little boy like that."

Danny lowers his arms and leans back against the bench. "If me looking at Penny bothers you, then just tell me. No need to call me a pedophile. Especially out here in public."

"Oh calm down. No one is paying attention to what we're saying."

"You never know. Earlier I heard a couple make fun of a guy behind his back for saying the word 'water' weirdly."

"You do know that you were the one who was eavesdropping, right?"

Danny pretends not to hear me as he blows his nose with a tissue from his pocket, each blow more superfluous than the last. We continue to sit on the bench, uninterrupted for a scant five minutes when a commotion erupts by the lake. More and more people gather about the edge, practically shoving each other out of the way in order to catch a glimpse of the spectacle. You'd think there was a 99% off summer sale over there from the rowdy noise overwhelming the usual laughter of children and quacking of ducks.

"What do you think is going on over there?" asks Danny with his binocular hands back up and in position.

I simply shrug in response, suddenly feeling too lazy to leave my perfectly comfortable seat that has slowly been gaining shade from a nearby tree. It's not easy to procure such ideal seating in the park during a weekend afternoon.

"I'm going to go take a look," says Danny.

"What about your super-vision?"

Without turning around, he waves me off, leaving me behind just as effortlessly as I'd left him. Not wanting to feel abandoned, I force myself to stand and follow Danny back to the edge of the murky water, where people are now flashing pictures left and right in order to document this momentous occasion. Danny and I are able to shove to the front layer of the crowd, where the splashing of water can clearly be heard. Towards the middle of the lake, there appears to be a stork flailing ferociously on the surface, wings outstretched well over six feet in length. It's white feathers glimmer as the sunlight bounces off the wet layers; the whole ordeal is almost blinding to see. And the more the bird struggles, the lower it sinks into the cloudy pond, until only its extended neck desperately holds its bare head above the water. People are in awe as children scream, tears rolling down their faces, begging their parents to save the poor bird. But no one dares to jump in to risk their life to save a mere wading bird from a potentially unseeable threat.

Towards the edge of the crowd, I spot a redheaded woman covering the eyes of her son as she gawks at the unplanned horror. I guess little Charles will have to find his scapegoat memory elsewhere—perhaps somewhere that doesn't involve the potential for sinking ducks.

16

April, 2005.

"Hey, you got a smoke?" Barry asks with his typical grungy expression.

I reach into my jacket pocket for my box of cigarettes and toss it over to Barry. He never carries around his own cigarettes, probably because he ends up smoking every pack the moment right after he buys them. Barry's a strange kid. He has an older brother who's studying medicine at some prestigious university and an even older sister who is already a successful patent lawyer somewhere in southern California. I guess you could say that Barry is the family "mistake," and he certainly gives his parents reasons to believe so. Just last week, they had to pick him up at the local precinct for getting into a fight with some other delinquents. I was there too, not partaking in the fighting, of course. Only fools fight with their fists.

"Did you see that new girl with the huge knockers?" he says with a cigarette already in his mouth.

"You mean Penny Bennett?" I ask as I flick the ash from my own.

Barry nods. "Yeah, that's the one. Man, she could be my lucky penny any day, if you know what I mean."

"No, I don't know what you mean," I say, and lay down comfortably on the bottom of the slide.

"You know, like," Barry stops and ponders for a moment. I guess he can't find the words he's looking for, because he grows silent and just continues to puff out smoke from his sharp nose. "Yo, how do you know her name anyways?"

I place my hands behind my head and give off a slight shrug. "I asked her. You know, you can talk to girls instead of being a pussy."

"Shut the fuck up man," says Barry jokingly as he kicks up sand in my direction. "Is she in one of your classes?"

"Precalculus, U.S. history, and band," I say casually, as if it's no big deal, which it really isn't.

"Damn man, you're lucky as hell."

"Not really," I say. "She could be in some of your classes too. You probably just don't know it since you skip so much."

"Man, it might be worth going to school just to find out," says Barry enthusiastically. I know for a fact that it'll take him a lot of motivation to make that visit. After all, Barry is pretty well known for being the skipping king of our class, with a less than 80% attendance record throughout his high school career. (The thing is, he skips because he wants to; a lot of the times I skip because I have to.) It's a safe bet to say that due to his frequent practice of truancy, dropping out is coming up very soon on his idle agenda.

"Yo, you wanna grab some grub, man?" he asks as he tosses his remaining filter. "There's a new burger place a couple blocks down. Best fries you'll ever have, man, I swear."

"I think I'll pass. I have to get back to school. There's a history test that I can't miss."

"Man, you just want to look at them titties again, don't you?" says Barry as he squeezes his hands in midair. "The waitress at the burger joint is hot too, man. Come on, you have to check her out."

"Sorry Barry, next time," I tell him as I bury my cigarette deep in the sand. We shake hands and part ways, leaving the playground as empty as we found it.

I quickly jog back to school, making it barely in time for my history class on the second floor of the main building. Besides band, Mr. Prescott's history class is my only class where seats are assigned to each individual student. It's pretty pointless from a student's point of view. After all, order naturally finds itself in a classroom setting. On the first day of class, the desk that people claim are usually the ones that they continue to sit in for the rest of the year. I can't remember one instance otherwise. But Mr. Prescott is an orderly man who takes pleasure from straightening folders on his desks and keeping the chalkboard flawlessly clean after every lecture, so trifling rules are to be expected of him.

My seat is in the far front, left corner of the room, almost grazing Mr. Prescott's sterile desk. Those poor overachievers would kill to have my seat. And due to alphabetical order, Penny sits directly next to me. Her enrollment in the class resulted in everyone else being shifted down a seat. She's wearing a purple skirt with long socks, or stockings, that cover up her slim legs. A white blouse covers most of her skin on her upper body, concealing her voluptuous figure, and her red hair waves softly over her shoulders. As she turns her head towards my direction, I quickly look away at Mr. Prescott's desk, where three sharpened pencil lay perfectly parallel to one another.

"You have the entire period to finish the test," Mr. Prescott says as he passes out multiple five-paged-double-sided packets to the front of each row. "Notes of any kind are prohibited, so put away everything except for a pencil and an eraser." Grant Yan, who sits in the back, still has his textbook opened and appears to be reviewing material until the last possible second. "Put away everything," Mr. Prescott repeats firmly, giving the perfectionist a cold look of authority through his horrid glasses. Grant quickly shuffles his textbook into his overstuffed backpack on wheels.

"You may begin" is followed by a rustle of paper being flipped over, as if a gust of vigorous wind burst through the open window. I look over to my right and see Penny already halfway through the first page. Pretty and smart, a nasty combo. With her body bent over the desk, her breasts push up in her blouse in a desperate attempt for air. Before I can turn my attention back to my own test, Mr. Prescott barks out, "Ashman, eyes on your own paper." My face turns red as I read through the first question. Well shit, now she probably thinks I was trying to cheat off her. At least that's better than letting her know that I was checking her out, right?

I continue to keep my eyes glued on my test. A question reads, "Name and describe a natural disaster that has affected a city in the United States during the past century." A pretty open question, which deviates greatly from the usual multiple choice and fill in the blanks that Mr. Prescott often practices. The first thing that comes to mind is the Great Fire of New York, something I read upon outside of class. Unfortunately, that happened centuries ago, sometime around 1776 or 78, but my mind keeps circling back to it. The fire happened during the military occupation by British forces during the American Revolutionary War. It was assumed that the fire was manmade, an act against the British occupation. So then, does that even count as a natural disaster? What the hell does it matter. I remember a different disaster, quickly scribbling down the 1989 earthquake which struck the San Francisco area, and how it killed over 50 people and left more than 12,000 homeless.

Midway through the exam, a student messenger appears at the doorway and hesitantly walks in, which summons Mr. Prescott from his perch. After receiving a note, Mr. Prescott calls my name telling me to pack my stuff and head to the front office. I reluctantly get up from my seat, handing over my incomplete test. He assures me that I can finish it later and requests that I gently close the door on the way out. Johnny, the kid who works at the front office for two or three of his periods, leads me down the hallway with mismatched steps.

"What the hell is going on, Johnny?" I ask, which compels him to stop walking. He turns towards me, his usual goofy grin absent from his face, and gives me a wide hug. "What the hell, Johnny." I push him away, careful not to push too hard and cause him to stumble.

"I'm sorry," he spouts. "I'm sorry."

We pass by a classroom where Mrs. Fields is popping in an educational video of sorts in Mr. White's classroom, and continue down the stairs into the main office where an officer awaits for my appearance. The officer is big boned with deep sunken eyes of blue. He has his burly arms folded behind his back, as if waiting impatiently for a junior officer who's gone to the restroom. My first thought is that I'm in some sort of trouble, that I've been caught on tape stealing a Jean-Luc Fillon record from the music store. But as I enter the room, I detect no malice from the officer's tense posture. He urges me to follow him to his patrol car, as if there's only so much time left before the sun were to explode. His urgency makes me very uneasy.

"Can someone tell me what's going on?" My voice echoes throughout the office, stirring an exchange of glances, not one person eager to speak up. The duty ultimately falls on the officer, who looks to the ground and fiddles with his hat in his bulky hands.

"There's no other way to tell you this, son," he pauses for a brief second. "Your family's house caught on fire, burnt right down to the ground."

My books! The first edition that I received from Ms. Finkland! I place my head in my hands and pull off my purple and black striped beanie.

"And my father?" I ask, with crocodile tears at the ready.

"Your father was caught in the fire," replies the officer. "Firefighters barely got him out, but unfortunately a bit too late. He's covered in third and fourth-degree burns. He's at the Keller Army Community Hospital right now." I stare at the officer as if he told me tragic news, but in my mind, I shake my head at the world's defiance against me. Of course, a simple fire isn't enough to completely kill off a monster.

"Officer Cory, sir," I say after checking his name tag, "it sounds like we don't have much time." My body shudders, convincing onlookers of my flustered emotions as fear and trauma. Only I know that I shudder at the idea of finishing the job.

I exit the building, trailing behind Officer Cory as Johnny chases after me. He gives me a pat on the back and says he's sorry once again to which I reply, "I know."

Officer Cory directs me to sit in the back, where a caged divider covers most of my view of the front. Not like there's anything to see anyways, besides the shaved back of the officer's head. The backseats are made entirely of plastic, and are more uncomfortable than the hard seats of public transportation. I guess this is what it feels like to be an arrested criminal riding in the back of a police car; the caged divider prepares criminals for the familiarity of the jail bars while the cold, hard seats keep them conscious and distressed. There's no doubt that I am wide awake and dismayed.

Traffic on the highway slows us down, despite rush hour having been two hours ago.

"I guess I have to," Officer Cory mutters to himself as he turns on his sirens. Blue and red lights reflect off surrounding cars accompanied by wailing whoop-whoops deafening to my ears. And like Moses splitting the ocean in two, cars in front of us start to pull off to the sides, creating a narrow passage in-between two lanes. We drive slowly along the dotted lines, coming to the occasional stop as some cars fail to properly respond in a timely manner. A couple of drivers visibly shake their heads in disgust, assuming that the cop behind the commotion is taking advantage of an ingrained institutional position. Officer Cory remains upright in his seat, casting back the unsolicited stares.

"I don't usually do this," he says to me, as if my opinion of him mattered to his unwavering ego.

"I understand," I say back.

It is completely silent for the rest of the drive to the hospital. I imagine Officer Cory isn't much of a talker to begin with, which is fine by me. It must be difficult to come up with something to say to a kid who has just heard his father was caught in a household fire. I can imagine.

Once at the hospital, Officer Cory leads me to the front desk, where we are then taken to the elevator to the third floor. The nurse leading us informs me of my father's situation: the critical condition of his appearance and his heart, and how he's on the verge of death. Her words slowly fade away as inaudible whispers while I grow tense in fear of what I'm expected to witness. Am I about to see my father draw his final breath? Or will I observe him rise from the ashes of a fatal blunder? I hope, with little remorse, that it will be the former of the two. If not, then I'm willing to do whatever it takes to ensure that is the case.

Officer Cory insists on waiting outside room 317 as I enter alone to witness the condition of my father. The moment the door opens, I am met with a foul stench of singed hair coupled with the expected vinegar-like smell of a sterile hospital. And there on the white bed, lies my father, barely recognizable with his bubbly flesh and multiple tubes connected to all sides of his mutated body. A breathing mask is strapped over his unsightly face, and for once in his life, he actually looks the part of a child-beating monster. An inconstant beeping grows fainter in volume as I watch my father's will slowly abandon his undesirable casket of a body. And I can't help but surrender to a sudden laugh, which I immediately attempt to swallow back down my bitter throat.

Oh, how the mighty drunk has fallen.

17

September, 2014.

"I'm really glad you didn't leave without saying goodbye."

"What are you talking about?" I ask after taking a generous drag of my cigarette. Penny continues to rub my stomach, unfazed by the cool breeze flowing through the open window.

"At the park, remember?" she says, pressing her body against my own.

It's only been a couple of minutes since we've made love, but I'm already sensing a raging desire to leave my mark once again. Her thin bed covers are still sprawled out on the floor, in an attempt to hide my clothes from sight.

"Yeah, me too."

Despite the despairing location of her two bedroom apartment, I must admit, the interior is pretty cozy with the Victorian style furniture and the hand sewn portraits of tulips and roses hanging on every side of the walls. It's almost as if I can smell pollen amidst the smoke in the air.

I pull Penny closer to me, pressing against her bare back with the palm of my hand. She responds by moving her hand down my stomach, stroking me gently in carefully measured motions.

"Looks like someone's ready for another round," she whispers into my ear. Before I'm able to force myself on top of her, she slips from my grasp and holds me tightly with both hands. And without warning, she fits all of me into her salivating mouth. I feel myself enlarge into her throat as I hold her head in place, surprised by her lack of resistance to withdraw. The sensation leaves me shivering with authority, as I twitch several times against the foundation of her tongue. And with a contrite conscience, I let her go, signaling for her to gasp for air before swallowing me whole once again, while this time motioning in and out steadily with imperfect rhythm. I pull back her lush, red hair to feel it taut within my grasp. And like the softest silk, her hair escapes through the gaps between my fingers.

Barely a minute goes by before a knock is heard by the door. Penny bends back her head as she calls out to her son.

"What is it, honey?"

A muffled voice cries from the other side of the door. "I can't go to sleep."

Penny throws the covers back onto the bed and retrieves her exposed clothes. "I'll be right out there, okay?"

I lay silently on the bed as passion wanes slowly from my body. Penny slides through the cracked open door with her gown and hair narrowly escaping the shut. I pull up the covers over my lower half, blocking the draft onto my moist parts. I bend my knees upwards, making sure there is plenty of space for my groin area to breathe. A couple of minutes pass by as I try to make out faces and animals from the rough patterns on the ceiling, like people usually do with clouds or the alignment of the stars in the sky. Just as I decide to get off of the bed and get dressed, Penny returns, softly closing the door behind her.

"I'm sorry about that," she says as she lets her gown fall effortlessly down her slender shoulders and back onto the wooden floor.

"Perhaps it's time for me to go," I say, unveiling myself from the covers.

"You don't have to go. Not yet. I just got Charles back into bed."

Penny climbs onto the mattress and kneels astride of my legs, inching herself closer and closer towards my chest. Commiseration of how life has treated her so far forces me to embrace her with both arms. And without thinking, I slide my hands down her smooth waist and grope her full hips.

"I'm ready when you are," she says with a devious smile. I am temporarily mesmerized by her perky breasts grazing my cheeks.

"I'm sorry, I really should be going." I give her a tight squeeze and lightly kiss her nipples goodbye, letting my tongue make a brief appearance. I then lift her up as I slide myself to the edge of the bed.

"That's not fair, especially after a kiss like that," she says as she tosses her hair so it cascades down her side. "Do you really have to go?"

A simple nod is all I can muster before I give her one last kiss on her red head. I get dressed quickly, and like the expert thief that I am, exit the apartment without producing even the slightest creak from the floorboards. Thirty minutes later, I arrive at the designated point where Danny is already parked and ready to go.

"Why are you late?" he says as he opens the van door for me.

I jump in and check the time on the dashboard. "I'd hardly call one minute being late."

Danny is about to toss his arms into the air, but refrains from doing so. "Oh, so if I'm one minute late, then it's all right to get upset at me for the entire night, but if you're one minute late, then it doesn't even constitute as being late?"

"Calm down, Danny."

"And what's that smell?" Danny says while sniffing in close proximity to my jacket. "Why do you smell like flowers?"

"I don't smell like flowers," I reply.

"No wait, more like," he takes another obnoxious whiff, "perfume? Did you put on some kind of perfume?"

"No, I didn't," I tell him with a stern look. "And just so you know, men use something called cologne, not perfume."

"I know that," he says as he slowly shakes his head. "So you did put something on then?"

"I already told you that I didn't. And if you must know, I left Penny in order to get here, so let's get started now, shall we?"

"Penny? You mean Penny Bennett?"

"Yeah."

"From the park?"

"Do you know anybody else with the same name?"

"This late?" he asks with his eyes wide open. "Was she naked?" It's almost as if Danny has completely forgotten about my earlier tardiness.

"I'm not going to give you any details, so can we just get rolling here?"

"If I was with naked Penny, then I wouldn't have left," Danny says in a daze.

"Don't be such a creep," I tell him. "And besides, her son sort of interrupted. It didn't feel right to be there after that."

"Her son? Wait, I thought you said at the park that the kid she was with was her nephew or something?"

"Yeah, well, I'm telling you it's her son now."

"So, she's single?"

"Of course she's single."

"Well, I don't know. I'd assume she'd be married if she has a kid, right? And I know you'd be okay sleeping with a married woman."

"That's not the point, Danny. She has a son. A son who knocked on the door while things were getting reheated."

"Well, it's not like the kid knew what was going on though, right?"

"Of course not, the boy's only five years old," I say. "It's just that, we were in the middle of something, and she had to put her son back to sleep. The whole thing didn't feel right. I can't help but think that she kissed her son goodnight—you know, with her mouth."

Danny raises his eyebrows in confusion. "Don't people usually kiss with their mouths?"

"Yeah," I say, "that's the thing. People kiss *things* with their mouths."

"Oh." And slowly, I witness Danny raise his eyebrows even

higher. "Oh!"

"Yeah."

"Well, maybe she didn't kiss him goodnight. Maybe she just patted him gently on the head. My mother use to do that, mainly because I used to complain about her breath smelling like raw fish all the time. She would always be eating lox with bagels and cream cheese, sometimes even without the bagels."

"That's really interesting, Danny. Please, tell me more."

My partner in crime goes back to shaking his head in disapproval. "One of these days, you'll miss my presence and my little anecdotes."

"Maybe," I say as I gather my gear in the back. "But I highly doubt it."

18

October, 2014.

"Hey, there you are."

I look up to see Josh peering down at me in his rented tuxedo, with his hands on his hips, while my hands are over my belly. We all rather preferred to wear our police dress uniforms today, but per Tiffany's request, the groomsmen went with matching tuxes.

"What're you doing sitting all alone over here? You should be dancing, having a good time," he says. "For goodness' sake, your best friend just got married."

I sit up and straighten my posture. "This whole best man business...all of the standing, greeting, talking, meeting new people...it's just taken a lot out of me."

"You did fine," Josh says. "And your toast was, um, good. Really good. I liked the part when you mentioned how Michael was the first friend you ever made. It was touching."

"Yeah, thanks." I know Josh is just saying these things to cheer me up; it's what he's always done, from the moment I met him on the first day of high school, when he offered me the seat next to him on the bus ride home.

"Let's go rejoin the celebration," he says with an out-stretched hand. "Maybe have some more cake."

"Maybe in a few minutes," I say. "I've just had so much to eat." I mean it as an excuse, but in reality, I do start to feel the lethargic effects of digestion pinning me down. I think back to only moments earlier when I was enjoying endless quantities of lamb chops and baked crab cakes, and washing them down with all sorts of virgin concoctions.

"What's going on over here?" April Green skips out from behind Josh into view, with her pink dress tracing her swift movements a half a second behind her.

"Apparently, Noel's had too much to eat."

"Well, I order you to order him to get back on his feet. Come on, use the chain of command, Sergeant Kapoor." When I saw April earlier today at the ceremony, I remember nudging Josh to tell him how surprised I was at how little she's changed in appearance. It looks as though she hasn't changed much in personality either.

"The thing is," Josh says as he scratches the back of his head, "I don't like giving out orders to officers from other pre-cincts, if I can help it. You know, my precinct is a lot small—"

"That doesn't matter," April declares. "If you practice now with friends, you'll be more comfortable barking orders at strangers."

"Well, you heard the lady," Josh says in what I can only as-

sume to be his new administrating voice. "Up and at 'em, Detective."

By sitting alone in the corner and drawing the attention of
two of the nicest people I know, I start to feel bad about keeping them from the festivities. Of course, I didn't mean to, but
in a way, keeping them hostage by their own free wills satisfies
my solitariness. So, I get up, with Josh's helping hand, and follow them back into the crowd.

"You still haven't said hi to Jamie," April says right before
we immerse ourselves back into the party. "You know, I
brought her along because I thought it'd be nice for all of us to
get reacquainted. We used to have so much fun together."

"That was a long, long time ago," I say. But, April's honesty
and good intentions make me regret my earlier behavior of
avoidance, so I agree to say hello. "Just give me some space."

"You heard the man," Josh says with the same awkward
voice as before. "Let's give him some space." They each pat
me on the shoulder and walk off to the dance floor.

I weave through pillars of people, most of whom I've just
met today, and many of whom I still don't know, when I find
myself at one of the open bars. From the lavish decor and
foods, to the three hundred and fifty plus guests, and the open
bars, I think it's safe to say Mr. and Mrs. Peterson have dished
out a lot of dough for this happy occasion. If I didn't know
Michael any better, I'd say he was marrying Tiffany for the
money.

"Could I get a cocktail, please," I say to the dark-skinned
bartender.

"What kind?"

"Anything," I say. "Try to surprise me. Just, no alcohol."

He nods and gets straight to work, pulling out a champagne flute. I continue to watch him until I feel a light tap on my back.

"Hey, Noel. Having fun?" It's Dan, with Pam standing right beside him, both of whom are wearing their dress uniforms. Why is it that everyone has to talk to me in pairs?

"Yeah, I think so," I say. "How about you two?"

"Oh honey, you don't have to lie to us," Pam says. "I can see right through you." She pushes up her thick framed glasses. "I can tell something is bothering you." A few years after Pam made the leap to Lieutenant, she's been teaching criminal justice as an adjunct professor at a nearby university. She made a permanent change in her appearance by adopting glasses to fit her new role and appear more studious. Recently, Dan has joined her in the ranks, being promoted to Lieutenant of Auxiliary Operations, and has also started to teach soon after at a different university. He's made a temporary switch to contacts, just for today.

"Here you are, sir." The dark-skinned bartender hands me a cloudy mixture. "It's a Bellini cocktail, which consists of peach nectar and spark—"

"Uh-huh, thanks," I say.

"You know," Dan says, "I know something that might help."

"Yeah, what's that?" I take a sip of the Bellini to find that it tastes more like apples than peaches.

"I don't know if you've noticed, but Emma came without a date. When I asked her about her boyfriend, she mentioned something about taking some time apart."

"You should go talk to her," Pam chimes in. "She's over

there with the little Girl Scout and the rest of your crew. She has on a blue close-fitting dress that I think you might find enticing. Who knows, this might be the only chance you get, Loverboy."

I roll my eyes, but in a good-natured sort of way, making sure I remain respectful. "Haven't we outgrown our nicknames by now?"

"You never outgrow your nickname," she says with a smirk.

"So, you wouldn't mind if people continued to call you Pamm-Pamm?"

"No, because it's a term of endearment."

"Right," I say, trying not to sound sarcastic. "I never found out what they used to call you," I say to Dan.

"Oh," he says, "that's because it wasn't very catchy." He places his hand on his chin. "It was 'Matsu.' There was a little misprint on my first ID, where someone put a space in the middle of my last name, so it read Aka matsu. So, I was Dan, also known as, Matsu. Needless to say, it never really stuck."

"Well, Pamm-Pamm, Matsu," I say turning to each of them, "I really appreciate both of your concerns, but I'm actually looking for someone else."

"We tried, I guess," Pam says, looking a bit dejected.

I politely excuse myself, leaving behind the poorly made apple cider. I spot Julie on the dance floor, uncharacteristically losing herself to the music, with Tommy-boy and A-Rod dancing awkwardly on either side of her. Emma is right beside them, swaying languorously. Pam was right about her dress; it is skintight, but not to the point where it becomes sensually inappropriate. What I like most about it though, is how it matches the color of her eyes. I feel tempted to go talk to her;

I mean, for some reason it'd make Pam and Dan happy. But then my eyes find Jamie in an equally beguiling burgundy dress, mingling with what looks like some of Tiffany's friends. She looks like her old high school self, but more mature—exactly like one would imagine her to look almost ten years later. I'm equally tempted to say hi to her as well. There are two beautiful, available women in front of me, but my insecure thoughts hold me back. On one hand, Emma already knows I'm interested in her, so now it's her move. I've bothered her enough already. And, on the other, Jamie has never tried returning my call way back when. Even if I didn't leave a call back number, she still could have contacted me some other way, but she didn't.

My line of sight is disrupted by the bride and groom making their way across the banquet hall with arms linked. Michael is still in the same tux, but it appears Tiffany has found the time to change out of her wedding dress and into a reception gown, which is just as white, but could easily be a hundred pounds lighter. I decide to go to them before they come to me and become the third couple in a row to disrupt me tonight.

"Hey, how's the happy couple?"

"Happy," Tiffany says beaming. She can't keep still, as if the illusory rollerblades I imagined her in back during my first visit at the Five Eagles have reattached themselves without her knowledge.

"We were beginning to wonder where you ran off to," Michael says. He too is wearing contacts just for today. "We wanted to thank you for everything you've done today."

"And in the days leading up to today," Tiffany adds.

"No problem," I say, turning to Tiffany. "It was my pleasure. So, now that you two are married, will you be taking his name, or keeping yours, or doing that hyphenating thing so it'd be Lee-Peterson or Peterson-Lee?"

"I've decided to stick with the traditional way and change my last name to Lee. It's actually a really pleasant name, don't you think?"

"Yeah, Mrs. Tiffany Lee really rolls off the tongue," I say. "By the way, I was meaning to compliment you on your choice for the centerpieces. The mix you have going here is pleasant. I never even knew orange roses existed, but they go well with the white hydrangeas. And I especially like the lilies."

"Thanks," Tiffany says as she performs her patented half twirl, facing a table to admire one of her centerpieces. "We actually decided on that together. When I asked Michael what he wanted, he said roses, while I wanted hydrangeas." Standing behind Tiffany, Michael shrugs to let me know he basically named the only flower he knew the name of. "The lilies were added by the florist to help hold the pieces together," Tiffany continues.

"So, I guess it's safe to say hydrangeas are your favorite flower?"

"You could say that," she says, turning back around. "They may not have any fragrance, but they're just about the prettiest flowers to look at."

Michael clears his throat. "So, how has the mingling been going?" he asks. "Met anyone interesting?"

Tiffany leans in and covers one side of her mouth with the back of her hand and whispers, "You know, you remember Jane, one of my bridesmaids. Well, from what I've heard, she has a little crush on you, and the best part is, she's single." As she leans back, she winks.

"Thanks Tiffany. But *I'm* just not interested right now. I know she's pretty, and just my type too, with long black hair, but—"

"No, that's Maggie." She turns around trying to find her friend to point out to me, but is unsuccessful in her quick search. "Jane's the one with the short, wavy hair."

"Wait, you mean the Black chick?" I immediately regret using her race as an identification tool.

"Yeah. Why? You have a certain preference when it comes to race? It's okay if you do. I know Michael is the same way." She sneaks a peek at Michael to see if she has embarrassed him.

"No, I'm just surprised, you know. That she'd be interested in me."

"Well, between you and me, she's not full Black; she's also part white. If that changes anything."

"Oh, I see," I say. "Thanks for the tip."

"So, are you going to talk to her?" Tiffany asks earnestly.

"Sure," I say. "As soon as I find her."

"Okay, good luck," they both say, as they wave me away. Little do they know, I have no intention of talking to another human being for the rest of the night.

The first chance I get, I slip out of the banquet hall to light a cigarette. I flick the flint wheel with a snap, which ignites a spark, but instead of immediately closing the lid to my lighter, I let the flame carry on as I watch it dance in the palm of my hand. And like a little pom-pom, the fire jumps up and down, encouraging me to let it free to spread and burn. Spread and burn.

"It's okay," I tell myself. "Everything is okay."

19

March, 2015.

The dimmed lights barely cover the surface of the room, but it's enough for me to spot the cracks on the walls. The lack of decent furniture is somewhat comforting, leaving space open to actually breathe. There are no noisy neighbors, or narrow hallways filled with cabinets like back at my apartment. Sometimes, I even think about moving in here. The abandoned building has only the bare essentials—there's a certain convenience to it. And the smell of fried chicken soaked deep within the structure of the ceilings and floors is an added bonus. Why aren't there any air fresheners that give off the scent of fried chicken?

Car lights beam through the windows, creating the atmosphere of a villain's lair. A couple minutes later, Danny comes in from the side door, followed by two men of strikingly different appearances.

"Hey, I brought them over," says Danny. "These are the guys I've been telling you about, Prissy and Miles." Before I have the chance to introduce myself, the smaller one of the two wearing a shirt portraying a turtle in chemical goo, comes right under my nose. His ridiculous hairstyle only brings more attention to his miniscule height.

"You must be the Reed Thief! I'm a huge fan, huge."

I take a step back. "Which one are you?"

"The name's Miles," he says with his hand outstretched for a handshake. The crevasses on his palm are moist with sweat. Where in the hell did Danny get this guy?

"So you must be Prissy," I say to the other man who's around my own height.

"That's my name," he says with his arms crossed. "But don't ask me how I got it."

"Uh, yeah, I won't."

Prissy puts his hands into his jacket pockets and narrows his beady eyes. "Hold on now, you're not even the least bit interested in how I got my name? Most fuckers don't let up on it once they hear it."

"Yeah, well, I'm not most fuckers now, am I?" I light a cigarette and take a seat on my favorite rocking chair. I can tell my apathy intrigues both the newcomers, because they follow my lead like curious dogs, obediently taking seats on the benches beside me.

"So," I say as my chair lets out a shrilling creak, "my partner's told me that you two have previous experience with the work we do."

"You bet, Mr. Reed Thief," says Miles. "We were in a couple of heists together, nothing as big as yours though--"

"Please, just call me sir. The Reed Thief is the name the public refers to me as. I'm not particularly proud of it."

"But why not? It's such a catchy name! And it grabs your essence perfectly."

"Because, I don't steal reeds," I say with a strict tone. "I steal jewels and diamonds." I stop myself from getting agitated with an extended draw of my cigarette. "If anything, they should be calling me the Jewel Thief, or the Reed Maker for all of the reeds that I've made and left behind."

"Of course, of course," says Miles, "the Reed Maker is such a better name."

"It's not though," I say. My discrepancy with the matter gives wacky hair a look of confusion. "The Reed Thief... phonetically, sounds much better, like perfect imperfect rhymes. Like half rhymes—as if the two words were meant to be, but never had the chance, until now." Sitting on his hands, Miles appears painfully confused. Prissy on the other hand stares at me like I'm some sort of special genius. It reminds me of the looks that people use to give Johnny back in the day.

"Hey, are you okay?" Danny asks. Tonight, he is wearing his oval frames that magnify his eyes in size tenfold.

"Yeah, why wouldn't I be?"

"You're kind of acting a little strange."

"Really?"

"Yeah. I mean, for Christ sakes, you high or something?" The newcomers sit quietly, nervously exchanging glances with one another.

"You know I only smoke cigarettes," I say rocking forward.

Danny shifts up to the edge of his chair. "Then what's gotten into you?"

"Nothing," I reply. Danny opens his eyes wide and gives me a long stare. "Shit, don't do that. You look like a fucking goblin working at a bank." Miles chuckles softly, but is silenced by Danny's varicose stare.

"Nothing changes around here, does it?" Danny says shaking his head.

"So Prissy and Miles," I continue, ignoring Danny, "what do you guys specialize in?"

Miles jumps in before the other even has the chance to think. "I mainly do lookout work, you know, making sure the crew doesn't get caught. And I'm pretty good at it, if I do say so myself, considering we never did get caught." He's practically beaming with pride, which I view as nothing more than misplaced embarrassment.

"So, were you ever part of the getaway?" I ask.

"Well no," Miles replies. "I never got my driver's license, you see. I've taken the driving test over six times, but failed each and every one. They had it out for me since the very beginning, those test drivers did with their ten dollar fees."

"But as a getaway driver, you don't really need a driver's license to begin with," I tell him. "Most getaway drivers don't even follow the rules of the road. The whole point of a getaway driver is to drive away from the scene of the crime and not get caught. If you do get caught, you'll have more to worry about than just the absence of your license."

"Of course, of course, Mr. Reed Thief, sir."

"I only ask because usually the lookout also acts as the driver."

"Well, if you'd like, sir, I'd gladly take the responsibilities of the driver."

"That's okay, Miles," I say, "we already have my partner here behind the wheel. No need to change that up."

"Of course, of course."

I blow smoke in Prissy direction. "So, what about you?"

"I think you can tell what I do from these," says Prissy while flexing his muscles. "It doesn't take a detective to figure that out."

"So, what do you usually do?" I ask. "Punch out security? Wrestle with the cops?"

"Naw, man. My body is the last resort. I just point my gun at whatever I need taken care of, when I need it taken care of." I give Danny an earnest look of disappointment.

"I'm sorry, Prissy, but we don't use firearms during our heists."

Prissy's face mimics Miles's earlier reaction of painful confusion. "You got to be kidding me."

"I really don't joke about work. Just ask my partner."

"Then how do you get around security?"

"Nothing good planning can't solve. You don't just bust in expecting guns to shoot away all of your problems. That's how the mob used to do things. That's not how we do things."

"If you expect me to rob a place without my gun, then you must be fucking crazy."

"Hey, watch it, Prissy," says Danny. "No need for that."

Prissy looks between both Danny and me. "You fucking kidding me? If the police have guns, then I'm going to need them too. If it ever comes down to it, I'm not just going to have my hands in the air like I'm at a fucking frat party. I'm going to be shooting my way out."

I lean in close to Prissy's face. His acne scars are now clearly visible under the thin light. "We don't use guns, because the way we do things, we don't need them."

"And I'm telling you I'm not doing a job without one."

Danny shakes his head. I should be the one shaking my damn head. Where in the hell did he get these guys.

"Then I suggest you leave," I say. "You're obviously too prissy to do things our way."

"What the fuck does that mean?" Prissy's on his feet, staring me down.

"I would have thought you'd know what your own name means." I flick the ash off the remainder of my cigarette onto what appears to be his newly bought shoes. Before Prissy has time to react, Danny grabs and pulls back his arms. Miles joins in, helping Danny keep the gun fanatic under control.

I light a new cigarette in front of Prissy's face. "You don't get it, do you? This is my operation, not yours. The door's right over there. If you don't like it, then just leave."

Prissy brushes off his oppressors and straightens out his jacket before storming out the side door with a "fuck this." The second he's out, I turn to Danny, ready to explode.

"What the hell, Danny! I thought you looked into these guys. I thought you knew whether or not they'd fit our procedures!"

"Look, I'm really sorry."

"You should be! Fucking hell. One guy is a useless lookout, while the other is a trigger happy idiot."

"I'm still here," Miles says, as if talking to himself.

"Christ, I know, I screwed up."

"We don't have that much time to prepare before the Diamond of Despair is taken out of the City. We don't have time for this."

"You think I don't know that?"

"Apparently not, bringing in a guy who gets off shooting down cops. You know why we don't use guns; they attract attention and leave behind *unwanted* evidence. And it's not just that. I mean, come on, Danny."

"Yeah, yeah, I messed up, all right?"

A silence long enough for two drawn out puffs fills the room. The scent of chicken is steadily overcome by the stench of smoke, re-entering my lungs for the second time. I open a window that used to be a portal for fast-food takeout. Danny follows me to the fresh air.

"So what should we do about Miles?" he asks.

"I don't know. What do you think we should do with him?"

"I mean, he looks useless, but he does seem like a guy who can follow orders without question. I think we should give him a chance. He *is* your number one fan after all."

"Why does my number one fan have to be such an eccentric guy? Doesn't it make more sense if my number one fan was a girl?"

Danny is shaking his head again. "Always with the jokes. Maybe you should get caught so your face can be on the news. Then maybe you'll get your wish."

I don't respond. Instead, I imagine my number one fan, young and pretty with nothing to lose. She's cute more than anything, but has the body of a goddess. Her short hair tickles the tips of her shoulders as she runs into my arms. I bury my nose into her dark hair and take a deep breath, the smell of fried chicken pleasuring my senses. Wait, what? Fried chicken?

"You won't regret this, Mr. Reed Thief, sir."

"Yeah, yeah, all right."

My stomach grumbles; it's been a while since I last ate.

"I'm going to get something to eat," I say.

"I can bring food here for you, sir," says Miles. "Just tell me what you want and I'll go get it." Miles takes out a blue pen and a notebook from his back pocket and holds the position of a newly hired waiter, with his face a bit too focused on the movements of my mouth.

"Uh, all right. You okay with chicken, Danny?" I ask.

"Sure, sounds good."

"All right, Miles, get us a fifteen piece bucket with two sides of spaghetti. You know that fried chicken place on Thirty-second?"

"Of course, of course," replies Miles. "Best fried chicken in all of New York."

"Yeah, here's fifty."

"How about drinks, sir?" I feel like I'm at an offbeat restaurant.

"We got a fridge here filled with drinks," I say. "Just hurry up and get the chicken."

Miles scribbles something in his notebook. "Should I ask them to put in more drumsticks than usual? I've done it before. More than half of my bucket had drumsticks. Was one of the best days of my life."

"No it's fine, Miles," I tell him. "I like a good variety."

"Of course, of course."

Miles sprints out the door with unnatural ease. It's just Danny and me again, like always. My shoulders relax as I take in a deep breath. Danny pops open a soda from the fridge and gulps it down, leaving no time for the fizz to escape. I finish my second cigarette and I'm about to start my third.

"You know you handed a guy you just met fifty dollars," Danny says in-between gulps. That's not like you."

"You mean that's not like *you*." I decide against lighting another cigarette.

Danny flings his hands into the air. "You're right, you got me once again."

"Not quite. You wouldn't even trust a guy with a dollar."

"You always have to push it so far." Danny takes a generous gulp and follows it with a restraint burp. "Sorry."

"No, I'm sorry. I guess you did your best with these guys today."

"Whoa, are you apologizing to me? Where's my tape recorder when I need it?"

"What's the big deal?" I say. "And who in the hell still uses a tape recorder? What are you, too stingy to get yourself a dictaphone?"

"And there goes the apology."

"Chill out, Danny. You know I torment you only because I'm close enough with you to do so. Take my mockery as compliments of our friendship."

"Well, that makes me feel so much better."

There's always that one friend who's always at the butt end of all the jokes. Danny's there because I know he can take it. He may not laugh it off like most do, but he takes it nonetheless. Does his feelings get hurt? Maybe sometimes, he's human after all. But I'm smart enough not to push it so far, despite what he may think.

My stomach grows louder and I become restive, rocking

vigorously back and forth in my chair. After about an hour of waiting, Miles comes in through the door, grasping two bags filled with chicken and spaghetti. I really should start eating healthy, but there's no one who cares enough about me to do so. Sure, I care about myself, but what's the point of living if you can't enjoy the little things in life, like fried chicken?

"I'm sorry I took so long, sir," Miles says, practically out of breath. The back of his shirt is drenched, and sweat drips swiftly down his disarranged hair, as if he was deluged with heavy rain.

"It's about time, Miles," I say. "What the hell took you so long?"

"I had to run back most of the way. I'm really sorry, sir."

"I've had enough apologies for one day. I gave you fifty dollars so you could take a taxi."

"I did, sir, but halfway back the road was closed, so I decided to just run the remaining blocks. Here's the chicken and spaghetti. And here you go." Miles sets down the food and hands me a $10 bill and a couple of coins.

"Whatever, at least you brought the chicken. Hey Danny, could you bring me a pepsi?"

The food is still warm, which is more than I can ask for. The spaghetti appears as if it came straight from the trays of my old elementary school cafeteria, which isn't necessarily a bad thing. Nostalgia in the form of an entrée—I wouldn't have it any other way. It's such a simple delicacy with the thick tomato sauce smothering the overcooked noodles, and the bottom of the to-go container hiding the one or two meatballs from view. I could eat just this for a whole week, no matter how cheap the meat is, but why should I when I can afford the upper-class quality of $40 prime ribs cooked to the fraction right before medium rare. Both meals are vastly different in price; however, only one can spark the memories from my innocent childhood. That's a taste even prime rib can't provide.

I split the bones of a wing apart and suck off the meat hanging from the top and throw the remains on a spread out newspaper. Danny does the same, with his bone cleaner than mine, as if a dog was taking time with his once-in-a-year treat. Miles sits idly by, refusing the take even the smallest piece, afraid that he'll fail some sort of test. He is proving himself even more worthy by the minute, although, there is an uncomfortable guilt in having someone, particularly a newly hired subordinate, watch you eat food that he himself delivered. But if you turn down an offer of fried chicken the first time, then I guess there really is no need to make a second gesture.

While I am not foreign to the silence of mealtime (Danny and I eat without words all the time), I feel obliged to start a conversation going in the midst of the new recruit. It's the least I can do to make Miles feel welcomed.

"Did I ever tell you about the time I stole a calculator?" I ask Danny, making sure I've caught Miles's attention.

"No," Danny replies, "must have been a really expensive one, like the ones we used for calculus class for showing graphs. I remember I installed games on mine and played during lecture all the time."

"Yeah, I remember those. But that's not what I'm talking about here."

Danny peels off the skin of a large breast piece. "There's a better kind of calculator than a graphing calculator?"

"Maybe, I don't know." I fling another bone to the pile.

"Anyways, that's besides the point. It was the last day of first or second grade. I don't really remember the details. But in our classroom, we had a box of calculators. They were solar powered, with the small squares on the top right corners. I don't think I've ever used or seen calculators before then, and the fact that they were powered simply by sunlight made me think it was magic. I was susceptible back then, so obviously I had to have one. So without even thinking, I took out a calculator from the box when no one was looking and slipped it into my pocket. It was that easy. I knew it was morally wrong to steal, but it didn't really seem like stealing at the time—more like taking a well-deserved prize. And when my dad came to pick me up, I remember showing him the calculator, telling him the teacher gave it to me as a gift. It was thrilling, to show off the product of a steal to another, especially to a man who would have easily beaten me for doing so. And my father said he would have to thank my teacher for it and was about to exit the car, when I quickly told him that Mrs. Noland had already left. Thankfully, my father's indolence prevented him from checking if she was still there. During that ride home, I was so complacent with my facade that the buttons on the calculator felt so rewarding to press, like the keys on a grand piano. You ever heard a fancy recital of a kid playing the piano? Well, that's how it felt like. It felt like I was a young prodigy performing in front of a huge audience: an audience who wanted nothing more than to watch me press the keys and play."

"Sounds like that was one special calculator," says Danny. "You still have it with you?"

"No, I don't know where it is. I lost it well before I realized its value to me. My father most likely threw it out during one of his spring cleanings."

"I know how that feels," Miles says, still dripping with sweat. "My mom threw away my limited edition figures when I was still in school. She said I was too old for such toys. Those figures were about sixty dollars a piece! She just could never understand their value. Not a day goes by when I think about how much I could make selling those babies right now."

"I think your story is a little bit different," says Danny, pushing up his glasses with his non-greasy palms.

"Yeah," I say, "just a little."

"Of course, of course."

20

April, 2015.

"All right, before we go in there, let's lay down some ground rules."

"Of course, of course."

"Okay, rule number one—talk with inside voices," I say. "There's no need to be loud or annoying. I know sometimes you get excited and you can't help yourself, but I'm not going to tolerate your incessant babble in there."

Miles nods with understanding. "I'll be sure to keep quiet, sir."

"Secondly, do not touch the jukebox. The owner doesn't like it when people play any music recorded after the 80's. It's silly, I know, especially since a fourth of the songs in the damn machine come from the 90's. But I don't want to ruin my relationship with this place and get kicked out."

"Of course, of course."

"And lastly," I say with a dry mouth, wanting nothing more than to sip a nice cool drink, "do not be rude to the barmaid, Rita. Don't flirt with her, don't talk to her, in fact, don't even stare at her. One peek, that's all I'll allow. Got it?"

"I got it, sir." Miles straightens out his shirt. "She must be quite a looker, to have the great Reed Thief be so infatuated with her."

"Not me, Miles. Him." I signal to Danny, who is kicking his feet against the sidewalk. I wince each time his recently polished shoes skid against the cement.

"I don't think this is a good idea," says Danny.

"What do you mean?" I ask. If I had a quarter for every time Danny expressed his doubts, then I'd be an even richer man. "Don't worry. I'm pretty sure Miles won't do anything completely stupid. It's just a bar, anyways."

"No, no, not *Miles*," Danny says. "I don't think it's such a good idea for *me* to see Rita."

"Well, why not?" I ask.

"Because, you know, of what you told me about last time you were at The Docks."

I let out a sudden laugh that even surprises myself, which immediately causes me to feel a bit guilty. I don't know how Danny puts up with me sometimes.

"Why do you always have to be so insensitive when bad things happen to me?"

"When bad things happen to you? Please. You had plenty of time to swoop in and charm Rita. Hell, years passed by as you just quietly sat on your stool, never striking the simplest of conversations with her. Maybe if you had some balls, you would have asked her out at least once when you had the chance. You really had nothing to lose."

"If I asked her and she said no, then we wouldn't have been able to keep on coming back. I didn't ask, so we wouldn't have to find a new favorite bar. It was the safe and practical decision."

"No," I reply with my arms crossed, "you didn't ask, because you are mortified of rejection."

"Okay, so you agree, it was the safe decision."

"Are you serious?"

Danny lets out a long sigh with a hint of wistful regret.

"Don't worry," Miles interjects, "you can just ask her out right now." Danny simply shakes his head in response.

I head towards the entrance of The Docks. "I don't think that's possible, Miles. You see, she recently got engaged, to some hotshot lawyer, no less."

"Oh..." says Miles as he follows me inside. Danny hesitates as the door closes, only to catch it right before it shuts completely.

The moment I step into the bar, I smell a scent of fresh mint, which strengthens in intensity which each step I take towards the counter. (There must be a hidden scented candle behind the bar.) Familiar paintings cover the golden-red walls with wallpaper peeling slightly around the edges. And in the corner stands the jukebox, playing a jazz piece I recognize as "In the Evening," mainly due to the featuring of the oboe. The Docks has slowly shifted its preference from classical to jazz music during the past year. Personally, I think the atmosphere fits with more of a classical rock vibe, but then again, it doesn't really matter all that much to me.

Danny and I take our usual seats while Miles grabs a stool uncomfortably close to mine. I decide to not make a big deal out of it as I flag Rita down.

"Hey guys," she says with a radiant smile. "Where have you been, Danny? I haven't seen you in a while."

"I was a bit busy, with family and all," he replies.

"Oh, I hope everything's okay."

"Well, not really—" I give Danny a quick kick to the shin to shut him up. There's no need for him to say anything stupid now.

"So, how are the wedding plans?" I ask. My question causes Rita's skin to glow even brighter.

"They're going great. Francis and I decided on having a compact wedding with only a handful of guests. We finalized the date for the second of December."

"An end of the year wedding, huh? That's pretty nice," I say smiling back. "So I'm guessing after you get married, you won't be working here at The Docks anymore?"

"I haven't really discussed it with Francis yet. But you know, I didn't quit working here even after I got the intern position at the firm, so we'll see. I like working here, it's fun."

"Well, I hope you decide to stay," I say. "We'd miss you if you left. And besides, I'd hate to be served by Kai over there. I don't think he likes us all that much. He always gives us these weird looks. I don't know, maybe that's just his resting face."

Rita leans in. "No, you're right," she says with a smirk. "He doesn't like anybody that much. Anyways, what are you guys drinking today?"

"Danny and I will have our usual drinks, and umm," I stare at Miles. "Get our associate, Miles over here a beer."

"All right, will do." Rita scurries off to her station surrounded by ingredients and alcohol.

I turn to Miles, who is looking down at his feet. "You're okay with just beer, right?"

"Of course, sir. Anything else would be too fancy for me."

The jukebox grows silent as the record switches out without command. An unfamiliar song fills the room with its mild rhythmic syncopation. Barely thirty seconds goes by when a drunk man in his forties sacrifices a quarter to change the tune to a blazing piece featuring a saxophone.

"So, um, sir, do you mind if I ask you a question?" Miles keeps his head angled so his line-of-sight doesn't meet with the back of Rita's slim figure.

"Yeah, sure, go ahead."

"Why is it so important to steal this particular diamond?"

Danny jumps in from his silent composition. "Are you crazy, Miles? You don't talk about these things out in public. What if someone were to hear you?"

"I'm really sorry. It's just that, I don't understand why we should go through so much trouble for a single stone, when we could just go to a local jewelry store and—"

"Miles!" Danny says with cold set eyes.

"Calm down, Danny. No one is close enough to hear us anyways. If anything, you raising your voice will draw in attention."

"Why does the reason even matter," says Danny, directing his concentration right past me and straight at Miles. "We hired you to assist us, not ask questions."

Feeling magnanimous, I decide to defend Miles before Danny says anything too damaging and accidentally scares off our hired aid. "Look, Danny, I know you're upset with the whole Rita situation, but that doesn't mean you can take it out on Miles. And besides, a little background information wouldn't hurt." Danny lets out a surly cough and resumes his position of secretly staring at Rita, who is now busy mixing drinks with a single hand.

"Well, you know about the Hope Diamond, Miles?" I ask.

"Of course, of course, the one they got from the Titanic."

"No, that one is a fictional diamond. The idea that the Hope Diamond sank with the Titanic is a complete myth."

"Oh."

"The Hope Diamond I'm talking about is now sitting in the Smithsonian Museum. But before that, it was passed on many times all the way back starting from the mid-1600s. It is said that the diamond is cursed, but that's a complete myth as well. Although, throughout the years, many people who have owned the diamond ended up being murdered. Some even committed suicide."

"Sounds like it's cursed to me," says Miles.

"No, more like it brought out the worst in people," I say.

Rita approaches with our drinks. The tray remains in perfect balance over her delicate fingers, yet somehow, under the hefty tray, her engagement ring catches the overhead lights, carving the rays into millions of pieces. Her fiancé must do very well for himself.

"Here you guys go."

We thank Rita, but before she has the chance to tend to other customers, Danny stands and asks to speak to her privately.

"I don't think that's such a good idea," I tell Danny. I give his jeans a sharp tug, hoping that he'll sit back in his seat and shut up.

"Please, just give me a couple of minutes of your time."

"Is there something wrong," Rita asks.

"Yes, well, it's no big deal really. It'll only take a minute."

And perhaps it's the pitiful sound of Danny's begging, or her own clueless naivety, but Rita agrees to hear Danny out and follows him in the hallway to the restrooms.

"Shouldn't we stop him?" says Miles.

"We should," I reply, "but at least he's finally taking action." I wave my concern for Danny away. "Anyways, back to the history lesson." Miles does his best to break his attention away from the restrooms. "This is not public knowledge, but the Hope Diamond rose as a set along with the Diamond of Despair. The Diamond of Despair—let's call it DoD for short—left a much more devastating path in its journey, causing the ruin of kings and the fall of civilizations. Eventually, the DoD was labeled so dangerous, that its sister Diamond, the Hope Diamond, was used as a scapegoat to draw attention away from the DoD. People suspected that the DoD was actually truly cursed. So it was kept hidden, and by the 1820s, it completely vanished from known existence."

"And now it has finally surfaced again?"

"Exactly, its whereabouts has finally been uncovered. George Henry Hope—whose ancestors once owned the Hope Diamond and named it after their own surname—is transporting the DoD across the US to New York, where it will be sent over the sea to his home in London."

"But you haven't answered why we're going after the DoD. Why not just steal the Hope Diamond instead?" asks Miles.

"Well, there are several obvious reasons as to why," I say before I take a sip of my Shirley Temple. "For one, the security around the Hope Diamond is pretty much airtight. It'd have to take superpowers to steal that diamond without getting caught. The Smithsonian security isn't something to laugh at, despite the incompetence of the higher-ups."

"Of course, of course."

"Second of all, it is rumored that the Hope Diamond displayed at the museum is actually a fake, and that somewhere along the change of ownership between Harry Winston and the museum, the diamond was stolen. This fact was kept secret in order to prevent embarrassment and mass panic. Even the directors of the museum are oblivious to this information. So it's really not worth it to go through the risk of stealing something that may have already been stolen."

"That reminds me of when I was little," Miles says. "I tried to sneak to the fridge past midnight to eat the last slice of pie, when I knew in the back of my head that my older brother was probably already stuffing his face with it while I was creaking down the stairs. Of course, the noise woke up my mother, and I ended up taking the fall for the missing pie." Miles chugs down the rest of his beer in an attempt to wash away his past memory.

"Hell, it happens."

"So sir, I know why you don't want to steal the Hope Diamond. But why the DoD?"

"Well, calm down, let me finish," I say. "The Hope Diamond is estimated to be worth approximately $250 million while the DoD is worth far more than that. But I'm not planning to steal the DoD for the money—I mean how would I be able to sell such an invaluable gem? No, I want it more as a gift. Imagine how famous I'd be if I were to steal the DoD and shared its existence to the general public. I'd be greatly accepted by the entire world and the whole ordeal would go down in history."

"But I thought you said that the DoD is actually cursed. Aren't you afraid something bad will happen?"

"You got to be a little kid to believe all that superstition. The only cursed thing about it, is that it's being held captive in George Henry Hope's personal collection. A diamond with such crimson beauty does not belong hidden behind closed doors."

Danny slowly returns to his seat, even more despondent than ever. Without hesitation, he downs his entire drink all in one go, including the bits of ice. From the slight fog about his glasses, I can tell things didn't go so well with Rita. It's probably best to leave him alone and not let him have anything else to drink for the night.

"Where did Rita go?" Miles asks.

Danny places his head in his hands. "She left."

"What happened?"

"For Christ's sake, what do think happened, Miles?" Danny's on the verge of making an ugly scene. A few heads start to turn in our direction.

"Miles, can you please read a situation before you speak?" I ask.

"Of course, of course. I'm sorry."

Danny shakes his head in a mocking manner. "Well, fuck you, fuck you."

Not wanting to become social pariahs in the bar, I suggest

for Miles to take Danny home, and that I'll take care of the business here. But Danny refuses to leave, spouting how he's not done drinking yet.

"I told you it was a bad idea for me to come inside," Danny says to me.

"Are you seriously blaming me for you being a complete idiot? Hell, what did you think was going to happen telling Rita how you feel about her? Did you really think there was a chance she was going to just drop her wedding and choose you over her fiancé?"

"No, of course not."

"Then why even create the opportunity to be automatically rejected?"

"Jesus, I didn't get rejected. I didn't tell her about how I feel. I mean, I was going to tell her, but—"

"But you were too afraid to?" I say.

"Can you just be a good friend and let me finish what I'm trying to say for once in your life? Jesus Christ."

"Yeah yeah, I'm sorry, go on."

Danny turns his focus back to his empty glass. "I was going to tell her, but then decided it'd be better if I just gave her a reason to hate me so then I'd know that there'd be no chance for us to end up together."

"And what exactly did you tell her?"

"I told her," Danny hesitates as his frustration steadily subsides, "I told her that I would prefer it if she would just quit working here as soon as possible, and that I've been avoiding coming here with you because I was getting sick and tired of drinking her drinks that literally taste like dog puke."

"Wow, what a mature thing to say."

"I know, I screwed up. I shouldn't have said anything at all."

"You know, part of the main reason why we come here, or at least for me, is because Rita makes pretty good drinks, especially on this side of New York. She's the secret bartender that only we know about. I think it would have been a lot better if you had just told her the truth instead of hurting her feelings. Being a bartender isn't particularly glamorous, but she loves her work and takes pride in what she does. She makes a lot of people happy with her drinks, and she told me that doing so makes her happy as well."

"I panicked, all right?"

"I guess facing rejection is as frightful to you as it is to me."

And with that, Danny stands and rushes for the door. Before I can ask where he's going, he shouts back that he's going to try to catch up to her and clear up the whole mess. And once again, Miles asks if we should go after him. And once again, I wave him off, saying it'll be all right. The two of us order another round of drinks, fully aware that the second round will be undoubtedly inferior to the first. Well, at least the beer will taste the same. I guess there are advantages to sticking with the malty brew.

Twenty minutes pass by when I hear my name being uttered from behind by an unfamiliar voice. I turn to see a young man in his early twenties wearing a sharp dress shirt paired with black dress pants. His hair is short and frazzled, like that of a scientist emerging from a failed experiment with barely a layer of hair left on his head. And from his anxious expression, it is almost as if he's in the midst of one of his experiments right now.

"Excuse me, are you two Mr. Ashman and Mr. Brackman?"

"Who are you?" I ask while Miles busies himself with his beer.

"My name is Tony Crawford. I was sent here by Mr. Davis to deliver this folder to you."

I take the documents from the delivery boy. "Jeremy sent you instead of coming here himself?

"Mr. Davis said that you would have liked it better anyways if he didn't have to personally make an appearance."

"I guess he's right about that." Having our meeting place at The Docks is the only thing that made it bearable to listen to Jeremy's wry jokes. I guess he's finally caught on to my lack of appreciation for his tacky sense of humor.

"Thank you, Tony."

"Oh, and there's a message that Mr. Davis wanted to me to relay to you."

"Okay, and what's that?"

"Mr. Davis strongly advises not to pursue this particular operation. He said that the success rate is far too low, and that you'll most likely fail even if the whole thing were to take place in the comfort of your dreams. It'd be best to set your eyes on something else."

"Well, thank Mr. Davis for his advice for me," I say while trying to sound as genuine as I can. "I'll make sure to take a good look over the files before I make my final decision."

And with a nod, the young mad scientist leaves the bar with a bit more confidence than he initially had upon walking in. Perhaps the completion of his mission is what drove his frazzled hair higher into the light, as if a puppet master pulled mercifully onto the thread connected to his head. A mad scientist puppet; what a peculiar way to describe a young, overly polite man.

"Do we take a look at what's in the folder now?" asks Miles, who now decides to make his presence known.

"No Miles, not now. We'll wait and take a look at these together with Danny."

"Of course, of course."

"And let's not tell Danny what Mr. Davis had to say. I don't want him to get any second thoughts."

"I'm good at keeping my mouth shut, sir."

"Oh, I hope so."

21

May, 2015.

There's no longer any pain in my left leg, and I've been told that the earliest I'll be free to go is by this afternoon or tomorrow morning, depending on how effortlessly I can walk. I was lucky nothing got broken, and that my stay has been a relatively short one.

I'm sitting up in bed now, enjoying a chocolate pudding Michael was kind enough to bring to me from the cafeteria. Unlike with most of my colleagues back at the precinct, Michael has come to visit me more than once since the accident, and he's the only one from our Burglary Unit to visit me at all. (Even Girl Scout from the Larceny Unit and my old partner, Tommy-boy, from the Missing Persons Unit brought me flowers on my first day here.) With each visit, Michael brings me treats and other goodies, and sometimes specifically requested items (that we like to joke as being contrabands). But, from the jump of his voice and his restive behavior, I can tell he's brought me something more besides a cup of dessert.

"So, have you heard?" he asks.

"Heard about what?"

"We have some new leads on the Reed Thief. Something may go down soon." I put the cup and spoon aside, and he continues. "Yesterday, we arrested a guy for petty theft, who claims to have met the Reed Thief. The boys who brought him in caught him with his pants down, like literally, since he was hiding in a public bathroom. It turns out, he was unlawfully carrying a concealed weapon, and has a past record with armed robbery. In case you wanted to know, the guy's name is Prissy."

I laugh. "Prissy, what kind of name is that? Isn't Prissy a girl's name? Like, short for Priscilla?"

"I said the same thing," Michael says, joining in on the laugh. "But, he told me it's a proper name for a man. Anyways, he shared with me some details about the next Reed Thief heist, hoping that would help lessen his punishment. He seemed very eager to."

I shake my head and say, "How would he know anything about the Reed Thief's game? It's not like the Reed Thief would go around telling everyone his plans."

"Well, Prissy said he has a friend working with the Reed Thief, and that his friend is actually very close with the Thief. He's also agreed to help with some sketches, but so far, they haven't been of much help. He said he's not very good with faces to begin with, and that it was dark when he met the Reed Thief."

I scoff. "Sounds like a long shot to me," I say, picking back up the half eaten cup of pudding and its accompanying plastic spoon. "It's most likely a bunch of bullshit."

"Yeah, he didn't seem too bright," Michael adds. "Not the type of guy someone like the Reed Thief would want to associate with. Still, I think we should check it out."

"No," I yell. Michael is startled by my involuntary outburst and goes to take a seat in the chair by the door. "I mean, don't do anything without me, unless you don't mind ending up like me, bedridden for almost a week." I take one last scoop of pudding before throwing it into the a nearby trash bin.

"You're right," he says, resting his head in his hands. "We'll leave the Reed Thief be, for now." I sense a hint of rancor in the way he said "Reed Thief," but before I can ask him about it and make sure he won't do anything without me, he pulls something out of his pocket and stands back up. "Here, I brought it like you asked." He hands me my Zippo lighter, the same one I've been carrying around since graduating from high school; the same one that once belonged to my dad. He had it in his possession the day he died. "I would have brought it sooner, but as I've just told you I've been a bit busy and haven't had a chance to swing by your place." He returns to the chair. "I'm sorry again about what happened. I should have been there to stop whoever it was that hit you and ran." His eyebrows tighten and his voice rises with indignation, but it's all just part of the way Michael offers his commiseration. I have yet to see Michael lose his temper since marrying Tiffany, and I'm glad he finally got over his truculent behavior.

"It's not your fault," I say, rubbing my thumb against the imprinted design of a four-leaf clover. The edges of the lighter are charred a brownish-black, giving the lighter an antique look and feel. "I shouldn't have chased that perp across the street like that, thinking the traffic would magically stop for me. But, there was nothing else I could have done, right? Although, I still can't believe both the runner, and the driver who hit me, got away." My thumb reaches towards the bottom of the lighter, where it traces the engraved initials, "G.A."

"Talk about having your share of bad luck," Michael says. He lays his head back and closes his eyes.

"Yeah." I flip open the lighter by squeezing the top and bottom between my forefinger and my thumb—the first trick I mastered even before I started smoking. The second time I perform the trick the lighter slips and lands on the floor close to the bed, between Michael and me. The resulting clatter captures Michael's attention, who sits back up.

"Hey, didn't the doctor also advise you to quit smoking?" he asks. "I remember her joking that, unless you quit, you'll be dead before you're thirty."

I nod. "Yeah, and I've decided I will. It'll be hard as hell, I know, but I promised myself I wouldn't be like those people who say they're trying to quit but still end up with a cigarette between their fingers. When I meet someone like that, I can't help but feel depressed. Either quit altogether, or smoke till you drop. Don't go halfway."

"Good for you," Michael says. "I know you'll be able to do it."

I lean to the side enough to pick up the lucky lighter and place it on the bedside table and smile at him. However, suddenly I feel depressed. I've replaced the wick and flint countless times on that lighter, each time marking an end of an era.

I'll no longer be doing any of that; I won't even need to buy more lighter fluid to refuel it.

"Well, I should get going," Michael says, stretching out his legs. "I'm supposed to pick up some groceries for the wife on the way home."

"Married life sure does sound fun," I say.

Michael briefly acknowledges my comment with a smirk. "By the way," he says as he opens the door, "you might want to change the water in some of those vases. I hear dirty water can cause them to wilt."

22

May, 2015.

For the first time in five years, I find myself going against my natural urge to smoke. The last time I did so, I had my wisdom teeth removed, all four of them. It was advised by the dentist to not eat or drink anything hot and not to use a straw. Smoking cigarettes is pretty much like using a straw to drink in warm smoke, so naturally, it was completely out of the question. After two weeks of recovery, I was never happier to light a smoke. Right now, I'm far over the edge with disappointment to even consider smoking. No amount of packs will be able to calm my jittery rage. And besides, right now, I need to be alert.

"Where in the hell is Miles? He should have been here ten minutes ago."

"Hey, don't worry about it," says Danny. "I'm sure he's almost here. The streets can be a bit confusing in this area."

"Oh please, how confusing can it be? Do you have his number?"

"Yeah, want me to call him?"

"No, I want you to delete his number from your phone, so you can never ever call him again. Of course I want you to call him!"

"Jesus, you need to calm down a bit. Go ahead and smoke a cig, I won't mind."

"Would you just call him already," I tell Danny as I contain my frustration.

"No need to be in such a bad mood." Danny takes out his phone and calls Miles, only to spot him running towards us a couple of seconds later. Miles opens the side door and jumps into the van, slamming the door shut as he lands in the back seats. Again, he is dripping in sweat; I don't think I've ever seen the guy without his shirt being somewhat soaked through. I let him catch his breath before I start the berating.

"Why are you late?"

"I'm really sorry, sir. It's just that, I heard some bad news."

"What in the hell are you talking about?" I ask.

"Well, you see, sir," Miles continues while wiping sweat off his forehead with the sleeves of his shirt. "I found out that Prissy has been arrested just a couple of days ago."

"And what exactly does that have to do with us?" I ask, fearing what might be said.

Miles senses my angst, which freezes him in place for a good second or two as a sweat droplet dodges his sleeve and rolls down his cheek. "Perhaps I should just go back home," he says as he reaches for the side door. The van locks with a loud snap before Miles even comes close to the handle.

"Miles, tell us what's going on," says Danny, sounding a bit more flustered than I am.

"It's probably no big deal," says Miles. "I sort of got into a discussion with Prissy about"—he hesitates—"well, about our plans. What we're going to steal, when we're going to steal it—"

"So you basically told him everything," Danny interrupts in a surprisingly calm manner. The worrier inside him most likely has yet to catch up to his natural reaction of shaking his head profusely. Or perhaps he's taking my role as the rational human being for once, providing me with time to quell my impatience of Miles being late.

The accused stares down at his shoes, which are tucked safely under my seat, as if his conscious being is hidden amongst his toes in attempt to hide from Danny's sight. It doesn't accomplish much, considering that most of Mile's plump body stands out awkwardly in the back seat. It's pitiful to see, so I turn forward to stare through the front window at a distant cab pulling over to pick up a lone stranger in the dark.

"I'm really sorry," Miles says, which causes Danny to narrow his eyes the way a drill sergeant would out in the blazing sun. Miles adds a late "sir" at the end, which seems to satisfy Danny's ego as he withdraws back into the driver seat.

"We have to call the whole thing off," Danny says to me. I was afraid that he'd jump to that conclusion, despite all the planning we put into this heist.

"We can't," I say, knowing that my rebuttal will only draw Danny back to his anxious self.

"What do you mean we can't? We obviously have to. You heard Miles. If Prissy knows of our whole operation, then what's stopping him from telling the police all about it? Prissy is small time compared to us, and I bet any information that idiot can relay about the Reed Thief will only lessen his small time charges. There's no doubt that he'll talk, especially considering the way you treated him."

"All of that doesn't matter," I say. "We have to go through with this. Right now is the only chance we've got to steal the Diamond of Despair. After tonight, that diamond is going to be across the ocean, lost somewhere among crumpets and tea."

"So it doesn't matter to you if there's a trap laying in wait out there for us?"

"There's no point in belaboring about it now, Danny. And besides, even if there *is* a trap, I'll be the one walking into it. I'll let you know well ahead of time to drive off without me. I know you can do that."

"Jesus, what kind of person do you take me for?"

"Well, considering you're the one questioning our success, I'd say from zero to Jew, you're being a real Jew." The second I utter my words, I shut my mouth closed, and massage my forehead due to my own temper.

"Wow, I've never heard that one before," he says.

"Danny, if I get caught, then your name will never come up. You know you can trust me on that. Hell, there'll most likely be no reason for your name to come up anyways, because I'll tell them that the Reed Thief is just me, and only me. And it pretty much is, considering I do all the actual breaking and entering. Come on, don't back out on me now."

Danny's shaking slowly turns into meager nodding. "I won't," he says. "I know how important this is to you."

"Thanks, Danny. I'll see you at the rendezvous point. Come

on, Miles, let's go." Before Danny has the chance to change his mind, I exit the van and gently shut the door close, despite the urgency in my head ordering me to save time and leave it open.

Miles pops his head up from his despondent position, surprised to hear me call his name in such an eager fashion. "Oh, wait. So, you still want me to go with you?"

"Yeah, hurry up. We don't have all night, you know."

Miles exits the van and follows my example, carefully closing the side door to the point where I'm not sure if it's actually completely closed or not. It's annoying to see someone so attached to you, attempting to copy every single move you make. I almost feel like the older brother Miles never had; at least I think he doesn't have one, although, I do recall some mentioning of a brother in some story involving pie.

We walk side by side towards the warehouses, which appear dark red under the pitch-black sky. Mile's shoes squeak each time he lifts his right foot, so I tell him to toss them aside, indifferent to whether he'll be able to pick them up later or not.

"But these were expensive," he says. "They were around a hundred dollars per shoe."

"Hundred dollars per shoe? I think you mean a hundred dollars per pair."

"No, sir, one hundred dollars per shoe. There's a special store owned by a guy named Leo. He gets his merchandise imported from different parts of Asia. He specifically sells each shoe individually, mainly because that's how his customers prefer to buy them."

"Well, you'll be able to buy plenty more after all this," I say.

Miles places his shoes behind a large bush, and shuts his eyes tightly as if making a mental note of the exact location.

Knowing him, I doubt his shoes will ever return to their original owner.

"All right," I say, "once we reach the roof, we have to quickly find the vent and remove the metal cover. I'll go down first and signal for you to come down after. When we're inside, I need you to stand ready by the vent and be on the look out. You know what you have to do, right?"

"Of course, of course."

"Good. Let's go then."

"I'm just curious, sir. What kind of reed did you bring?"

It's a question that I wasn't quite expecting to hear, but I'm not surprised that Miles has asked it; he is my number one fan, after all. I shuffle through my pocket with the thought of giving him a glimpse, but it doesn't seem right to unveil such a significant possession, especially before committing to the actual deed. So I keep my bride of a reed safely tucked in my pants—it's bad luck to reveal the bride before the "wedding," anyways.

"I have a very special reed planned for tonight," I say as I pull down the ladder to access the fire escape on the side of the building. "It was one of the first reeds given to me by my oboe instructor when I was a little boy. He made it for me as I watched him carefully, and it was only recently that I finished what he started, carving the tip to perfection and changing the colors."

"So, are you saying that this reed symbolizes the end of the beginning?" Miles asks

"In a sense," I say. "More like the beginning of the end."

"Sir," Miles says with a lump in his throat, "are you telling me that this is going to be your last heist?"

My last heist? It would certainly be nice to move away from the artificial lifestyle in the city and leave behind the risks and stress that come along with it. I could buy a convenient house in the suburbs, rescue a dog from the shelter, and live the rest of my days mowing my lawns and doing my best to avoid my neighbors (who I already imagine to be the prying types). I guess that new lifestyle will give me plenty of time to explore my older interests that I've abandoned many years ago, such as playing the oboe and drawing meticulous portraits of un-touched landscapes, although I may need to relearn the basics to both.

"You know what, Miles? It all depends on how this heist turns out."

"I will give it my all, regardless, sir."

"Of course you will."

We climb up the rusty ladder to the fire escape without much trouble, aside from Mile's occasional wince in pain as his feet meet the cold metal of each step. Apparently his socks, despite their thick appearance, are considered close to being nonexistent. We are met by a surprising wave of sweet air at the top of the building, which is rare in this part of the city where the nearest bakery is more than three or four miles away. The smell reminds me of the time I mistook the scent of car gas as the redolence of delightful pastries from a nearby shop. I was three and a half gulps of air in before I noticed the Ford Crown parked next to where I was standing, emitting toxins right under my nose. If only I had stayed ignorant just a little while longer to enjoy that last half of breath, instead of cough-ing profusely like I was dying from some sort of lung disease.

I check around the base of the buildings for any signs of an automobile with the engine left on, but there is not a car in sight, which I find to be a bit ominous. My eye twitches from my suspicions, and I'm about to tell Miles to stay quiet, when he abruptly yells that he has found the vent. I can feel the varicose vein on the side of my head pump an unusual amount of blood as I attempt to withhold myself from yelling back at him for his stupidity. We start to loosen the cover of the vent, bolt by bolt, when all of a sudden, a voice rings out from the other side of the roof top. Miles drops the cover, which vociferously swings by a single screw, back and forth, back and forth, screeching all the while.

"Freeze," the voice shouts. "Stay where you are."

And like the obedient kid that he is, Miles sprints in the opposite direction, going as fast as his socks allow. The following rush of boot-to-floor steps propels me to chase after Miles, without glimpsing back at our pursuer. Gunshots fire from behind, but I keep on running, slightly reassured by the ricocheting clanks immediately following each shot. The voice keeps on shouting, but I'm running so fast, all I can hear is the sweet air whooshing by my ears. Miles is close to reaching the edge of the rooftop, and just when it appears like he's going to dig in his heels, he instead adds to his speed, flipping the switch in his mind similar to how a driver does when faced with an indecisive yellow light. Much to my surprise, he jumps over the low curb and lands on the adjacent building with plenty of room to spare, though he tumbles with little to no grace, skidding both the palm of his hands and his knees. His success makes me think, If Miles can do it, so can I, so I run to the point well past the feeling of a runner's high and press myself off the curb at a slightly lower angle than I initially calculated. The moment I'm suspended in the air, I fear for the worse as I sense the force of gravity already pulling me down, closer and closer to the ground. And like an optical illusion, the alleyway below grows nearer in proximity, and all I can do to survive the moment is shut my eyes tight and reiterate the word "shit" over and over in my head. And before I know it, the top half of my body slams on the edge of the lower building, knocking the wind out of me briefly before I have the chance to climb up safely and regain my orderly stature. I look ahead to see Miles, still running but at a considerably slower pace, too self-absorbed in his own wellbeing to check on his boss. And I look back and spot a looming figure preparing to jump my way. I continue on my sprint to catch up with Miles, when I hear a thunderous thump followed by a cry for help. The man must have miscalculated the jump worse than I have, judging from the desperation in his voice. I only make it a couple of yards forward before my diminishing sense of humanity turns me around and forces me back towards the edge of the building. And over the edge, approximately two feet down, the man is barely hanging on by the tips of his fingers, his gun obviously already a victim to the 48-foot drop.

"Grab on!" I tell him, as I lay flat and reach down as far as I can. "Miles, come back and help me here!"

The man lets go of his right hand and swings it up a couple of times before being able to grab onto my extended hand, squeezing it so tightly that I can feel my glove leaving deep imprints onto my palms. And that's when I realize, from the faint light shining down from the crescent moon, that the man clinging for dear life, is none other than Michael Lee. Assuming that Michael probably weighs close to 200 pounds, the burden at the end of my arm grows even heavier.

"Pull me up. Pull me up!" Michael says while staring down at his inevitable doom.

"I'm trying, okay? I'm trying," I reply as I grab onto the edge of the building with my free hand, not wanting to be dragged down as an extra victim. "Miles! Get your ass over here, now!"

But Miles is most likely too far to hear me, so I shift my attention to pulling up Michael alone. And as I attempt to tug up my right arm, his beady eyes meet mine, and for a second, time freezes as his pupils expand with recognition.

"Noel?" he says softly.

I ignore him just as I ignore the growing pain in my arm.

"No, wait," he continues. His eyes grow wide and within that same split second, my glove slips off my hand and falls rapidly to the ground in his unyielding grip. A resonating thud follows as Michael's body lands sprawled in an unsightly position next to a garbage disposal. I pull myself up in an astonishingly calm manner, as if I planned for all this to happen. And without a sense of urgency, I walk in an eminent fashion towards where Miles has disappeared to.

"Fuck," I mutter under my breath as I fight the urge to light a cigarette.

Danny is not going to like the sound of this.

23

November, 2013.

This is the second time I've set foot in the Five Eagles. Michael has once again, invited Josh and me to his favorite late night eatery to celebrate another achievement in our lives; our successful completion of three years on the force. And, since we're all part of the promotional fast-track scheme, at least in varying degrees, we're now eligible to apply for promotions to either become sergeants or detectives, something we are only able to accomplish thanks to our four-year degrees.

Before I can take another step, I'm stopped by a large Black man, who holds me back with one hand on my shoulder, as he asks to see my ID. I take his request as a compliment of my youthful, Asian looks. As soon as he sees my NYPD ID card, the bouncer removes his hand, and with a polite "thank you, sir," sends me on my way.

It appears I'm the first one of the group to arrive, so I decide to wait at the bar and get a drink. "A club soda, please," I say. The bartender is a sharp looking young man who gives me a strange, judging look; it's probably the first time he's had someone order a club soda so late in the evening. He probably thinks I'm an A.A. member who misses the atmosphere of a bar; in other words, a loser.

"Got a problem?" I say to him. He just looks at me like I'm some sad sap, and continues to wipe down the countertop with an old rag. I can tell he's eventually going to get my drink by the way he finally throws the rag over his shoulder, but he sure is taking his sweet time. So, I decide to speed things up by placing my hands on my waist, thus pulling back the flaps of my jacket and revealing my 9mm service pistol. Normally, I wouldn't do something like this, but my time patrolling the streets have made me lose my patience with others, instead of building up the one I already had. I turn, facing my profile towards him, to make sure he sees it, holster and all. The sight of the firearm causes him to jump, and he fetches my glass of carbonated water in mere seconds.

"Thank you," I say. "I hope the next time I ask for something it doesn't take you nearly as long."

I sit on a stool and lean back on the counter, observing the rest of the bar. It's surprising how much the place has changed in such a relatively short amount of time. There's no longer any young college kids hanging around in the tables towards the back, despite it still being a Friday night. (The place isn't empty though; there are still a fair number of patrons scattered about.) The lighting is so dim, almost nonexistent. And, although I don't remember much about the general decor, I'm certain it has been completely redone. Simply put, there's nothing left hanging on the walls except for molding skyblue wallpaper. Even the people working here are a lot different from their predecessors.

I light a cigarette and decide to explore, taking my club soda with me, trying to find something that's remained untouched—like a lost relic resting on the bottom of the Atlantic Ocean—but there's nothing. I even wander into the bathroom, hoping to find a bowl full of potpourri, but instead find an automatic air freshening dispenser hanging above the toilet. The dispenser sprays its chemicals as I leave, as if it's giving me a consolation prize, but it only manages to enervate me. And I don't know why, but I suddenly want to leave the bar and never come back again.

"Hey, kid. Did you lose something?"

I step out from under the low ceiling of the bathroom hall and take a second to look for the owner of the voice, and spot an old man eyeing me from the bar counter. A shadow is cast over his eyes from his deep sunken sockets, which do well in hiding his developing crow's feet. And like a wild mushroom, brown spots cover the top of his bald head. He has on a dark leather jacket, with a matching trilby hat placed in front of him, and is holding a beer in one hand and a pen in the other. The way he holds the pen, with his thumb covering his first and second fingers, resembles that of a child, which is the only thing about him that catches me off guard.

"Did you hear me?" he says.

"Uh, yes, I did," I say. I walk up to him and take the seat adjacent to his. "Sorry, I was having a hard time finding who was speaking. You have a sort of, um, ubiquitous voice."

"Ha. That's the first time someone's told me that," he says. "I'm Paul by the way."

"Noel." We shake hands.

"So, what were you doing earlier? It looked like you were looking for something, or someone."

"Oh, no," I say, somewhat embarrassed. "I was just checking the place out. It's been a while since the last time I've been here."

"Same with me," Paul says. He takes a sip of his beer and I finish off my soda. "In fact, I don't remember the last time I've been here, but I know I have."

I signal to the young bartender and he makes himself available right away, leaping directly in front of us, and leaning in ever so slightly.

"Can I get a Roy Rogers? And hold the cherry."

"Right away, sir," he says.

Old Paul scribbles something down on his notepad, looks up, and says, "I see you're not much of a drinker; that's good."

"Yes, but I'm still a smoker," I say, holding up my cigarette butt. I drop it into an ashtray and pull out my pack for another. I make sure to offer Paul one first, which he accepts, and I help him light it, before lighting my own.

"So," I say, "what's that you're writing?" Again, I find myself stepping out of the bounds of my usual actions, asking a complete stranger something about his personal business.

"Oh this?" Paul slides the pad over to me. "It's a letter. Or at least the beginnings of one." I read the scribbled notes, at least what I can make out from Paul's chicken scratch. Besides the greeting, there's nothing much else.

"Who's this for?" I ask, showing as much interest in my

face and hands as I can manage.

"My estranged son."

The barkeep places a tall glass filled with a refreshing mix of cola and grenadine syrup on a neat napkin in front of me.

"Oh, well I didn't mean to pry. I'm sorry I asked."

"No, that's all right. If I didn't want you to know, I wouldn't have told you." He smiles a genuine smile, with the prints of his crow's feet making a brief appearance. He enjoys his cigarette for a while. "I could actually use some help. You see, I'm stuck. I'm not really sure what it is I should write. I think it's because there's just so much I have to say."

I nod slowly, buying time to think of a suggestion. "It might help to address each issue one at a time. You'll be surprised at how quickly, easily, and painlessly it can be done." I take a short drag. "Image a mile long cigarette. It certainly would take a long time and a heck of a lot of effort to smoke something like that. But, if you think about it, it can be done, one puff at a time. I mean, I've probably smoked enough cigarettes to make a mile—shit, maybe even four or five times as much, and I'm only twenty-seven."

"Ha. That's the best analogy I've ever heard." He reaches over to reclaim his notepad. "I guess you could say *the man who removes a mountain begins by carrying away small stones.*"

"Sure," I say. His insertion of an aphorism irks me since it seems as if he's turning my suggestion around and trying to preach it right back at me. "Of course, *it's easier said than done,*" I add. Two can play at that game.

Paul finishes his beer, so I call over my new friend behind the bar to order him another.

"Thanks," Paul says, "but I have to get going. Don't want

to get on the wife's bad side." He stands and pockets the pen and pad before zipping up his jacket. "Thanks for the help, and for the smoke." He grabs his hat and makes his way to the exit.

"Good luck," I say back as the bouncer gets up to hold the door open for Paul. He tips his hat at either the bouncer or me (or both) before stepping outside and disappearing out of my life forever.

I enjoy the next few minutes in solitude, sipping away at my drink and my smoke, when I hear the bouncer's voice again welcoming someone.

"Hey, Mikey, it's good to see you again." I turn around in my seat and see Michael sharing an intricate handshake with the man. "And Miss Tiffany, it's good to see you too."

"Thanks Tyrus," Michael says.

"How's your mother doing?" Tiffany asks.

"A lot better now, thanks for asking," Tyrus says as he takes Tiffany's overcoat and hangs it on a free peg of the coat rack.

I turn back, not wanting to be the one to have to call out to the happy couple.

"Hey, Noel. It's good to see you've made it, man." Michael pats my shoulder. Just a second ago he was at the entrance; I always forget, for such a big guy, he sure does move fast.

"Hey, it's good to see you too," I say as we hug. "And it's nice to see you again too, Tiffany." She initiates a hug, which I follow through with.

"I hope you weren't waiting long," she says, her hair is short now, but still as yellow as I remember.

"Nope, I just got here. Why don't we move to a table."

We pick out a table in the middle of the floor, which could

be the exact same one we sat in more than three years ago.

"Any idea when Josh'll get here?" I ask them.

"Actually," Michael begins, "you're the only one we told to meet us here."

"Oh. Then we're not meeting up with Josh?" I ask.

"We are," Michael says. "Later at the karaoke bar on Korea Way. We just wanted to talk to you first—about the wedding." He pauses as he takes off his jacket. "I was wondering if you'd like to be my best man."

I choke on my sugary drink, and start to cough uncontrollably. Tiffany rummages through her purse and hands me a napkin. I use it to cover my mouth and wipe up any splatter I may have created before thanking her. I was sure Michael was going to ask one of his brothers to be the best man at his wedding, but I guess, now that I think about it, he's not very close with either of them. In fact, I don't remember a time he's ever talked about them.

"Of course, I'd be honored to," I finally say. Both Michael's and Tiffany's faces beam back at me. "How about a drink?" I snap my fingers and hear the scuttle of my sycophantic friend.

"Hey John, I see you've met our friend Noel," Michael says to the young man.

"Yes I have. So, what can I get you both?"

"Just a beer for me," Michael says.

"And the same for me," Tiffany says. Little John scuttles back to the bar.

"So, I was meaning to ask," I say, "what's up with this place? It reminds me of a dungeon, and the staff is rude, well at first anyways."

"Yeah well, ever since Tiffany left, this place has never been the same. It's like she was the one good thing holding this place together, and I stole her away from here. The only reason we come back is because it's where we met and got to know each other." Tiffany makes an endearing sound, and the two kiss. They're interrupted when John comes back with their beers.

I pull out my pack again and offer it to them. I think maybe with a cigarette in their mouths they won't have the chance to flaunt their love in front of me in the form of PDA.

"I'm actually trying to quit," Tiffany says.

"Maybe later," Michael says. "When we change locations."

"And when will that be?" I ask.

"We're supposed to meet Josh in"—he checks his phone—"about twenty minutes. We should probably leave after we finish our drinks." He takes a few gulps followed by a satisfied, contained belch. "So, how's preparations for the detective's exam going?"

"It's going," I say with a shrug. "I'm just not getting enough time to study, with all of the ongoing investigations. Did you know, I've helped with over fifty cases of burglaries and robberies since completing my trial period with Dick, and about a fourth of those have gone unsolved. Those cases don't include any of the overlapping kidnappings cases. To top that off, at a majority, or I guess plurality, of the unsolved cases there's always a new oboe reed left behind, each more detailed than the last. We've been calling the perp of those cases the Reed Thief back at the precinct. Whoever this guy is, he's been driving some of the senior detectives mad."

"Sounds like an interesting character," Tiffany says.

"I'll say."

248

Michael takes a final chug of his beer and stands up. "Let's get going, don't want to have poor Josh waiting all alone for us." Tiffany follows his lead, leaving behind an unfinished bottle of beer.

"Actually, I asked some of the guys (and girls) back at the station if they'd like to join us. I told them to meet us here, so I'll just wait to see who shows up and catch up with you guys. I'll give them a few more minutes." Since Michael's bid to transfer to my district has been accepted, I thought it'd be a good idea to introduce him to a few members of the 53th precinct before his official transfer date.

"Okay, sounds good, best man," Michael says. He throws back on his jacket and goes over to the bar with his wallet out.

"Hold on, let me pay for the drinks," I say. "I already sort of have a tab going anyways."

"Thanks, Noel," Tiffany says as she kisses me on my cheek. "I know you'll be the *best* best man any friend can ever ask for."

24

May, 2015.

It's getting to those days when the sun stays out well into the late evenings, but it's hard to tell if today will be one of those days. I park my unmarked Crown Vic outside of a mess of cop cars. It's close to eleven in the morning when I exit the vehicle and drag my feet to the congregated group of officers and fellow detectives. Strangely, their faces do not become more distinguished with each step, but instead appear murkier. The heavy clouds play a part in the masking by blocking out the sun, as if it never existed, and keeping the air damp. Of course, the shadow of the dark alleyway doesn't help the situation either. I throw the end of my scarf that has come undone over my shoulder as a cool breeze hits my face. The air is surprisingly bitter to taste, if that's even possible.

"Detective Ashman." A stiff voice calls out. When I enter

the cover of the shadows, I see it's Sergeant Alexander. He's standing with Detective Wheeler, Detective Lieutenant Brown, and Deputy Inspector Salinger. I've never met the Deputy Inspector before, but I know it's him from photographs on the walls of our station. Brown's favorite Detective Sergeant is nowhere to be seen; I guess Megan has taken Stephen's place.

"We'll have press on the scene any minute now," the Sergeant continues as I join them. "Captain Ramirez and Lieutenant Hendricks are on their way to help with that. And this is Depu—"

"I know who the fuck this is," I say. "I've seen his smug face every day for the past five goddamn years hanging right inside the front door of our precinct. What I want to know is what the hell happened here."

"Watch yourself, Ashman," Sergeant Alexander says back with stolid indifference. Even on a day like today, the Sergeant's face remains frozen like a figurine's, just like on my first day at the station. It's no surprise he's remained as the precinct's Operational Sergeant for so long, opting out on promotions in favor of remaining in his comfortable position.

"It's okay," Salinger says. "Let the young man vent." The old man carefully places his hand on my shoulder and says, "I'm real sorry about your friend." His white bushy eyebrows lower with sympathy, but I ignore him and turn to the Detective Lieutenant.

"So, what happened here?" I say again, opting out on the repeated use of profanity. Brown walks further into the alley where detectives from the Crime Scene Unit are already positioned and working, and tells me to follow him. He keeps his head lowered, and I know, despite his usual arrogant behavior, he has been affected by this event; like me, Michael is (or I guess now was) one of his men, so he must feel some responsibility for his death. Megan moves to follow us, but I stop her, holding up my hand.

"Please, I don't need your sympathy," I tell her.

"I'm sorry Noel, I really am. But I'm not here for you. I'm here as the Detective Lieutenant's new SDS trainee. I'm going to make Detective Sergeant someday." She shows me a weak smile.

"Good for you." I'm trying my hardest not to unleash my pent-up anger at her. "I want to be left alone is all."

White Serena complies with my wish, taking a step back and allowing me to follow Brown into the alleyway alone.

From the looks of things, Michael's body has already been moved, and what's left of him here is a puddle of coagulated blood. Brown walks up to a tall woman taking pictures of the tainted ground, side of the warehouses, and bags of miscellaneous items. "Detective Janssens," he says to her, "I need you to tell Detective Ashman here what you know so far pertaining to Detective Lee's death."

"Yes sir." She leaves her bulky camera hanging on her neck. "We know Detective Lee died from a tragic fall from this warehouse," she says pointing to the one on her right. "We also know the event occurred sometime between twenty-two hundred hours and oh two hundred hours. The scene was called in by a passerby about an hour and a half ago." She takes a second to look around. "I should have Detective Yoo explain the rest to you since he's in charge of fingerprinting." She looks around again and calls out, "Yoo. Detective Yoo."

A man of slightly below average height walks over, carrying

a black forensics case. His brown jacket ruffles from the alley-way wind as he attempts to button it up with his free hand.

"Yoo, could you tell Detective Ashman about the finger-prints you found? And the glove?"

"Of course," he says. Janssens excuses herself to take some more photographs. "So, I had a look up on the rooftops of these two buildings, and from what I saw, it's apparent Detective Lee attempted to leap from this warehouse to the other, most likely in pursuit of a perp. However, he didn't quite make the jump, and instead, found himself hanging from the lower edge of the roof of this building." He mimics Janssens by pointing to the one on his right. "I know this because I found fingerprints matching Detective Lee's on the edge. But this is where things get even more interesting."

"Is this a fucking game to you?" I snap.

"I'm sorry. I didn't mean any disrespect." Yoo makes some sort of gesture akin to a bow. "So, when we investigated Detective Lee's body, we found a single glove clutched tight in his right hand. This leather glove." He picks up a sealed bag with a black glove inside from the ground. "The left pair is nowhere to be found. This means he came into possession of the glove while hanging on the side of the building, which leads me to believe there was someone else up there with him the moment he fell. I think the glove most likely belonged to the perp he was chasing. I know it's hard to believe, but from this conclu-sion, the perp is either a compassionate person, or is someone Detective Lee personally knew that would try to help him up." I feel a tinge of anguish surface on my face. "So, it's hard to say if this was a homicide or an accident."

"Thank you, Detective Yoo," Brown says. With a slight

lean forward, Yoo nods and joins the rest of his unit. Brown places his hand on my shoulder and guides me back out of the alleyway. "Come on, Ashman," he says. "How about you take the rest of the day off."

"No."

"Then let's head back to the station and get some lunch after. It'll be my treat." It's the first time Brown has ever offered to buy food for me, much less offered to eat with me. But, I still decline.

"Well then," he continues, "if it'll make you feel better, you can come with me when I go to tell his family the news."

"No," I say once more, imagining Tiffany's plaintive cries as I attempt to provide her with some solace. "I'll go tell them alone."

"Look, Ashman, I know he was your friend, and you two knew each other since—"

"Hey!" I yell out as I run towards a suspicious character inspecting the street. We're in the middle of nowhere in terms of the city, and criminals have been known to return to the scene of the crime. (Sometimes they just can't help it.) I catch in the corner of my eye, Brown shaking his head as he walks off in the opposite direction.

"Freeze right there," I yell again, still yards away. The little man obeys me, and freezes with his back arched and his face in the bushes. When I get close enough, I lower my voice. "What are you doing here?"

The man keeps his position. "I'm just looking for my shoes," he says. "I left them somewhere around here last night."

"And why did you hide them in a bush?" I ask. "Are they

even worth the trouble?"

"They made too much noise," the myopic fellow says. "And yes, they're expensive. About a hundred dollars per shoe."

"You mean per pair," I say.

"No, sir, one hundred dollars per shoe. That's the way they're sold."

The man starts to wobble, so I tell him it's okay to stand up and face me slowly. He does so, and as soon as he sees my face, he smiles.

"Thank goodness, sir. You've got to get me out of here before the police over there figure out I was here last night."

And at this very moment, my suspicions are confirmed. I can't arrest the man without losing my opportunity to end all of this once and for all. So, I decide to play along.

"Okay, no problem. That's why I'm here. It's too dangerous for you to be here." I push him away from the rest of the officers and the parked cars, making sure not to touch the soaked patches of his shirt. "Do you have your phone with you?"

"Yeah, why?"

"I forgot mine at home."

He places his cell phone into the palm of my waiting hand. "You know, this reminds me of the time when I lost my binoculars—"

"I'll tell you what," I say. "I'll stay here and find your shoes. What I want you to do is call this phone in about, oh let's say an hour, and I'll come to you and drop off your boots and return your phone. Sound like a plan?"

"Of course, of course," he says. I watch his ridiculous

spiked hair sway back and forth as he runs off in nothing but his mangled socks.

25

March, 2008.

"How're we doing with the sauce?" Big Joe asks.

"It's coming along," I say, stirring the concoction, the lumps of tomatoes and bell peppers have by now coalesced into a smooth, oily texture. "It should be done soon. I'm basically waiting for it to thicken a bit."

"Good, we want to have everything ready, with plenty of time to spare before opening," he says, and walks out of the kitchen.

Today, Big Joe has me helping out in the kitchen for the first time; throwing out the kitchen trash doesn't count. I'm usually tasked with managing the register, or cleaning up the dining area, or playing waiter. I think the success of my suggestion to start having Friday specials, where we would add a new menu item for just one day, helped to get me initiated into the kitchen, though it's also probably due to the fact I've been working here for almost five months now. I've been here long enough for Big Joe to finally trust me with his secret recipes. He has it in his head that his competitors would go to any lengths to cheat him out of the restaurant business, even if it means going to lengths such as planting a spy in his kitchen.

Joe's Bistro is popular with the college kids, seeing how it is located right outside of the campus's main gate and provides a quiet study area. We serve several different blends of coffee (and on occasion, wine, when older patrons visit), with moderately priced entrees that remind the students of rich, home cooked meals. The place may be a small hole-in-the-wall establishment, but I have to admit, if I wasn't working here, I'd still probably find myself eating here almost everyday, enjoying the varying dishes of sandwiches, soups, Italian pastas, American casseroles, and French cassoulets.

Big Joe waddles back into the kitchen and pretends to check the coffee machine, but I know he's keeping an eye on me. He calls to Daphne to help him make last minute preparations with the casseroles and soups. Out of the seven people Big Joe has on the bistro's payroll, I prefer working with Daphne the most. She's a bit older than I am—she being a graduate student and me just starting my third year as an undergrad—and therefore acts as my mentor, on school, work, and personal matters. When she enters, he excuses himself to go set up the salad bar. As he exits, I watch as he squeezes himself out of the kitchen door. I guess there was a time when Big Joe was just Joe, otherwise he would have named the place *Big* Joe's Bistro.

"Well, he seems a bit anxious, doesn't he?" Daphne asks

once Big Joe leaves.

I shrug. "He always gets nervous before opening." Which most likely led to his crapulous habits of overeating and his eventual weight gain.

"I know," Daphne says, "but today he seems more so than usual, don't you think?" She takes off her oven mitts and takes a second to stare at me, waiting for my response.

"It *is* the first time I'm helping out in the kitchen," I remind her. "And, it's Friday."

"It sounds like a combination of both," she says as she finally turns away. "By the way, what is the Friday special? I haven't had a chance to ask Big Joe what it is yet, and I haven't seen him prepare anything for it."

"This is it," I say, pointing at the pot of red sauce with the end of the ladle. "It's chicken cacciatore. Big Joe has already prepared the chicken, which is sitting in the fridge." I walk over and open the refrigerator door to show Daphne the pile of sauteed chicken breasts and thighs on the bottom shelf. "I saw the recipe in one of those home styling or country living magazines and suggested it to Big Joe. I thought it'd—"

"Hold on, you buy those magazines?"

"No," I chuckle. " I've been getting these magazines in the mail from an old subscription of the previous tenant ever since I moved in. I skim through them before I throw them out, since you know, it'd be a waste otherwise."

"Oh okay. Yeah, I get a whole lot of junk mail like that all the time." She goes back to lifting the lids to the soup pots, peering into them and adjusting the heat accordingly. "You were saying?"

"I thought it'd be perfect to serve on a Friday, seeing how

it's an Italian dish we don't have on the menu, but at the same time, it's very similar to the hearty meals we normally serve. It seemed simple enough to make; we have the ingredients laying around, and I thought it'd be popular with the students."

Daphne takes a whiff of the sauce, and I can almost see its pungent aroma seeping into her nostrils. She sighs heavily. "No kidding. I bet they'll love this." She then dips her little finger in the pot and tastes it, making a smacking sound with her lips. She gives me a thumbs up and walks to the door and says, "Okay, I'm going to see if Big Joe needs help with anything else. Keep up the good work, Noel." She's about to leave, but instead she hangs by the doorframe and says, "Though, you might want to add a bit more white wine. It'll help bring out some of the more subtle flavors. Okay, bye."

I watch her disappear out the doorway, her narrow hips easily slipping out of the passageway. Daphne is not a woman I'd consider to possess the standard qualities of feminine beauty. However, over time, I've come to see her for the attractive woman she is. Of course, there's no romantic interest, just safe admiration.

I add a few tablespoons of wine, lower the heat, stir for a few minutes, and place the lid over the pot. I'm proud of my creation, and almost can't wait to try it during my lunch break—I just hope there'll be some left then. Back at community college, I was able to secure a work-study position to fill some of my free time, when I wasn't out raiding the city. I later convinced Josh and Michael to apply for the job as well. We managed the front desk and library of the Justice and Criminology department, which eventually became the home of our majors. The repetitive work had a stultifying effect on us, so we eventually quit, one by one. There's a stark contrast between the work-study and Joe's Bistro; here, I've been given sort of a creative license.

Daphne walks back in, now wearing the restaurant's uniform, the design which Big Joe has been circulating amongst his workers since the bistro's opening almost twenty years ago. Our uniforms now are not as old, but have still been through their fair share of owners. The blue color of the shirt pockets has faded, while the rest of the originally white garb has turned into a light beige—still, the outfit remains respectable and strangely charming.

"Missed me?" she says in her offhanded way, with an open posture, always expecting a reply.

"What do you think?" I say without delay. "By the way, I've been meaning to ask you why you choose to work here? I mean, why not teach an undergrad class, or work as a reader?"

"I have. I was one of the many GSIs for the introductory chem class a year ago. It was the most boring job I've ever had. Working at Joe's is a whole lot more fun. Plus, the pay is a whole lot better."

"No kidding."

"If you're done here, you should probably get into your costume soon too."

"Right." I pick up my backpack I left leaning on the back door.

"By the way, have you heard from Benny yet? He should have been here by now." She registers my clueless look. "I mean, gosh, we're going to have our hands full in less than ten minutes."

I leave Daphne alone in the kitchen and head to the bathroom to change. As with Daphne's uniform, mine is also old and worn out, but I put it on with pride. I lace an apron over my jeans and mentally prepare myself for the rest of my shift. I wash my hands and clean my nails.

"Noel. Noel!" I hear Big Joe calling for me.

"One second," I say back. I open the bathroom door to find Big Joe waiting impatiently outside.

"I'm going to need you to wait on the tables again. At least until Benny shows up."

"No problem, Big Joe." I say, faking a smile.

He disappears into the kitchen, and I go about, setting the tables and regressing back into my old routine and duties as the waiter. A minute before eleven, just as I flip the sign to read open and unlock the front door, a young kid scurries in. His untidy, long hair, tacky I love NY t-shirt, and torn jeans, which are embarrassingly two sizes too short, lead me to believe that he's a new arrival to the campus, and most likely, to the city as well.

"Welcome to Joe's Bistro," I say. "Are we expecting anyone else?"

"No, just me," he says.

"Okay, no problem." I lead him to a table against the wall and hand him a menu. "I'll give you a few minutes to look that over, but I highly recommend our Friday Special. It's chicken cacciatore over rice, which is chicken braised in a tomato-based sauce with onions, bell peppers, and mushrooms. I'll be back with some water, unless you'd like something else to drink?"

The boy steadily shakes his head.

Before I get to the kitchen, the door opens and Benny enters, his shirt is soaked with sweat.

"You better get changed," I say to him, without any greetings.

He heeds my advice, whether he wants to or not, and runs into the bathroom. He's nothing if not obedient. I take this time to let Big Joe and Daphne know of Benny's arrival. Big Joe nods and Daphne is relieved.

"It's a good thing he finally showed," she says. "I know you don't want to be waiting anymore, and besides, we're going to need you in the kitchen. It's always been three in the kitchen and one waiting tables."

Benny enters with his uniform on. "I'm sorry I'm late, Big Joe" he says with a stolid look on his face. "I was finishing up a semester exam."

"It's all right," Big Joe says in a calm voice as he slices onions with deft, immune to the reflex tears effect. During my time here at Joe's, I've never witnessed Big Joe reprimand any of his staff members once. I think it's partially due to the fact that he only hires students—those of us who are in need of a fair paying job. He chooses to run his restaurant with a magnanimous approach, a philosophy that has worked for him for many years.

"Why don't you go ahead and take over waiting on that young man out there," Big Joe says to Benny.

"Actually, if it's okay with you, I'd like to finish what I've started," I say.

"All right," Big Joe says. "Knock yourself out."

I return to the dining area with a glass of water and find the kid reading a book. "So, should I put you down for today's special?" I say as I place the glass in front of him.

"No," he says. "I want the salmon cassoulet." He pronounces salmon correctly, but says cassoulet with a hard "t" sound at the end.

"Okay," I say, "but you're missing out." I leave him to continue reading whatever book it is that he's chosen over bringing along a lunch companion.

"So, one order of your chicken cacciatore?" Daphne asks as soon as I enter the kitchen.

"No, he wants the salmon cassoulet," I say, emulating the way the boy pronounced the French word.

Big Joe immediately starts putting together the dish, taking out a bowl from the cabinets.

"Don't worry," Daphne says. "He's just the first customer. There'll be plenty more I'm sure. And besides, it sounds like he's a seafood person anyways."

"Yeah, you're probably right."

I try not to worry about it, but I can't help but take the initial refusal of my chicken cacciatore as a bad sign. And I really need my dish to sell well, or else Big Joe might just decide that it was too early for me to move into the kitchen. I need to be in the kitchen, working the stove, turning on the fire, and watching the vegetables burn slowly under my control.

"Perhaps the kid out there needs just a bit more convincing," I mutter under my breath. But I abandon the thought and decide to take the highroad, resisting the impulse.

26

May, 2015.

With a lighter tucked snugly in his pocket, Noel waits in the third floor hallway of the abandoned house behind the Fulton Market. Needless to say, the outside air is rancid with the smell of raw fish, but he prefers the suspicious scent of freshly caught salmon and week-old scraps to the stuffy stench of collective dust and aging wood. With the windows cracked open, he takes in a deep breath, as if he just sat down to a recently made Thanksgiving dinner, complete with turkey gravy and homemade pumpkin pie.

The abandoned house was discovered from one of Noel's old cases, where a gang of thieves used it as their underground auction house, selling mainly stolen art. It's a wonder how the thieves were able to use the house as often as they did, considering its precarious state of missing beams and battered floorboards. It's almost as if potential mines have been laid out, waiting to detonate with each daring step taken.

A voice calls out below from the front door, which causes Noel to shoot up into position.

"Hello? Miles, are you here? What the hell is this place?"

Noel grows tense as each footstep grows louder and louder up the steep stairway. His fingers clamp tightly around his metal lighter.

"Miles, there's no need to hide. It's just me. Let's talk everything out, all right?"

"Miles isn't here," Noel says as a purple beanie slowly surfaces at the opening of the stairway. "Hello, brother."

Leon finishes his last step and points contemptuously at Noel, bravely stomping closer over the mines. "What the hell are you doing here?"

"I had Miles invite you here," Noel replies. "Well, I actually did, sending you a message from his phone." Noel strolls into the closest room, leading Leon into an empty quarters that was once a bedroom. "I caught him near the site where Michael was found. Apparently, he was looking for some sort of shoes. Interesting guy."

"That fucking idiot."

"So it *was* you then?" says Noel. "You were there when Michael died."

"Look, I don't know what Miles told you, but I never meant for anyone to get hurt—"

"But someone did," Noel suddenly snaps.

Leon edges closer towards his brother. "That guy was shooting at us! You'd think I'd get a medal for turning back and at least trying to help him up."

266

"What were you trying to steal, anyways? What was so important for you to put lives in danger?"

"Oh no you don't," Leon says with his finger back to pointing. "You don't get to say shit to me."

"I get to say whatever the fuck I want!" Noel shouts back, briefly losing his composure and dropping his lighter. It lands between two loose floorboards, emblem side up. "You really think I didn't know who the great Reed Thief was all this time? I could recognize those reeds anywhere. You left me quite a collection, or rather, the department. I kept quiet, all these years, for you, because I didn't want you to get caught. I was looking out for my little brother."

"Don't do that. You know just as well as I do that a hundred fifty seconds doesn't make you the older one. Don't act like you care about me. Don't act like you did anything for me. You left me with our father, remember? While you went off and scared our mother to God knows where."

Noel scoffs at the remark and paces back and forth by the balcony window. Dust and dirt act as a filter, shaping yellow distorted patches of light from the outside rays. "You know they say that the bigger person does things for others without telling anyone," he says. "Well, I don't want to be the bigger person anymore, the bigger brother. You think the fire started all by itself?"

"What the hell are you talking about?" Leon asks impatiently, already knowing a hint of what his brother is about to tell him.

"That day, before I left for school to go on a field trip, I left the stove on and dad's can of lighter fluid a little too close to the flame, knowing it'd eventually catch fire. I knew dad was going to be passed out all day on his fucking couch. I made it look like an accident, and the insurance company was none the wiser. I did it, for us. More particularly, for you."

"You mean you did it for yourself. After mother was gone, you were left with no choice but to join me and face those daily horrors. Where were you before all that, when I was the only one in that house to satisfy father's violent urges? Oh, that's right. You were living the good life with mother. Because of a mere hundred and fifty seconds, she chose you. Well, I didn't exactly get to choose who I wanted to live with. But lucky for you, you ended up with mother, while I got father."

"You want me to take pity on you?" asks Noel. "You didn't have to turn to criminal life. You could have easily made something of yourself like I did. But because of you, someone got kill and the lives of others will never be the same because of it. And because of you, I'm just as guilty of your crimes. I tried so hard to live an honest life. A good life. But you held me back with each heist you pulled."

Leon turns and starts for the staircase. "I'm not going to stand here and take this shit from you. If you want to stop me, then go ahead. If not, I'm leaving."

"Don't take another step," Noel says. He walks back to where his lighter lies and picks it up, raising it high above his head. The sound of flint sparking a flame causes Leon's head to turn.

"What the hell are you doing?"

"Don't tell me you didn't notice the sweet smell of gasoline when you stumbled in here," Noel says with a wistful smile. He then takes an even deeper breath than before, reaching the hidden odor of cheap fuel that was hiding underneath the overwhelming layer of fish fetor. "You and I, we don't deserve to live in this world amongst people like Michael, Tiffany, Josh, and...Jamie. Because of you, Tiffany is a widow, and I let that happen. I cared for you too much and I let that happen. The best we can do now, is ask for forgiveness."

"Noel, don't do this," Leon says. "I'm sorry, all right. You were right. It wasn't your fault. None of it was your fault: Mother, Father, me, Michael, none of us."

"I wish I could have seen him the moment he died. I wish I was there with you."

Leon takes a small step closer. The yellow light barely reaches the bottom of his pants. "It was quick, Noel. He died a painless death." He takes another step closer, submerging himself in the yellow light.

Noel pulls out his gun with his other hand and shoots Leon in the leg. It's the first time he's ever shot another human being, much less, the first time he's ever had to use his pistol out of training. "No," Noel whispers over Leon's cry of pain. "Dad. I wish I could have seen the result of my work." Noel lets out a chuckle and mutters something inaudible to Leon. The flame continues to burn incessantly in his hand, causing the lighter to become uncomfortably warm.

"Your work?" Leon snaps. "You mean mine! All you did was toast his outsides, you fucking psycho. I had to actually go to his hospital room to finish the fucking job!" He's bent over, leaning on the inside of the room's door frame, applying pressure to the wound with both hands, wincing from the pain. Blood flows down his leg, and under the yellow light, shifts into a rare shade of orange. "You think killing us will solve everything? What the hell do you know about what we deserve.

I did nothing wrong. Absolutely nothing. You have such a God complex, thinking that you have the power to condemn me, to judge me, to control me, to take care of me. I am not some little thief who needs looking after, who deserves justice."

"Goodbye, brother."

Noel's final impulse takes over as he tosses the lighter into a thin pool between himself and Leon. Instantaneously, fire travels in all directions, reaching the stairs before Leon is even able to turn away. And within minutes, the abandoned building that was once used as an underground auction house, is swallowed in unrelenting flames.

27

August, 1990.

It's a really hot and sunny day. The lions are hiding in their cave. They're not really doing anything.

"I want to see them eat," I tell my father.

"They're too hot to come out," he says. "Let's go see the elephants instead. Maybe they're out playing in the mud."

We pass a pond that daddy calls a "marsh." There are ducks and fishes swimming around. There are also two big cranes standing in the water. A group of people stand by and watch. We stop and watch too. A mommy duck is followed by a bunch of little chicks. People take out their cameras and take pictures. Daddy and I just watch.

"That one looks lost," I say as I point to a chick alone on the water. The mommy duck keeps on swimming and leaves the lost chick behind. The chick paddles around in circles and peeps for help. The mommy duck doesn't hear. She doesn't seem to care.

The crowd starts to get louder as the chick swims out of the water and waddles towards the fence—towards me. Before the chick escapes the marsh, daddy picks it up and drops it back over the fence, into the water. People cheer but my father acts like it's no big deal, because it isn't; I could have done the same thing.

The lost chick swims back to the middle of the marsh. The mommy duck and the other chicks are long gone. But the lost chick keeps swimming. It just keeps swimming, trying to find its family.

All of a sudden, a crane swoops down and gobbles up the lost chick. A small lump moves down the crane's throat and disappears into its stomach. People gasp. I begin to cry. The mommy duck doesn't care. She is swimming with her other chicks. She doesn't care about me.

28

May, 2015.

There's no time to think. Just run, just go. Blood continues to trickle down my legs, beneath my jeans as I stumble out of the room towards the staircase. Fire bursts in all directions; I can feel the heat begin to dry up my blood-soaked socks. I've never seen fire travel so fast, from one corner of the room to the other, and out the door. The flames dance in front of me, taunting me to throw myself into their burning arms. I hesitate as I look back towards Noel, who appears mesmerized by the growing fire on the verge of swallowing him whole. There's no time, I tell myself, no time to look back. I anticipate my first step through the fire, only to plummet down the stairs, landing face first onto the second floor with blood gushing out from my nose as well.

"Fuck."

Noel howls above the crackling fire. "Where are you going? Don't leave me here. Don't leave me here to die alone."

I'm not dying here. Not here. Not today.

I drag myself across the scorching floor as the fire races by me, infecting the walls and the forgotten doors. I already find myself longing for the previous fishy stench over the intoxicating burning of deteriorating wood. You'd think I'd be used to the smoke, from all the cigarettes I've enjoyed over the years, but I find myself choked out of both thought and breath. What the hell is there to think about, anyways. Just keep moving. Just keep moving before everything comes crashing down and it all turns to ash.

Fresh smoke and dust enter my lungs, as a familiar voice echoes in my head. "How's it going there, Gestas?" Danny emerges down the narrow hallway, wearing his favorite pair of glasses.

"What the fuck do you want?" I say as blood dribbles into my agape mouth.

Danny shakes his head as a faint smile appears below his crooked nose. "I'm just here to see how you're doing, Gestas."

"Leon! My name is Leon, you idiot!"

In a blink of an eye, Danny is crouching in front of me, with his head still shaking side to side. "No, your name is Gestas. You've got to stick to the codenames, remember?"

"Fuck codenames," I tell him. "And fuck you!"

Danny retreats to his original position. "All right, all right. Jesus. You're obviously in a bad mood."

I ignore him as I continue to inch myself closer and closer to where he stands, away from the burning fire. Somewhere nearby, I can hear the collapsing of walls, the shattering of glass, and gunshots. And like a whipped horse, I push myself to move even faster, collecting splinters from the unkempt floorboards. But no matter the gap I close, Danny continues to stand the same distance away, unmoving with his head shaking as it always does.

"What's the hurry Gestas? The Diamond of Despair isn't going anywhere, you know." Smoke fills the better half above the floor, gently obscuring Danny's upper body, but I can still make out his head moving incessantly back and forth, just like a grandfather clock.

"That diamond is long gone by now."

"You can still steal it," he says through the smoke. "You're the infamous Reed Thief, are you not?"

"Yeah, I am."

"You need to steal it. You have to. I mean, how else will you get her attention and gain back her love?"

The pain in my leg suddenly disappears as I raise my head to take in a deep breath. All around me, the framework shimmers brightly in a fusion of red and orange. Red and orange. Red and *red*.

"You know, you're a good guy, Gestas," he says with what I imagine to be a smile. "You never ratted me out. Even when you got caught."

"No," I say. "Why the hell would I?"

And for the next couple of seconds, Danny grows silent, leaving the flames to whisper their plans of destruction to one another without interruption. The whispering slowly turns into mellow chitchat, and eventually grows into boisterous chatter. I continue down the hallway, acting ignorant to what they have to say in their foreign tongue.

"Fuck." I stop abruptly in my tracks. "I need to get my book," I say as I try to turn my head around. "I can't let it burn, not again, not this time. Ms. Finkland let me borrow it, and it's a first edition. Hell, a *first edition*! I have to return it in a better condition than I got it in. I have to, I have to, or else father will find out." I look back towards the end of the hallway. "Danny? Danny, help me find it. It's a first edition. I don't want father to know. Please, help me. Help me...brother."

The smoke is now too thick to see through, so I close my eyes and call upon my precious memories, believing they can withstand the violent inferno in my stead. And I pray, hoping someone will come and save me.

Someone will come for me. Someone always does.

29

March, 2012.

I wrap my hands tightly around my cup of hot cocoa, absorbing as much heat as I possibly can. Despite it being close to the beginning of April, the weather is still as cold as it was during the holiday months, growing more and more stubborn as the years go by. The café is considerably crowded, with people flooding in just to escape the unusual chill of light snow that children undeniably welcome with open arms (and tongues). All around the counter, people are lined up, circling one end to the other, obscuring the visible order of exactly who's next in line. Customers seem to grab whichever drink becomes available, and in some cases, minor arguments break out over which drink belongs to whom. I must commend Danny for procuring our special-of-the-day hot cocoas as easily as he did. It is in his job description, after all, to get in, and especially out, as fast as he can.

"Good stuff, huh?" Danny says as the fog on his glasses from an earlier sip dissipates.

I scoot in my chair a little, trying to make room for the crowd developing behind. "It's all right, I guess. Although, I can't say I particularly like the marshmallow all that much. It tastes like nothing and takes up about a third of the cup."

"Really? I'd have thought you'd like the marshmallows. They're what makes this place special."

"No kidding," I say while eyeing the constantly growing line to my right. It's no wonder no one has slipped on the wet floors yet, if you consider how tightly packed everyone is. An old woman practically floats over the floor while being scrunched between three large men in thick winter coats. This is definitely a fire hazard, if I ever saw one.

"This place needs a better layout," I say. "I mean, just look at that counter. Why in the hell is it smack in the middle of the shop? And why is it taking up so much damn space?"

"I don't know," Danny replies, "I think that's just the style of the café."

"And why do they have the lines start from the very back of the store? People who come in have to fight their way through the people who want to get out. And let's not forget the ridiculous line circling about the room. Instead, they should have the line start at the front of the café, so people can order what they want there, circle around the counter, and exit as they get their drinks."

"I guess you're right," says Danny with his glasses still clouded. He takes another sip, adding onto the fog which makes it look like he's wearing sunglasses of a unique shade.

278

"I wouldn't be surprised if someone were to die from this mess."

"You think so?"

I do my best to point out behind me without accidentally poking someone's eye out. "There's probably somebody dead out there already, but nobody knows it yet because it's so damn crowded."

Danny shakes his head slightly as he takes another sip of his cocoa. I can't tell if he's shaking his head in agreement, or if he's just doing so out of habit. "You ever think about dying?"

His sudden question catches me off guard. "What?"

"When you're on your deathbed, about to die, do you think you'll be able to accept your fate, or be too scared to close your eyes?"

"Uh, way to ruin the mood, Danny. Hell, I'm just trying to enjoy some hot cocoa here."

"Jesus Christ, can't you just take my questions seriously for once? I listen to your ramblings all the time, but you never listen to mine."

"Okay, okay, calm down. Jeez."

A pause follows as we both take a sip of our drinks.

"So?" he asks.

"So what?" I say back.

He shakes his head in obvious frustration. "Forget about it."

"Of course I've thought about dying before," I tell him. "I mean, who hasn't? I think the first time I've thought about death was when I was seven or so."

"Jesus, that's kind of early," Danny says as he pops off the white plastic lid of his cocoa.

"Yeah well, my father had a dog when I was little—a German Shepherd named Chum. Luckily, it was just old age that got him. But I remember the day that he died, how a new side of the world ironically came to life and opened up to me, and it was then that I fully understood the meaning of death. There's a certain time in your life when you think that life will last forever, but all it takes is the death of a family pet to wake you up from your naive dream."

"Why a pet?" asks Danny, who has finally decided to remove his glasses and enjoy the rest of his cocoa undisturbed. It's a rare occurrence to witness Danny's eyes unwarped, so I take the opportunity to maintain eye contact and study the color of his dark pupils.

"Well, pets usually die first," I say with an intense gaze. "That's how it usually goes, right? Pets, grandparents, then parents."

"I don't know about that," Danny says while shaking his head again. "I think you got that order all wrong. Just take a look at you and me."

"Well, I guess there are always exceptions."

After Danny finishes his cocoa, we decide to get out of the cafe, but the thought of re-entering the belated cold convinces me to gladly get lost within the crowd, becoming part of the problem. And as I cling onto my hot cocoa (which is still plenty hot), I feel like an emperor penguin huddled amongst its colony, unmoving in either direction. I tuck my flippers to my sides and take little, awkward steps, which is the best I can do in the current situation. The doors swings wide open as two fellow penguins become lost into the abyss, allowing in the chilling arctic winds. My fantasy is cut short as someone bumps into me from behind, causing me to spill some hot co-coa onto my jeans. Before I have the chance to turn around, the culprit shoves his way past me, pressing open the doors just as they're about to close shut. And before I know it, I'm outside the café with Danny right behind me. The wet patch on my pants makes it unbearable to move, so I decide to take a chance and catch a cab before my jeans freeze over and stiffen.

It doesn't take much effort to procure a taxi by the main road. As the taxi driver starts for our destination, I take a sip of my cocoa, which is now lukewarm at best, but I still reluctantly down the rest in order to prevent future spillage.

"You know when you die," says Danny, "do the moments right before really matter?"

"What are you talking about?" I say as I stare out of the side window. The snow has picked up quite a bit, which reas-sures my decision to avoid the slippery streets and the grimy subway.

"Let's say a woman is raped before she's murdered. The moment she's raped doesn't really matter, right? Because a short while afterwards, she's killed anyways."

"What? Of course it matters. She experiences the rape, doesn't she?"

"But then she dies," Danny says. "So it doesn't really matter to her after that. It matters to people who are alive to hear about it. But it ultimately doesn't matter to her, because she's dead."

"So if you were raped before you were killed, would that not matter to you? Would you be completely fine with it?"

"Of course not," Danny replies with a disgusted look on his face. "But it wouldn't matter to me anymore, because I'd be dead. And when you hear about my death, you'd be even more upset by it all."

"What makes you think I'd care if you were to get raped or not?"

Danny just shakes his head quietly. It's an endless loop with this guy.

"Okay, okay," I continue, "so are you saying that, really, it doesn't matter what people do with their lives because they're just going to die anyways?"

"That's not the point. I'm saying how someone dies matters more to the people around him than it does to the person himself. Dying a quick, painless death is better news for people who care about you than for you yourself."

The taxi driver moans, signaling his discomfort which immediately kills the conversation at hand. And for the next couple of minutes, the only thing I can hear is the slight jingle of the ornament hanging from the rear-view window.

Danny decides to break the silence as we take a sharp right turn. "Jesus, what are we doing on thirty seventh street?"

I knew I shouldn't have taken the chance.

30

June, 2015.

The walls and ceiling are completely white and barren, with only a single window providing color with its view of the outside. The smell of plastic overwhelms me, and I realize that I'm strapped to a bed with tubes lodged deep into my nose. An unbearable itch forms on my left arm and spreads to my shoulders, neck, and resonates throughout my face. I try to move my hands to quell the fever, but I only end up squirming in place, unable to properly move a single joint.

"Just try to relax."

I look over to my left and see a woman in a distasteful light blue uniform. She gives me a quick glance, then resumes her work, checking the beeping equipment of my vitals. Her dark hair is short, barely reaching her shoulders, where a stethoscope hangs on both sides of her neck, favoring one side more than the other.

I do my best to speak, lingering on each word that passes through my dry lips. I ask her about my brother, but she doesn't know what has happened to him or about anything else. Her answer is so vague, that I begin to wonder if I even have a brother. I can't help but surrender to a sudden laugh, letting it all flow out, letting it all go, when I notice flowers in the corner of my eyes, sitting on the table to my very right. I ask her whether she knows who sent them.

"I'm not sure, I'm sorry," she says without even taking a look at the bouquet.

I pull my head closer to the bedside table and inhale through my nose, expecting to smell an opulent aroma, but the stench of plastic overwhelms me once again.

Of course, I should have known.

No. *She should have known.*

If only she had stayed, she would have been showered with jewelry and flowers. Diamonds and hydrangeas.

A. C. Ahn wrote *Hydrangeas on Fire*, his first novel, while pondering what the moment before death is like. He writes short stories for both enjoyment and publication. His work, "The Dragon and the Snake," won First Place in the Crime Category for the Writer's Digest Popular Fiction Awards. He splits his life between the San Francisco Bay Area and Seoul, Korea.

Visit his writing blog at www.TheAhnBros.com.